THE CANDLE SPUTTERED AND THE ROOM WENT BLACK.

The wind rose in violent fury, beating against the glass doors as if something outside were trying to force its way in. The strange and delicate music of a harp vibrated through the room and the sickeningly sweet scent of lavender rose from every corner of the darkness. Amanda trembled and instinctively clung to David. But the grip that held her had suddenly turned vise-like and fiendish. Her arms were pinned to her sides, her body crushed down painfully into the bed.

Amanda tried to scream, but no sound could be forced through her lips. She tried to call out David's name, but suddenly she was unable to breathe. Devilish laughter surrounded her. In the pitch black darkness and confusion, the glass door blew open. Crashing against the walls, they splintered into a thousand pieces.

"The third Mrs. Whitcomb . . ." a hollow voice cried. "The other two before you, strangled in their beds. . . ."

Then she heard the shrill, bone-chilling sound of someone screaming, calling out for help. But there was none. . . .

KATE CAMERON

EVIL AT WHISPERING HILLS

LEISURE BOOKS ❧ NEW YORK CITY

*For my mother,
who was born in Southern Indiana
and passed on the heritage of these hills
to her daughters.*

A LEISURE BOOK

Published by

Dorchester Publishing Co., Inc.
6 East 39th Street
New York, NY 10016

Copyright ©MCMLXXIII by Dorchester Publishing Co.,
    Inc.

Printed in the United States of America

EVIL AT WHISPERING HILLS

1

Amanda saw herself in a strange room lit by a single taper. The furnishings and draperies were hidden in deep shadows and she stood by a set of French doors that opened out onto a balcony. The wind rushed through the trees outside with an eerie moaning sound—the sound of a woman crying. Amanda struggled to close the doors but the wind rose in force and fury, moaning louder, fighting her with a preternatural will. Her long thick hair blew wildly around her head, the damp air molding her thin muslin nightgown to her body like a second skin.

Suddenly, she felt someone come up behind her and a man's heavy hands rested on her shoulders. "Come away from there now, Amanda," a darkly seductive voice implored. Powerful arms encircled her body and led her deeper into the shadows. Warm lips pressed against the smooth bare curve of her neck. As if by magic, the wind abated and the doors closed by themselves. Amanda's heart beat wildly as she turned in her captor's embrace.

It was David, her husband of barely a few hours. And yet, it was not. . . . The candle, flickering on the bedside table, cast his golden hair and handsome face in ominous shadows. She brought his familiar features into focus for just an instant and then his image seemed to cloud and transform into someone else. Some malevolent looking stranger. Only his eyes remained the same, dark eyes lighted from within by a look of desire that was frightening in its intensity.

He swept her up and carried her effortlessly to the canopy bed. He laid her down gently and soon stretched out beside her. His lips met hers in a deep, soul-searching kiss, his hands roaming over her body as if to memorize each sensuous peak and curve. Amanda felt suddenly drained of all free will. She knew little of what happened between a man and a woman. Her sheltered upbringing and vague imaginings had hardly prepared her for the sensations that now seemed to shatter her very soul.

She wound her arms around her husband's broad shoulders, feeling herself sink into the soft bed beneath his weight. She surrendered herself to him totally, writhing and tossing in response to his caressing hands and lips. Her body trembled, the pleasure so intense that she could hardly stand it another moment before she cried out. "David . . . Oh, David," she sighed, burying her face against his shoulder.

"Hush," he soothed her. "You mustn't be frightened. There is so much pleasure yet to come between us on this night. In the morning when you wake, you will truly be Mrs. David Whitcomb."

At his words, the candle sputtered and the room went black. The wind rose in violent fury, beating against the glass doors as if something outside was trying to force its way in. The strange and delicate music of a harp vibrated through the room and the sickeningly sweet scent of lavender rose from every corner of the darkness. Amanda trembled and instinctively clung to David. But the grip that held her had suddenly turned vise-like and fiendish. Her arms were pinned to her sides, her body crushed down painfully into the bed.

Amanda tried to scream, but no sound could be forced through her lips. She tried to call out David's name, but suddenly she was unable to breathe. Devilish laughter surrounded her. In the pitch black darkness and confusion, the glass doors blew open. Crashing against the walls, they splintered into a thousand pieces.

"The third Mrs. Whitcomb . . ." a hollow voice cried. "The other two before you, strangled in their beds. . . ."

Then she heard the shrill, bone-chilling sound of someone screaming, calling out for help. But there was none. . . .

Amanda woke, moaning aloud in her sleep. She sat bolt upright and pressed her hands to her face. Panting, she pushed back her thick hair and tried to catch her breath. Someone had already opened the heavy drapery and dawn's cool grey light filtered into the unfamiliar room. It was the bedroom of the master suite. She had never even crossed its threshold until last night, her wedding night.

She turned and looked beside her, but the other half of the bed was empty. The covers had been pushed back; the impression of David's head still remained in the pillow. He must have risen before dawn to ride out to the far side of the plantation, Amanda thought. David . . . my husband. It was all still so new, almost shocking to think of herself as married to her employer. But they were truly man and wife. She leaned back against the pillows, remembering how her husband had so passionately taken possession of her the night before. The memory of her own naive, but surprisingly ardent response, made her flush. But when she had finally fallen asleep in David's arms, she'd been visited again and again by the same terrifying dream.

All through the night, David had woken her from the nightmare. He had held her in his arms and soothed her back to sleep as if comforting a small child. "The day's excitement must have upset your nerves," he had said.

He was angry with himself for not showing greater restraint and consideration, even though it had been their first night together. Then it was Amanda's turn to comfort her new husband, to assure him that she would not have traded her pleasure-filled initiation into the mysteries of love between a man and wife for anything. David pulled her close then. Settling her head on his broad chest, he murmured tender words until she slept.

Now Amanda found herself alone, with no one to comfort her or drive the vicious, haunting images of the nightmare from her mind. The dream had filled her with a chilling sense of foreboding.

Not for the first time, Amanda wondered if she had done the right thing by marrying David Whitcomb. Though he treated her respectfully and even desired her, Amanda knew he had not married her for love. Accepting David Whitcomb's proposal had been an impulsive decision on her part. Not like her at all. Ordinarily, Amanda was a level-headed person who always thought through the consequences of her actions. Her father, a practical minded merchant seaman, had raised her that way. "My girl Amanda has got as much common sense in her little finger as any bloke's got in his entire head," he liked to brag. The well-bred ladies of the family's acquaintance believed it was unattractive and even unnatural for a woman to be so clear thinking and plainly spoken as Amanda. It would certainly prove a hardship when she tried to catch a husband, they whispered among themselves. But to Amanda's thinking, she wanted no part of a man who desired a wife prone to flightiness and swooning spells.

From the first, David Whitcomb seemed to respect her powers of judgment. And like her father, he encouraged the straightforward way Amanda expressed her opinions. Amanda knew she could never seriously consider marriage to a man who treated her as some drawing room ornament. In that way alone, David had won her esteem.

Nonetheless, Amanda had surprised even herself by finally agreeing to marry the master of Whispering Hills plantation. But looking back, her life had taken many extraordinary turns ever since her father's death, almost a year ago.

Amanda had never known her mother. All she ever knew was that her name had been Honore, and she had died when a baby boy was born. He'd been put to rest alongside his mother, and Amanda's father had taken her often to put flowers on the grave.

Arthur Kendall was away from home for two and three months at a time, but he saw to it that his daughter did not lack companionship or in-struction. She had been firmly grounded in history, geography and mathematics; since she'd shown a flair for languages, her father had hired a Latin master, then a French tutor. Amanda had been studying with her French teacher when the news of her father's death had been brought to her by Jeremy Tomlinson.

The transition from being a sheltered darling who had lived in the lap of luxury to a penniless orphan had almost shattered her. And would have, she thought ruefully, if it had not been for Mr. Tomlinson's steady shoulder during the days that followed her father's funeral. She could still see his face before her when he said kindly, "My dear, if I could see my way clear to supporting you, God knows I would do so. But unfortunately, your father and I just recently sunk every farthing into a new business venture. It seemed a sound invest-ment at the time. If things had worked out, we both should have retired within five years. As it happened, your father's ship met disaster, and we've lost everything. In order to satsify debts, I must sell everything I have; likewise, I must sell your father's house and all the furnishings. Now, your education will stand you in good stead, and I've just the thing for you. I've found suitable employment that will take advantage of your learning."

"And what is that, Uncle Jeremy?" Amanda pressed her small hands together and kept biting her lower lip, unwilling to allow herself to go to pieces in front of Jeremy Tomlinson. Not when he had lost everything he had, too.

"I have found a position for you with an elderly French lady who needs a companion-secretary. Hates men. Won't allow one to set foot on the place. She's a spinster."

"Hates men?" Amanda had experienced an im-mediate picture of herself living in some remote French village with a crotchety old woman who kept herself surrounded with screeching parrots and peppermint lozenges. For her part, Amanda liked men, and her father had often told her he wanted her to meet a good man and true, some day, and hoped she would find the same kind of happiness he'd known with her mother. She rather doubted that she'd find anything but unhappiness and boredom with a French lady who hated men. "But haven't you something . . . maybe with someone who doesn't hate anybody?"

Disappointed, the solicitor had drummed his fingers on his desk top. "Well . . . there is my old friend, Mason Whitcomb's son. He's lost his wife and has two small children, for whom he needs a governess. But that would mean leaving England."

"I should have to leave England if I went to live in France," Amanda pointed out.

"To be sure you would. But one can easily cross the Channel and get back home. I don't know about America." Mr. Tomlinson poked out his lips and shook his head. "It seems to me a wild sort of place, from all I hear. Indians with their infernal tomahawks . . . it wouldn't be as though you'd be living in a civilized place, regardless of what young Whitcomb says. He writes in his letter that he lives on a plantation in a new state called Indiana. That brings to mind darkies, and I've heard Indiana is an unhealthy, swampy place."

Amanda kept objecting to the French lady. Mr. Tomlinson objected strenuously to her decision to go to America. She was sure she preferred a post with children over one with a lonely old lady. After all, it was 1817. How wild and uncivilized could this place Indiana be? Finally, after making her promise she would write to him if she needed help or wanted to return to England, Mr. Tomlinson gave in.

The journey to Whispering Hills had been long and rough. During the tedious hours of travel, Amanda wondered if she would have ever accepted the position in the Whitcomb household had she known beforehand just how difficult the trip would be. First, there had been the crossing from Liverpool to New York. Next, a coach carried her inland where she met a wagon train that rumbled over the rugged countryside at a tortuously slow pace.

Though she had traced her journey on a map, Amanda had not been able to imagine a country so vast and wild. But she soon learned that those thin lines that marked the distance she was to travel were deceptive. The wagon train ride to Cinncinati had taken all of three months.

Amanda now recalled how she had finally chosen a barge instead of a flatboat once she had reached Cincinnati. She didn't know which would be better, but when she learned that pigs and chickens would be among the passengers on the flatboat, she decided against it. Besides, the barge left the banks of Cincinnati an entire day before the flatboat was due to depart. Once again the map's finely drawn curlicues that made their way south to Louisville appeared to be much shorter than the real distance was. Two weeks after leaving Cincinnati, the barge arrived in Louisville.

Amanda remembered a woman named Twilight McInnes, who had talked endlessly about nothing all the way from Cincinnati. "That-there's Indianny. Right across the river." She had told Amanda as they stood on the dock the morning the barge finally landed. "A ferry boat, hit'll take ye. Cain't hardly see nothin' through the mist, but hit's thar, all right, less'n hit's chunked off into the Ohio River." The woman then threw her head back and exposed a great expanse of long, stringy neck, chortling in a manner that reminded Amanda of a braying donkey. "Hee-yaw, don't that take the rag off'n the brush? One of them-thar cyclones could a come along and chunked all of Indianny off'n the ground, right into the river." Fortunately for Amanda, who hardly knew what to say to such a disastrous announcement, Twilight McInnes' brother pulled her to one side. But before he was able to drag the woman out of earshot, she screeched, "And who be ye goin' to work fer? Never did say, all the livelong time we was on the River."

"It's . . . it's a place called Whispering Hills," said Amanda. She didn't want to answer, but even the noisy woman's brother had his head tilted at an expectant angle, and it seemed to her that all of the other people who were gathered in the little group who had just stepped off the barge were listening for her answer. "I'm to be governess to Mr. Whitcomb's children," she added. The last sentence came out unexpectedly. Later, when she was on the ferry boat and going back over the incident, she realized she'd added the last part because there had seemed to be a shocked kind of silence after she'd said she was going to Whispering Hills.

It was Twilight McInnes who had finally spoken again. "Well, then! And will it be Mr. Whitcomb's pleasure to wed yet another girl, only to murder her in her bed when he tires of her? Twice wed, with both wives dead. The last one was governess to his young'in, too."

"Sister!" The talkative woman, who Amanda had more than once felt was not in her right mind, was jerked roughly to one side by her flustered brother. "Pay her no mind, Miss," he said as he tapped his temple with his index finger.

"She's lost her mind. McInnes had her up to Cincinnati to a doctor for her silly ways," said a pleasant masculine voice at Amanda's side. "Come. I'll help you into the ferry."

Amanda was grateful for the sound of a normal

voice and an accent that didn't grate on her well-bred English ears. It had been hard to follow the torrent of words that Miss McInnes babbled throughout the tiresome two weeks since she'd left Cincinnati, and it hadn't taken her long to come to the conclusion that the poor woman wasn't quite sensible. Yet she couldn't ignore the small shiver that raced up and down her back at the woman's shrill voice, and those final words had set the hair at the nape of her neck on end.

She felt the same reaction now, a month later, as she recalled the incident in her mind.

At the time, the young man who had spoken to her on the dock gave her a hand onto the ferry. "You musn't pay any attention to Miss McInnes," he said. "It's very sad really. She was a school teacher before she . . . before she became what people call 'daft.' She was thrown from her horse and landed on her head. Hasn't been quite right since, poor lady. Won't you let me help you to a seat? There seem to be plenty."

Amanda was a little flustered at having such a young and decidedly handsome man acting in such a forward manner toward her without proper introduction. She felt inclined to show him her haughty profile and refuse to answer, which would put him in his place at once. But people in America appeared to pay less attention to the proprieties than did the English. She didn't find it nearly so offensive now that she saw such behavior as the custom in this bold new country.

Besides, the rough current made the ferry rise and fall so rapidly it was like going over a series of bumps. Amanda was swaying from side to side, her knuckles white from clutching the railing with both hands. She accepted the hand the young man offered and murmured her thanks. When she was seated on the hard wooden bench she strained her eyes through the mist toward the Indiana shore.

"I'm Lochard Whitcomb," the young man said then. He seated himself at her side. "Please accept my apologies for not introducing myself sooner. My brother, David, asked me to come for you. You are Miss Amanda Kendall, aren't you?"

"Yes . . ." She extended her hand to him. "I'm Miss Kendall. How do you do?"

He took her hand and smiled. She hoped she wasn't staring impolitely. He had a great deal of chestnut colored hair, she noticed, and hazel eyes. The light sprinkling of freckles across his nose gave his face a friendly look. He appeared to be around twenty-five years old and was dressed in elegant breeches of dove-colored material. His boots were made of soft, fine leather and were very clean. So were his fingernails. A trifle ruefully Amanda remembered her father telling her often that the mark of a good man is not always his clothes. But she still appreciated people who were careful of their appearance.

"How far is it to the other side?" she asked him then.

"Oh, we'll be across within a half hour. Then we're almost there. My brother's house is not far from the riverbank, but far enough away to keep his house from being flooded. Was your journey long and tiresome?"

"It took forever," Amanda replied. She didn't want to remember the shipboard days and nights of rainswept terror or the lightning that had burned so brightly the prairie sky was fiery. Great claps of thunder had shaken the very earth under the endlessly rolling wheels of the wagon. Nor did she want to think about the two-week journey down the Ohio River with that awful woman and her silly chatter, to say nothing of the unbearable heat, the filth, the swarms of insects that tried to devour everyone on the barge.

"And how is old Tomlinson? Well, I hope."

Amanda turned puzzled eyes upon Lochard Whitcomb. Because of her extreme state of exhaustion, she had quite forgotten about the solicitor who had obtained her post in America. The young man smiled. "I was born in England, you know. No, of course, you couldn't know, could you? You see, I'm five years younger than my brother, David. Mother was not well. She felt she hadn't long to live, so she asked my father to take her back to England. She lived until I was seventeen. We remained in London for two years, then father decided David and I must return to America. I knew Mr. Tomlinson well; he was a round little man, as I recall, with white sideburns and a long beard. So good of him to send my brother a well-bred young lady to teach his little ones some manners. I'm afraid you'll be shocked at their lack of discipline. It's been a long time since a woman has been on the place—one they can talk to, that is. There are servants, of course, but they're illiterate as well as inclined to spoil the children."

Amanda wanted to ask if it were true that Mr. Whitcomb had buried two wives. She looked down at her hands and choked the words back, knowing full well that if she asked he'd know she was dwelling on the other thing the demented creature had said. She wondered how she could be expected to *not* think about such a startling statement, though. She wished she were older and had more experience. All the time that she was telling him Mr. Tomlinson was in good health, and asking him the ages and names of her charges, she was aware of the dark question that kept climbing up to the surface of her mind and the equally dark answer that Lochard Whitcomb might give her.

The water was lapping more gently against the edge of the ferry, but the mist seemed to be thickening. When she couldn't think of any more polite questions, she began to fidget, thinking surely they had been crossing the Ohio for much longer than it should have taken. Then she realized the ferry wasn't moving. Lochard Whitcomb stood up. "I'll just go to see why the ferry has stopped. We're all but there."

When she was alone, Amanda felt her strong imagination begin to play tricks on her. She looked into the mist and saw that it seemed to be lessening. Tiny little feathery tendrils rose in wispy curls, then danced under a faint rose and gold light. Her mind wanted her to dismiss the last few months, to pretend that nothing she had endured during her long journey was real. It didn't seem possible that she was now truly sitting on a ferry boat bound for Indiana and a plantation. She was dreaming it all, and soon she would awaken in her own pleasant room in London. Tilda would come with her morning tea and toast, after which she would run downstairs to see if her father had sent her a letter. But before she was entirely carried away into a wishful dream-world where everything was exactly as she had known it and felt secure, she set her soft mouth into a hard line and forced back scalding tears.

I'm here. This is a real ferry boat, and something absolutely natural and normal has caused the boat to stop. A man named Lochard Whitcomb has come to fetch me in the place of his brother, David Whitcomb, for whom I am to be gainfully employed as governess of his two children. Andrew, a boy of twelve, and a girl, ten, named Nelda. I must not allow myself to believe this is the end of the world and that when that scary fog lifts, the ferry boat will dash over the edge of the earth into nowhere.

Amanda now recalled how much she wished just then that she had taken Mr. Tomlinson's advice and become the companion and secretary to the old French woman. For all I know, she had thought, the mad Miss McInnes was speaking the truth. And this is a desolate place. So chilly in spite of the heat. Her arms had broken out in chill bumps and her head was swimming with dizziness. A wave of nausea came over her and she hoped she wasn't going to have to lean her head over the side and be sick. Lochard Whitcomb came back and told her all was well. She felt the boat beginning moving towards the shoreline again.

"We hit a snag," explained her escort. "The river is low this time of year." Then his voice changed and he lifted a hand toward the opposite shore. "But look! The mist is lifting!"

It was true. Amanda's disbelieving eyes swept over the Indiana shore line and found it verdant and lush under bright midsummer sun. Now that the rolls of fog were clearing, she could see that the river itself was transparent as glass. Great elms and sycamores overhung the bank, the emerald green of the leaves reflected in true color in the river. There was a fairyland quality in all that untamed beauty, she thought, with a rush of appreciation. The last little tendrils of vapor rose high in a blue, blue sky just as the boatman shouted to someone on the other side. After his voice was nothing but a distant echo, a hush settled over the peaceful scene. The only sound was the slip and riffle of the long poles that were used to push the boat through the water, accompanied by a thrilling trill of birdsong.

"Oh! It's beautiful," said Amanda.

To the west was an unbroken stand of trees that stretched as far as she could see up the bank and along the river stretched as far as she could see up the bank and along the river's edge. To the east was a clearing that boasted a cove and a small dock. As her eyes traveled from the shore, she saw a wide expanse of dark green lawn that appeared long enough for bowling on the green. And it was flat enough too, she mused as she noticed how the bank leveled off as though it had been terraced. As her eyes swept upwards along the lawn, she saw dazzling white stepping stones bordered with brightly blooming flowers. High on a hill stood a magnificent house, sparkling white under the sun. She drew in her breath in amazement, totally unprepared for such a grand building in the midst of the wilderness. Even from the little cove she could see that the house was enormous, built along architectural lines that made her think of home. Lochard Whitcomb explained that the view from the front of the house was even more impressive. There were fluted columns that supported the wide veranda which was accessible from both floors, he said.

"But to think I'd see white brick! Like in England!" Amanda cried. "And such big bricks, too."

Lochard Whitcomb smiled. "What you see is Indiana limestone. My father's acreage includes a quarry. He built the original part of the house, which included the great hall, library, keeping rooms, kitchens and upstairs bedrooms. My brother added the wings after he was married. He inherited the plantation, of course. My land lies to the southeast, beyond the ridge. It's possible to see my home from the nursery as well as your bedroom. Of course I could ill afford a grand dwelling like Whispering Hills. But I'm quite content with what I have."

Remembering Lochard Whitcomb's words,

Amanda now wondered if there had been bitterness in his tone. Right then she was conscious of a ripple of disappointment in his voice that both surprised her and embarrassed her. It occurred to her that if he had a home of his own, he was probably married; and she couldn't quite understand the disappointment he felt, especially since she'd just met him. But then she told herself she felt that sinking sensation and sudden sense of loss only because Lochard Whitcomb was the only person she had met yet from Whispering Hills. All of her days to come were cloaked in unanswered questions, so she could forgive herself for impulsively feeling dismay at the idea of her escort being married. And even though the sight of the very civilized house was cheering, she still felt a dark cloud of foreboding. It didn't seem right on the hill . . . not in the face of all that dazzling white beauty. Yet she did, and tried to find a reason for her sense of nameless fear. She finally came to the conclusion that she was worn out from traveling, for again she was acutely conscious of a sudden chill, dizziness and nausea.

That's it. But what a deplorable time to come down with an attack of vapors! The very first in my entire life! Well, I'll just have to try to ignore it. I won't give in to it. But that's no doubt why I feel so awful about this place. She thought of the dear, careworn face of Mr. Tomlinson and reminded herself that the Whitcomb family were his friends. She knew he'd never have allowed her to come if the Whitcomb family had not been reputable people. But the fact that she'd promised to keep in touch with the elderly solicitor was small comfort when she contemplated the idea of going back to London in defeat, unable to adjust to a new country. Worse, to consider a return trip over perilous roads, then back across the sea. She didn't even want to think about that. As she turned her attention back again to the magnificent house where she would live, a wash of homesickness for England and all the friends she had left behind came over her.

Just then two small forms appeared on the rolling green lawn, and she brightened as Mr. Whitcomb explained that the children had come down to meet the ferry.

The ferry boat had slipped into the little cove and the solid timbers groaned as the ferryman jumped out and made the boat fast with a chain. The boat lurched a little and Amanda was grateful for Lochard Whitcomb's steadying hand around her waist, but she made her own footing firm, and drew away to show him that she was not accustomed to having a strange man touch her. "I'm all right now," she said in the cool, polite tone of a well brought up English girl. "It was a sudden jolt, though."

Young Whitcomb laughed, then called tenderly to the golden haired children, who were running down the bank. "Watch it there, Nelda! Don't go so fast, I say."

It was the boy who stumbled and fell in his pellmell rush, though. Amanda watched the graceful way the child accepted the tumble, then the quick, embarrassed grin that brightened his charming features when he stood up. He smiled directly into her eyes. In a formal voice, he called across the ten feet or so that separated him from the ferry boat. "Miss Kendall, I believe? We're so happy to have you here, Ma'am." He held out a hand to his sister, who had turned suddenly shy, with downcast eyes and flushed cheeks. "And this is my sister, Nelda. Say how-do-you-do to our new governess, Nelda."

The little girl raised startlingly blue eyes and

met Amanda's gaze in honest appraisal. In that moment, an answering pang of sympathy was in Amanda's heart, for she fully understood what was on the pretty little girl's mind. Surely, she thought, little Nelda is thinking the same thing I am: *Will she like me? Will I like her? What will she be like? Will she be stern and strict? Will she stay, or will she run away, back to the safety of England. . . .*

After the exchange of greetings, once she was off the ferry boat and walking along the gentle slope of the riverbank, Amanda became so much in sympathy with the motherless children that she quite forgot her own turmoil. She also tried not to pay too much attention to a towering figure that strolled with the same kind of grace as the little boy, down from the house. It was not until Lochard Whitcomb made the formal introductions that Amanda forced herself to look her new employer full in the face.

The family resemblance between David and Lochard Whitcomb was immediately apparent. Yet, as Amanda now recalled, at their first moment of introduction she had found the differences in their looks far more intriguing than the similarities. Her new employer looked very much like his brother, but a version drawn by a bolder, more hasty hand. The two men stood at about the same height. Yet posed beside Lochard with his hands locked behind his back, David seemed bigger and more powerful. His broad chest and shoulders strained against the fabric of his dark waistcoat and unlike his brother, he wore high black riding boots, caked with mud. While Lochard looked dressed for high tea in the drawing room, David looked as if he were typically most comfortable in the rough, vital outdoors. He had not gone to any great trouble to prepare himself for her arrival, Amanda noticed, and she doubted if he would see fit to apologize for it. Altogether, he struck her as a man uninclined to apologize about anything.

Lochard's features had impressed Amanda as smooth and untried. But in David's face she saw the effect of experience, the mark of life's victories and sorrows. Where Lochard had sensitive, finely drawn lips, David's mouth was more generous and set in a way that suggested he didn't smile much. His eyes, unlike Lochard's clear hazel ones, were dark as a gypsy's, which contrasted oddly with his thick gold hair. Those eyes appraised her boldly, from head to toe, without being actually impolite. She wondered if he found her wanting.

Although he was a gentleman like his brother, David's bearing suggested a more reserved personality and a more discerning intellect. Amanda, who considered herself a good judge of character, sensed that her new employer's respect and acceptance would not be as easily won as Lochard's had been. Yet, something in David's expression challenged her. As Amanda politely took his hand, she met his dark gaze spiritedly. *"I will prove to you, David Whitcomb, that I'm worthy of your respect,"* was the message her glance conveyed.

"We shall see, young lady," he seemed to reply. The corner of his mouth turned upward in a reluctant smile.

"You must be exhausted, Miss Kendall," David said aloud just then. "Come along up to the house and we'll see you properly settled in your room. I'm sure you would like to rest awhile before the children are let loose to crawl all over you."

Looking faintly amused, he glanced down at his daughter, Nelda. Already clinging to Amanda's hand, the little girl looked up at her new governess shyly, her incredibly blue eyes filled with awe and adoration. Well, at least I can be sure that I've won over one member of the Whitcomb household, Amanda thought, suddenly feeling very weary. With little more conversation, she followed David to the house, Nelda on one side and Andrew, skipping along like a frolicsome colt, on the other. Only Lochard did not trouble himself to keep up, lagging some distance behind them.

In the house, a sea of black faces wavered in front of her suddenly swimming eyes and she stumbled through a greeting or two, knowing she'd never remember the names of any of the servants. Her legs were trembling, and even the little jewel box that she carried with her reticule felt so heavy she feared she might drop it before she was allowed to go up the wide, curving staircase to her room.

"I'm Becky," said the slender dark girl who showed her the way. "I'm your maid. Just a few more steps, Ma'am, then down the hall. Such a big house, but the Master has made it a pretty sight, don't you think?"

Stumbling along, holding herself together by sheer will power, Amanda nodded. She wondered why she'd suddenly been taken with such extreme exhaustion and was only too grateful when Becky opened a door onto a cool, dim room. Her fingers dropped the little chest and the reticule on a marble-topped lowboy and she was only vaguely aware of the black girl kneeling and removing her boots. Her hands were shaking uncontrollably.

"I don't know why I'm so weary," she murmured. The room gave her the impression of swaying back and forth. Windows curved inwards, then outwards. The bed rose into the air and the floor spun under her.

* * *

Her next lucid thoughts were confused and dark, but she was almost able to sort out the reality from what she knew was the delirium of a fever that had possessed her from the time she set foot inside of Whispering Hills.

The gentle brown face of Becky came into focus and broke into a smile. When she spoke, her voice was soothing and soft. "You feel better now, which is good. Mostly, the fevers go on for days and days. But you're young and strong in spite of the tiring journey. No, now. Don't try to sit up just yet, Miss Amanda. You'll have some broth and a bit of fruit first."

Amanda felt unbearably weak, but in possession of all her faculties. Through cracked lips, she croaked, "How long have I been sick like this?"

"Three days, Miss. You spoke of your papa often, and his death. It's sad when the papa dies and there is no mama left. You also spoke of the long, hard journey and the little Miss and Master, and other worries on your mind. But don't let that scare you. Only I was allowed to remain at your side. You feel clean and neat? You just had a bath." The brown-skinned woman continued to smile, and Amanda nodded. Her skin was fragrant and clean and her hair had been brushed.

"Yes. Thank you. I . . . things are coming back to me now. I was dizzy and weary . . . and . . . you say you were the only one in the room with me while I was ill? How dreadful of me to get sick on my very first day here."

"It's best to get it over with," said Becky. "Everyone gets sick sooner or later. Yes, I was allowed to be here with you—nobody else. The Master's decision. You see, I have already had the fever, and I, too, am strong." Her brown eyes, both intelligent and curious, continued to look at

Amanda expectantly. "Why you ask if anybody else here, Missy? You see somebody else? You said you did. You said she come by the window, flew in at night. Give me a start, too, for you called her by name—and she's dead."

"Charity," said Amanda. "She had bright golden hair, like Nelda . . . like the young Mistress."

"Yes. That was what you said, Charity, but I tried to not pay you any mind. You under the crazies with hot skin and glazed over eyes, but you said it. Charity. You know a woman by that name where you came from, across the water?"

"No. But it was a dream, I think." Amanda frowned. Her tongue felt thick and scalded, but she was conscious of gnawing hunger. "I suppose I dreamed of a woman who looked—or rather somehow who Nelda looks *like*—because I had the little girl on my mind right before I became desperately ill."

"Yes, yes," answered Becky in/solemn agreement. "Only how did you know her name? It was Charity that you spoke aloud. Just like you heard her tell you her name. And then you said—*Oh, yes . . . the children's mother*. But then you went to tossing and turning and carrying on. Hollered that you wouldn't leave the house, you didn't believe in ghosts. Well, listen, Missy, maybe you don't believe in ghosts, but I do. I saw that shade once before, and I don't like it. If she's going to come in the window and fool around here, I'm glad you're better, for I want to go back and live with my man. I don't like no ghosts. Especially when they come back from the grave to tell a nice girl like you to go away. In the grave is where dead folks belong. It isn't decent of them to be up and running around, flying in and out of windows, I tell you!"

2

Amanda would never forget how quickly Becky backed out of the room, her eyes wide open with fear. In a near-whisper, she said she would get the broth. Apprehensively, Amanda looked toward the long, narrow windows where she remembered seeing the misty form slip into the room.

It was just the fog, she told herself—*mist, like the day I arrived. With the sun shining against heavy, swirling vapors, combined with my fever, of course. That would account for the gold of her hair, the billowing of her dress. The rest was simply my feverish state combined with my abominable imagination.* Already, the memory of what she had actually said to the ghostly figure was fading from her mind. She was almost—but not *quite*—content to deny she'd seen an apparition.

In the first place, I don't believe in such things, she told herself angrily. Even as a child, she had made fun of her playmates when they spoke of ghosts and goblins, of headless horsemen and things that go bump in the night. But she wondered if David Whitcomb's wife had truly been named Charity. Then the memory of the demented woman who had screamed so wildly about two murdered Whitcomb wives came back to her all of a piece. She shivered, trying to blot the ugly memory from mind.

If one of those wives of David Whitcomb was named Charity, I shall leave here immediately, she decided. And then she shook her head to clear it of cobwebs and tried to laugh at herself. *No you won't. You'll stay right here, because Becky could just as well have imagined you gave your ghostly visitor a name. She would know, after all, if one of the Whitcomb wives had been named Charity.*

Silly girl, she kept upbraiding herself. *You don't even know if there were two wives. And certainly you don't know they were both murdered. And young Mr. Whitcomb assured you the woman who spoke of murders was daft. Her own brother tapped his temple in that unmistakable way that denotes insanity, so stop this ridiculous doubting and calm yourself.*

Footsteps sounded in the hall outside the bedroom door, and Amanda was pleased to see Becky back with a steaming bowl of broth. "Your first spoonful of nourishment in three days," said the maid. "And this. I brought you something right nice from the garden."

Amanda looked at the bright red object that contrasted glaringly with the white plate under it. It was shiny, but the skin looked soft, like a plum. She decided if it was a plum it was certainly the biggest one she'd ever seen, for it was larger than her closed fist, and she'd never seen one so red. "Is it a plum, then? In England we have only purple and green plums. No red ones. At least not this bright color of red."

Becky laughed. "A tomato. You never ate a tomato? They're good for what ails you."

A well-modulated male voice spoke from the door. "You don't need to taste the tomato, Miss Kendall. They take a bit of getting used to." He smiled and continued, "I'm afraid the servants look upon the new fruit recently come up from the south as somewhat of a cure-all for anything from gout to the plague."

He turned to Becky then. "If you want Miss Kendall to taste the tomato at all, I suggest you serve the infernal thing properly. Bring it back down to Flora and have her slice it very thin," he instructed in a firm, but not unkind tone. "And add a dash of salt on top as well."

"Yes, Sir." With a slight nod of her head, Becky took the strange fruit on its plate and departed.

Now that they were left alone, Amanda felt keenly aware of David Whitcomb's presence. It didn't strike Amanda as altogether proper that she should be left unchaperoned in her bed. But neither David, nor Becky seemed to notice.

"Here, let me help you take this broth," David said, sitting down on the edge of the bed. As Amanda lifted herself up against the pillows, she was suddenly conscious of her state of undress. The neckline of her summer nightgown was low and trimmed with French lace, exposing what Amanda considered a thoroughly indecent view of her creamy white shoulders and bustline. She hurried to cover herself with the bed clothes, but David quickly tucked a wide linen napkin under her chin, thereby saving her from further embarrassment. His rough fingertips brushed her throat and arms, sending strange sensations coursing through her body. When she looked up at him, she could see his dark eyes lit with mirth. There was another look there too, one which was exciting

as well as frightening to her. Although Amanda
was naive and inexperienced, she knew very well
when a man's blood had been stirred.

He lifted a spoonful of broth to her lips and
Amanda took it. "You look very well indeed," he
said in a hushed voice. "Another few days and
you'll feel as though you've never been sick."

"I'm sorry to have caused you all this trouble,
Mr. Whitcomb," Amanda apologized. "I can't
understand it. At home . . . In England I mean, I
hardly catch so much as a cold." She was more
than a little ashamed of having given in to the
sickness immediately upon arriving. Now, having
her employer tending to her like a nurse seemed to
make matters even worse. Amanda didn't want
him to think he'd been stuck with some sickly chit
of a girl who would prove more trouble than she
was worth.

But he quickly waved away her apologies with a
gentle insistence that he was only happy the fever
hadn't come upon her while she was still traveling.

"I don't like to think of what might have happened to you if you'd been stricken on that
dreadful journey." His dark eyes met hers with
such a look of possessive intensity that Amanda
felt herself flush. She quickly looked away. Her
employer was a man of deep feeling, to be sure.
From all indications, he seemed extremely protective of both his family and the servants at Whispering Hills who depended upon him for their
welfare.

He put down the bowl of soup and leaned over
to look at her closely. "Your eyes are clear. That's
a good sign."

She was amazed at his tender smile. Her
memory of those first few harried moments after
her arrival were hazy at best. But she had the
distinct recollection of thinking that David Whit-

comb was somewhat cold and reserved. The man who looked at her so warmly now seemed anything but.

"The light still bothers my eyes a bit, but I suppose that's to be expected," Amanda replied.

"For a day or two. It's nothing to worry about. I understand from Tomlinson that you are a great reader. But you mustn't strain your eyes while you are recuperating," he warned.

"Oh . . . I can't read?" Amanda asked, sorely disappointed. How would she amuse herself alone up here all day?

"My word . . . what a look! One would think I'd said you couldn't eat," he laughed. "Don't worry, Miss Kendall. Andrew is quite a proficient reader. He'll come and entertain you. It will be good practice for him. . . . I might come and read to you myself," he added.

Amanda was surprised. "You mustn't go out of your way on my account, Mr. Whitcomb. I'm sure you have better things to do."

"Let me be the judge of that," he said with mock severity.

Amanda smiled in response. The effect of his nearness was so disconcerting, she felt light-headed all over again. She could recall thinking that David Whitcomb's looks were more impressive than his brother's. That was partly due to the difference in their ages, of course. But she did not recall feeling so attracted to the man. Yet her attention to him just now was almost over-whelming. She told herself that it was merely the fever's lingering effects. But as David reached over and gently fingered a lock of her hair, she knew it was not her illness that made her heart-beat quicken so.

"I see Becky has been taking good care of you. I like the way your hair looks, combed down around your shoulders like that." He gently smoothed back a strand that had fallen across her cheek. "It's such an unusual color, your hair," he commented thoughtfully. "It's got red and gold, and even a kind of whiskey color, all mixed together. It was the first thing I noticed about you when you stepped off the ferry."

Even though he had leaned back in his seat a safe distance away, Amanda struggled to regain her composure. Was he being so attentive and paying her these compliments because he admired her, she wondered? Or, did he speak to everyone who worked in his household in such a candid manner? She was quite a bit younger than he. Perhaps he felt it was his duty to amuse her, the same way he might amuse Nelda if she were confined to her bed.

"I've been told that I have my mother's coloring," Amanda replied finally. "I've only seen pictures of her though, so I couldn't say for sure."

"Yes—Tomlinson wrote me about that. How sad for you never to have known your mother," he said, quite sympathetically. "But I must admit, it was part of the reason I hired you. I knew you would understand why I am so concerned about having the right type of governess tend to my children. They not only need a sound education, but a special kind of warmth and care that has so far been lacking in their lives." He smiled, and his brooding features were remarkably brightened. "Andrew and Nelda are quite eager to have you up and about again. It's all we can do to keep them away from this door so that you can get your proper rest."

"I can't wait to begin spending time with them. Perhaps you can send them in later to visit me."

"We'll see," David said, giving the idea some consideration. "If they're careful not to tire you out . . . My cousin, Sarah, who lives with us, is also looking forward to meeting you. But that introduction will have to wait until you are feeling stronger."

"Sarah?" Leaning back against the snowy white pillows, Amanda blushed as David lifted the corner of the napkin and dabbed at her chin.

"She is my mother's sister's daughter," he explained. He had picked up the bowl of broth again and offered her another spoonful. "You'll meet her in time, but I must prepare you. Although Sarah is highly intelligent, she can't speak. When we were children, we were told she was deaf and dumb—but dumb she is not. Of course, as a child, my brother and I took the word literally. We'd heard our cousin was dumb, so we thought she was stupid. Nobody told us . . . I hope you won't think I have a strange way of bringing up my two, while we're on that subject. I don't believe that children should be seen and not heard. Of course, I want them to learn proper behavior. Manners and all that . . ." Amanda had to smile at the plainly irreverent attitude he had toward the subject. "I understand from Tomlinson that your father allowed you to speak up without being discourteous and I was most impressed with your backround in languages and literature. You see . . ."

Although she was listening attentively, David cut himself off abruptly. Becky had just entered the room and was making herself busy, arranging the silk comforter at the foot of Amanda's bed.

"But I must be tiring you, Miss Kendall. We'll have plenty of time to discuss these matters soon." He was about to put the soup bowl down when Becky appeared at his side and took it from him. "Thank you, Becky," he said to the maid. He got up from his chair and motioned for her to sit

there. "I'll go now," he said to Amanda. "If I may,
I'll bring the boy and girl after you've rested
again."

Becky held the spoon while Amanda nodded.
"Of course. I'm most anxious to know them, and I
do feel very well. But it's quite safe? I don't even
know what made me sick. They're not in danger of
catching my disease?"

"Some of the bad water you drank on your
travels, no doubt. It's said it causes swamp fever.
But if one regains one's strength within three
days, all is well." He frowned. "Too often, a
sickness such as yours ends in death. I'm glad
you're recovered, Miss Kendall." He gave her a
serious look, followed by a pleasant smile and left.

During the next two days, Amanda began to look
upon her recent illness as a mixed blessing. Her
upbringing kept reminding her that she had
caused everyone a great deal of inconvenience,
which upset her. Somehow, she felt as though her
body had betrayed her at a time when she'd
wanted to appear at her very best. Yet there were
certain rewards in being confined to her room for
a few days longer; in that way, she was able to
meet each member of the household on a one-to-
one basis. After they left her room she had time to
think about them in solitude and sort out her
impressions at leisure.

Most important to her were the children, ten-
year-old Nelda and twelve-year-old Andrew. They
proved to be as charming as her first, feverish
impression. Andrew had inherited the tall, lean
body that apparently ran in the Whitcomb family.
His hands were beautifully shaped, with long,
tapering fingers that immediately made Amanda
wonder if he'd been given instruction in music or
in other artistic pursuits. When she asked him if

he liked music or drawing, he sighed and said a shade sullenly that Nelda was the talented member of the family. "She plays the harp, you know, like her mother. But I like to do plays."

"Do plays?" Amanda was sitting by the window feeling pampered in a great, soft chair with a matching footstool.

The boy's eyes sparkled. "Yes. I want to be an actor man. My papa takes me to Louisville sometimes. It's only across the river—remember, when you came across on the ferry? Well, they have a theater there, and I go to watch them play-act. I made up a play of my own, too. All by myself. We were going to do it for you, Nelda and I, when you came—but then you got sick, so we couldn't do it. We can do it pretty soon, though, when you're well. Nelda will play the harp while I do the narration. Then we'll—but I don't want to tell you about it because then you'd know what's going to happen."

Amanda's heart quickened. It was a joy to look into those great big liquid brown eyes and see all the different expressions that came and went with such speed. The boy had a face that reminded her of paintings by the old masters with his sensitive mouth, dark, wide-apart eyes and oval face. One of her own favorite amusements was the theater, and she made up her mind to encourage young Andrew all she could if she met with no objection from his father. "And does your papa like your plays, Andrew?"

"Sometimes he does. But sometimes he doesn't have time. I don't think he likes to hear Nelda play the harp because it makes him sad. You know. When he hears the music it reminds him of her mother, who died. But then, sometimes he *does* like to hear her play it. Otherwise, why would he ask her to play songs for him in the evening after supper? It's most confusing.''

She plays the harp like HER mother . . . it re-minds him of HER mother, who died. Andrew's words, carelessly spoken, pounded at her consciousness. Uncomfortably, because she was opposed to asking children questions that she felt were better put to an adult, Amanda heard herself saying, "Then your mother and Nelda's mother were not the same?''

"Oh, no. My mother died when I was very little. I remember her, though. I've a miniature of her in my room. Shall I get it for you? Then there's a painting of her in the great hall. There's one of Nelda's mother there, too. But you aren't quite well enough to go down the steps yet, are you? So I'll just run and get the little picture for you." The boy darted from the bedroom and was back immediately. He held the picture out to Amanda with a proud smile. "She was very beautiful, wasn't she? I remember when she combed her hair. It was long and black and shiny. She could sit down on it." He laughed, and spoke of other memories of his mother. "She always wore a lilac scent. Sometimes I go into her room and I think I can still smell her in there. Nelda's a scaredy-cat. But *I'm* not afraid of my own mother like she is *hers*," he said in a childishly proud voice. "Dead people can't hurt you, and even if they could, what's there to fear from my own mother? Still and all, sometimes I get all goose-pimply when I think she might still be in there in her room. But I've never seen her. Papa says I can smell the lilac perfume only because she was in there for such a long time—he says I don't remember her, too. That I was too little when she died. But I do remember her.

"Papa couldn't bear to have anything changed. He wouldn't let anybody take anything away from her room, and I'm glad. But Uncle Lochard said it was a sign of madness to keep everything around for both wives as though he expects them to come back." Andrew's laugh, sudden and shrill, came as a shock. Then he added in a light, teasing vein, Besides, Papa would have a hard time of it if two wives came back from the dead. Which one would he choose? My mama would never allow him to have two wives like men do in some places. She was half Italian you know, and half French. Papa says she was explosive sometimes, but I think it amused him when she stamped her little foot and lost her temper." He walked across the room and picked up Amanda's hair brush, and his next words left her speechless. He spoke like an adult, and the words and tone of voice sounded vindictive. "Nelda's mother was named Charity. She didn't have it in her to get mad at anybody. Too stupid, I'm afraid."

Amanda's hand clutched the gilt-edged frame of the ivory miniature. All the time the boy had spoken she had continued to look into the pure, classical features of the portrait. It was easy to see where Andrew had inherited his perfect features. His mother had been a great beauty with her dark hair piled on top of her head, her enormous dark eyes and her firm, yet sweetly curving mouth. But in spite of the softness, the artist had captured, there was a subtle haughtiness in the woman's expression, she thought. And again she was stricken at the remarkable resemblance between mother and son. Before she answered him, she thought out very carefully what she was going to say, sensing a vulnerability in the twelve-year-old boy in spite of his offhand remark about Nelda's mother.

"She was very beautiful, Andrew. And you resemble her very much. I'm sure she wouldn't want you to say Nelda's mother was stupid, for such remarks are cruel. Your mother doesn't look as though she were a cruel woman."

"Cruel?" Andrew quirked one eyebrow and grinned. "Oh, no. She wasn't cruel. It was just that she was strong-minded and brave. She didn't want anybody else to be mistreated, either. You know my papa buys the servants at the auction in Louisville, don't you?"

"Buys the servants?" Such an idea had not occurred to Amanda, although the servants were all brown or black, and she'd known, of course, that America was involved in slavery. There were few blackamoors in the part of London where she'd lived, but she'd gone to lectures against human bondage. Her father had been an avid abolitionist, and she had shared his views. It struck her that she should have known she would encounter the horror of slavery in America, but until that moment she had not thought of it. She remembered that both Lochard Whitcomb and David had referred to the staff as "servants," not "slaves." Yet she winced at the appalling idea of her employer standing in front of an auction block and bidding for blacks like those newspaper cartoons she'd seen of such vile practices.

Andrew laughed. "You've lost all the pink in your face, Miss Kendall. And your eyes are big as saucers. But don't worry. After my papa buys them he gives them their freedom." He lifted his chin proudly. "And what I was going to tell you is, it was my mama who figured out a way he could do it, too. Hah! Nelda's mother didn't care a whit about the poor slaves. All she wanted to do was sit close to my papa and look at him and smile so she could show her silly dimples. And play the harp for him. She couldn't even *read*!" This time there was no mistaking the contempt the child held for his stepmother's memory.

"Everyone doesn't have an opportunity to learn how to read, Andrew," Amanda said mildly. "Especially ladies. Many men believe it isn't necessary for a girl to have an education. But you must admit that your stepmother was capable of learning. It takes a great deal of talent as well as perseverance to learn to play a harp."

"Talent is not the same thing as intelligence," said the child. "My papa told me that, and he ought to know."

Amanda handed the miniature of Andrew's mother back to him, her mind whirling. From the moment he'd first said the name, *Charity*, she'd wanted to scream. Becky had refused to discuss the incident concerning a ghost Amanda had supposedly talked about during her illness, although she'd volunteered the information herself. Until that moment when Andrew spoke the name of Nelda's mother, she'd not been sure a woman named Charity had existed. When she'd grumbled at Becky, tried to question her, the maid gave her a sullen look and said she didn't want to talk about "shades." So although Amanda wanted to learn more about Nelda's mother, she felt it wiser to let Andrew speak his own mind, come back to the subject of Charity without her prompting. The child was clever as well as sensitive. She couldn't allow herself to ask questions that would arouse his suspicions, or worse, cause him to become fearful of the walking dead. In order to take her own mind off her burning curiosity, she deliberately replaced the question in her mind by wondering if the boy made the girl's life miserable by his constant reference to her mother's inadequacies. She sincerely hoped not, and made up her mind to put a stop to such behavior if that were the case. "What was your mother's given name, Andrew?"

"Celeste Andrea Marie. I have her second name, except I'm a boy, so it got turned into Andrew. My middle name is Mason, after my Grandfather Whitcomb. He was a soldier during the Revolutionary War. I bet he killed a lot of the bloody English."

Amanda was reminded of her position. "Andrew, we do not use swear words."

The boy pierced her with a mocking, deliberately daring expression in his almost black eyes, but his words were all innocence. "Bloody? Is that a swear word?"

"You know full well it is," she retorted. "Look. You'll not be able to wind me around your little finger, my boy." And his expression turned instantly contrite, then his face became wreathed in smiles. Again she was surprised at his adult-like ability to say the expected words and choose the perfect facial expression.

"Just testing you out, Miss Kendall. You can't blame a lad for trying. I say—must I always call you Miss Kendall? I've told you lots of things, so I think it's only fair that you tell me your first name."

"Amanda. If you like, you may call me Miss Amanda, but we must not forget our manners." In spite of her earlier puzzlement, she found herself melting under another fresh onslaught of his charm, during which time he told her how glad he was that she was there, how he had longed to get back to lessons.

"Even Nelda wants to learn. We've missed having someone to read with us and teach us things. We shall have wonderful times together, and you'll love Whispering Hills, I promise," he said as he left the room.

Becky, she learned quickly, was obviously putty in the hands of the children and their father. Without probing, Amanda found out that all of the servants looked upon David Whitcomb as a combination prince and savior. Becky had been born on the plantation, which explained her ease with English, as well as her tendency to disregard the social barriers between her employer's family and herself. At times Becky slipped into a regular patois, especially when excited or overwrought. Amanda found this out when Becky told her about David and Lochard Whitcomb's father.

"He was a hard man, Miss. No, what he really was . . . was a mean old devil! Used a free hand with the whip, too. Killed my father and two other slaves on that same day, mad as a hornet because the rains came before they got all the crops in. But after the young Master took over, all that changed. My man and I live in our little house and Master Whitcomb pays us wages," she said proudly. "Cash money, just like all the rest of the niggers. Even the fiel' han's is free to go off if they wants to, but they doesn't. They go across the river into Kentucky, they likely to get theirselves hung. They go north, they apt to get hung, too. Here, they don't have to do nothin' but work reg'lar and gets paid reg'lar. Do what they want with their money. Fix up the house—things like that. Us niggers just like anybody else; we don't have no grand place like this-here one, but we plenty well off, me and my man Jimson. Oh, Missy, they treats niggers *bad* most places. Killin' and buyin' and sellin'—my ole mammy tole me it almos' as bad to get bought or sold as to die! An' there's plenty of them white devils that pleasures their nigger women and has babies by them, then sells *them*, too! 'Course, some of 'em makes their own little babies into house slaves, but it shows you what kind of meanness is borned and bred into their bad ole bones, them gittin' little nigger babies and sellin' them off like they was hogs!''

Becky's earlier attempts at behaving herself and pretending to be lady-like quickly melted during Amanda's convalescence. When Amanda objected to some of Becky's colorful expressions, the servant merely chuckled tolerantly. "Oh, lawsy, Missy, what difference do it make what you calls it?''

"The children," Amanda pointed out. "Surely you don't use such words around Nelda and Andrew!''

Becky's rich hearty laughter rang out. "Them little dickenses—they knows plenty of words. They don't need to learn any from *me,*" Becky said in her own defense.

"And I don't *either,*" Amanda wanted to reply. She wanted to protest that she'd been a sheltered young lady. It upset her when Becky said outlandish things in her presence. But she didn't mention her distress, just as she held her tongue when she wanted to ask Andrew more about her employer's second wife and how she had died. Because she could never quite get the crazy woman's words about murder out of her mind, any more than she could completely disregard the possibility of a ghost in the house.

One at a time, the rest of the servants were brought up to Amanda's sickroom by Becky and introduced. There was Flora, the cook, whose husband was named Herbert. Flora was chocolate brown and weighed at least fourteen stone. She kept her hair covered in a snow white linen turban. Herbert stood at a discreet distance from Amanda's chair, a tall, slender man with grizzled hair and skin so black that it had a bluish tinge. Matilda, who was fifteen and inclined to something Becky called "flipperty ways," was giggly, pale bronze and lovely. She had hair that was almost straight instead of nappy, and when Amanda looked into her eyes she was startled to see that they were the same clear blue as a summer day. Matilda was the upstairs maid. Faylodene, who looked halfwitted and sluggish, took care of the downstairs rooms along with several younger girls. Faylodene had a new baby ever nine months, Becky informed Amanda, all of them by different men on the place, mostly the "han's."

"Hans?" Amanda, perplexed, repeated the strange new word, one of many.

"You know. Fiel' han's. They works in the fiel's and lives in the compound, a bunch of wuthless no-good skonks if they ever was any," said Becky indignantly. "Shifflesses' niggers ever lived on the face of this earth! Not wantin' to get ahead, live in they own house like somebody. They spends all they money on corn likker and trim."

"Becky, you must speak more clearly. I don't understand half the words you use," said Amanda weakly.

"Shif'less, that means no-account. Sets aroun' when they not workin'. They gets them some jugs of likker then strum on ole strings to make music. Dance and get dronk as skonks."

Amanda worried endlessly about the child, Nelda, during those days she spent getting her strength back. One afternoon as she looked down on the bright green lawn under her window, she was distressed to see her charges engaged in a fist fight. Andrew was taller than Nelda, but the little girl was quick and she was obviously enraged. Her pretty little face was bright red and her small hands were flying. Fingernails raked Andrew's face across his cheek. Andrew howled and shoved his sister to the ground, but the little girl jumped up and raked the boy again across the other cheek. At the same time her other hand grabbed a hank of hair and pulled mightily.

Amanda leaned out the window, commanding the children to stop fighting, but her voice was lost in their wild, screaming taunts. The cook came dashing out of the house and pulled the children apart, her deep voice shouting all kinds of threats as she did so. To Amanda's open-mouthed astonishment, sweet Nelda screamed swear words at her brother that would have been more fitting to fall from the lips of a harlot. Andrew's answer was equally vulgar, and the cook shouted angrily, "You little varmints stop that cussin', you *knows* them is bad words! What's y' new gov-ness gonna think of you if she hears dirty words like that?"

As the cook led both children into the house, Amanda saw that Andrew's cheek was bleeding from Nelda's fingertips. Shaken, she wondered how in the world she would cope, and remembered Lochard's warning that they were undisciplined—something she felt was an understatement. For her point of view, it just wouldn't do for children to grow up in such a wild, rowdy environment where they overheard swear words and other unsuitable talk from the servants.

She decided to speak to David Whitcomb as soon as possible about her concerns. Ever since he had visited her room the first day her fever broke, he had made a habit of coming by in the early morning to check on her recovery. Sometimes his visits were very brief, and they only exchanged a word or two. More often than not, however, he found the time to sit and talk with her in that same quiet, candid way he had the very first day. There was no doubt in her mind of his intelligence. Further, he'd shown her a glimmer of his sense of humor and his great love and understanding of his two children; and he'd pleased her by talking of literature, a common bond. He'd also interested her by speaking of political affairs. He seemed to enjoy it when she expressed her opinion on such matters, or merely related her impressions of "outlandish" America. Amanda found it amazing that they never seemed to be at a loss for lively, interesting conversation.

Once Amanda was well enough to leave her room, David offered to take her out into the garden for short walks in the morning air. Looking back, Amanda was now willing to admit that these walks had been a very treasured part of her day. Though, at the time, she never would have admitted the extent of her growing feelings for her employer. They would walk slowly along the carefully groomed gravel paths, David pointing out various flowering shrubs and native plants that Amanda had never seen before.

Although their conversation drifted from one topic to the next, they spoke of the children most frequently. David was concerned about preparing them for the future. "This country is an entire new world. A disorderly world," he had told her one day. "In order to have what they need—even to *keep* what they have—they must be well educated and strong willed. Encouraged to think for themselves."

Amanda had to agree that it was very important for the children to develop sound moral judgment and an independent will.

"Yes—I imagine you'll be an excellent instructor on both those subjects, Miss Kendall." David graced her then with one of his rare smiles. "You seem to have such a composed, logical way about you. Quite rare in a woman. 'Horse sense' they call it in this country. And as for an independent nature, your journey alone from England has proved that. A considerable feat, wasn't it?"

Amanda smiled too. "Sometimes I think if I'd known how hard the journey was going to be, I never would have undertaken it."

"But you are not sorry that you've here now, are you?" he asked quickly. Amanda thought she had detected a note of alarm in his tone. At first, she was flattered. Then she chided herself for thinking in such a silly way. As if David Whitcomb were some young country squire who had come to call on her after Sunday service. He was her employer. His concerns were for the well-being of his children. He was obviously afraid that once she regained her full strength she might decide to return to England and leave him without a governess.

"I have no thought of returning to England, if that's what you mean, sir," she assured him. "The beauty of this place aside, I have grown quite attached to Nelda and Andrew. Now that I'm here, I won't abandon them. That would be most irresponsible, I think."

"I'm afraid that I have offended you now, Miss Kendall." David Whitcomb stopped walking and looked down at his boots, his brow creased with concern. Amanda could not help but notice just then what a strong, fine profile he had. Like that of a marble Roman statue she had once seen in London's National Gallery. His lashes too were incredibly long and thick for a man. They served to make his dark eyes look even more mysterious, as if they were filled with secrets. "Please forgive me," he said, turning the full force of those dark eyes upon her.

"Of course . . ." She didn't quite understand why he should show such concern over the matter.

"I imagine that you do miss your home though.

It's only natural." They had reached a small foot bridge and he took her hand to help her over. "You can tell me if you do," he added.

"Sometimes I do miss England," she admitted. "Not often, but . . . sometimes." David Whitcomb had a most uncanny way of drawing the truth out of her, she realized. Or perhaps it was the warm pressure of his hand on hers that had made her speak so heedlessly.

Although they had crossed the bridge he continued to hold her hand. "We will do everything in our power to make you feel welcome here."

"But you have been so kind already, Mr. Whitcomb. I didn't mean it that way at all."

"I know exactly what you meant, Miss Kendall," he assured her. "But I can't impress it upon you too strongly . . . I want you to think of Whispering Hills as the place where you belong now. This is your home."

Amanda truly believed David Whitcomb meant every word he had said. It seemed more than the concern the master of the house should show a mere governess. But Amanda brushed such questions aside. It was just that the children had gone so long without a stabilizing force in their lives. He wanted to be sure that with Amanda's arrival, they had finally found one.

It was a few days after this conversation that she told him of the squabble she had witnessed between Nelda and Andrew. From the look on his face, she gathered that it wasn't the first time such behavior had been reported to him.

"I have warned them time and again about fighting. Andrew is older. He should know better than to behave in such a manner."

"It was very difficult to say who started it." Amanda didn't wish to lay all the blame on

Andrew unfairly. "I believe they need attention more than discipline, and someone to set a good example for them." Without looking up at him, she added, "Surely you can't be unaware of the rivalry between them?"

"Rivalry?" He stood at her side and she was very conscious of his warmth, of his commanding presence.

In a faltering voice she forced herself to speak what was on her mind. He had never once mentioned his two marriages, and Amanda had certainly felt it was not her place to bring up such a topic. But now, the issue seemed unavoidable. "Mr. Whitcomb—some children compete in horsemanship or foot races. But Nelda and Andrew seem bent upon battering one another over the relative merits of their respective mothers. Andrew, in particular, seems resentful of your second wife. Was there any reason for him to dislike her? May I ask you about the circumstances of your remarriage?"

"Oh." To Amanda's unease, a smile was in his voice as he spoke, just as though she had never mentioned the awkward topic of his two wives. "There was nothing unusual about my second marriage."

"Mr. Whitcomb. I'm sure you must realize that people gossip," she said coldly.

He shrugged. "Surely *you* must realize, Miss Kendall, that you can't believe everything you hear. I was lonely, and my son needed a mother."

"But your second marriage must have come indecently close upon the heels of your first wife's death. I'm well aware of the difference between the ages of your children. Or should I say the *little* difference in their ages!"

"Oh. That." Whitcomb stuck his hands in his pockets and whistled tunelessly. "I had a perfectly good reason for acting in haste. Andrew was a sickly child. Has nobody told you this, then?"

"No." In spite of herself, Amanda was interested. Looking back, she could see how eagerly she'd hoped he could explain away her doubts. "I didn't know Andrew had been ill as a young child."

"We thought he'd never make it. I can see that I'm going to have to tell you everything, but right now I can't. My son has just left the house, and within a few seconds he'll be here. There are some things that it's best not to discuss in front of a child. We'll talk together about this as soon as we can."

His words were abrupt, almost cold. Once again, he had taken on the reserved manner she had first encountered upon her arrival. It continually amazed her, the way David Whitcomb could be so warm and open at times and then change so drastically. It made some inner voice whisper a word of warning. *This man is not to be trusted. Don't let yourself fall prey to his charms.*

But as Amanda watched him greet his son with a tender embrace, she knew in her heart that she had already been charmed by David Whitcomb.

He did not come to her room for several days after that meeting. Amanda could not help but feel disappointed when the mornings passed, one after the other, without the sight of his tall, imposing figure in the doorway. She assumed that she must have offended him by bringing up the topic of his past marriages. But she failed to see how it could have been avoided any longer.

One morning after breakfast, Amanda decided she would not sit and wait another minute for David Whitcomb's visit. After Becky had left the room, she took a silk shawl from her trunk and went downstairs. Just because David had not come to fetch her, it didn't mean she couldn't walk in the garden by herself.

She had been strolling the grounds for some time, enjoying the sunshine and crisp air, when she heard a stern voice call out behind her. "Amanda! . . . Miss Kendall . . . what do you think you're doing out here?"

She turned to see David Whitcomb striding angrily toward her. She adjusted the shawl around her shoulders and faced him calmly. "Why walking, sir. Taking some air. It's much too nice a morning to spend cooped up in that room."

"You're not well enough to be outdoors alone. The doctor said . . ."

"But I feel very strong and completely recovered, Mr. Whitcomb," she cut in, not caring to hear once again about the lengthy confinement the overly cautious local doctor had prescribed.

"I am happy to hear you feel so fit, Miss Kendall. But a fever is deceptive. You could grow tired and become ill again outdoors. With no one here to help you. When I came by your room just now, neither Becky nor the children knew where you had gone. I must insist that you do not walk out alone until we are sure you're entirely well."

"Yes—I understand," Amanda said, lowering her gaze. He seemed sincerely concerned about her safety, which touched her. She could not help but feel that she had disappeared almost as a spiteful child would, hoping he would come to fetch her and find her already gone. Now that it had happened just that way, she was sorry. "It's just that I do feel myself again. I am eager to take up my duties, Mr. Whitcomb."

His lips pursed, he looked down at her thoughtfully. "I am sure you are. Maybe you can begin at the end of the week. If I see the doctor in town this afternoon, I will ask his opinion on the matter."

His anger forgotten, he reached out and lightly fingered the rose-colored silk shawl. "Very pretty," he commented. "The shade goes well with your coloring. But are you sure it's warm enough for you?"

Amanda nodded. "I'm very comfortable, thank you."

"Good . . . let's walk a bit then, shall we?" Lightly taking hold of her arm, he led her toward one of their favorite spots in the garden.

"There is something I've been meaning to speak to you about," he began. "But I thought it best to wait until you were well again."

"Please tell me what is on your mind, Sir." She felt alarmed at the serious tone of his voice. She wondered if he would tell her now that her frankness had displeased him during their last conversation and that that was why he had not visited her for so many days. "I feel quite well enough to hear whatever it is you have to say."

"You do, do you?" he replied, now faintly amused at her brave front. "Then I won't beat about the bush. I want you to be my wife, Miss Kendall. To be mistress of Whispering Hills," he bluntly replied. He stopped walking and looked down at her.

Amanda was shocked by his words. In spite of her insistence that she was healthy, she did feel suddenly lightheaded. "You'll forgive me if I seem surprised, Mr. Whitcomb. But I've barely just arrived here. . . ."

"I know it seems precipitous of me. But I believe a marriage between us would be best for all concerned. Especially for the children. It is on their part that I entreat you to consider my proposal carefully. You were right the other day when you observed that they need attention more than discipline, and someone to set a good example for them. I think you are just the person to give them the kind of nurturing they need."

Amanda did recall saying such things. But she hardly thought it an appropriate reason to get married. "You will excuse me for speaking so candidly, but surely you and I don't need to be married for me to give Nelda and Andrew such attention. I consider it part of my job here."

"As it should be, of course," he agreed. "But for how long, Miss Kendall? A year or two at most? They need such attention from a woman like yourself until they are fully grown." He paused and took her hand. "I am not such a fool that I can't see what an attractive woman you are. That is one thing Tomlinson did not warn me of in his letters." He smiled ruefully. "If not by your looks alone, then surely with such a fine mind, you will soon garner many proposals of marriage from the young men hereabouts. Frankly, Miss Kendall . . . *Amanda*," he corrected himself, "now that I have you under my roof, I refuse to lose you so easily."

His words were both thrilling and unsettling to her. She didn't know quite what to say. But the look in his eyes as he gazed down at her demanded some response.

"This is all very sudden. . . . I must agree that it would be in the best interest of the children." She did wish to marry someday. She could never promise David Whitcomb that she would give up the chance to have her own home and husband in order to stay on in this house as a mere employee.

He smiled. "Then you will at least consider my proposal?"

She ran her tongue over her lips and nodded. "Yes—yes, I will," she said, her voice almost a whisper.

He moved toward her then, and taking hold of her slim waist, pulled her closer. Before Amanda had time to realize what was happening, his lips met hers in a searing, passionate kiss. Instinctively, she raised her hand to touch his cheek, her fingertips lightly brushing his thick golden hair.

She had been kissed once or twice before by awkward, hesitant boys. But those experiences did not compare even remotely with this. Feeling herself crushed against David's warm, broad chest, she felt breathless, thrilled to the very center of her being. She found herself responding to the touch of his lips on hers in a way she had never imagined possible.

When they finally parted, David looked down at her. He appeared deeply moved by their embrace, but then quickly masked his feelings with an expression that was impossible to read.

"We had better be getting up to the house now," he said gruffly.

Amanda nodded and raised her shawl on her shoulders. With her arm lightly cupped in his hand, she allowed him to lead her back.

Amanda spent the rest of the day with the children. Their constant chatter and activity provided a perfect distraction from her thoughts about their father's proposal. At times, she found herself fantasizing about being mistress of Whispering Hills, being stepmother to Nelda and Andrew, wife to David Whitcomb. She knew her life would not be perfect. There would be minor difficulties like helping the children to resolve their differences. A more definite problem would be dealing with a trait she had noticed more and more in Andrew—there were times when she knew he wasn't telling the truth. It troubled her each time he spoke of his mother, insisting he could remember her very well. Once Amanda had gently tried to suggest that he didn't really remember his mother; that he just thought he did.

She told him she was sure he had heard so many wonderful things about her that he'd confused actual memory with having overheard pleasant remembrances. Andrew had not grown angry with her, though she'd half expected him to. Instead, he'd look at her with a frown and inform her that she was mistaken.

That afternoon, however, her time with the children had passed quite peacefully. They never seemed to tire of hearing stories about her journey and about England. When Andrew left Amanda's room to ride into the state capital with his father, Nelda seemed pleased to have their governess all to herself.

In spite of what Andrew had said about his half-sister's lack of intelligence, the new governess found her alert and curious, with an amazing understanding.

A few minutes after Andrew left, the adorable little girl turned those beautiful azure eyes on Amanda and asked if she'd like to hear her play the harp. "Papa said he was going to get me a pianoforte. That maybe you could help me learn real notes. But I'd like to show you what I've learned to play on Mama's harp."

"Tomorrow, I plan to come downstairs," said Amanda. "You can play for me then."

"Oh, but I'd like to do it *now!* While Andrew is riding with Papa. When we're by ourselves, Andrew *likes* to listen to the music, but when we're with Papa or anybody else that's old, Andrew gets mad when I play the harp. Then he says ugly things to me and sings silly songs. He's a nasty little show-off. Honestly, sometimes I *hate* that boy! So please have the harp brought upstairs now. I want to see if you like the way I do it without anybody else to bother us."

The lovely child looked so earnest and anxious

that Amanda gave in. Nelda's voice broke pitifully as she spoke, and tears brimmed in her eyes, but they didn't spill down her cheeks. When the harp was brought upstairs and the dimpled, golden-haired child seated herself behind it, Amanda was stricken with an aching sorrow. To think of two little motherless children brought back memories of her own childhood. One time she'd overheard her Nanny say, "A child doesn't miss its mother unless there's a memory of the way it was to have one." The nurse had been talking to a friend, no doubt unaware that Amanda was listening. She'd wanted to cry out that she did miss having a mother. It didn't matter that she couldn't remember how it felt to have the comfort of the loving arms of her own mother around her; what did matter was that she knew other girls had mothers. As a child she had always felt cheated when she saw that special look of love in a woman's eyes for her child.

In a way, she felt just a little closer to Nelda than she did Andrew, probably because of the bond of sisterhood that exists between women even when one is a child and one is an adult. Then too, she was reminded of herself as a child in the lightning-quick way Nelda's moods changed. Like Andrew, Nelda's temperament was unpredictable. Both of the children might change from stormy tears to mirthful joy in the twinkling of an eye, which was similar to the way Amanda had been as a child. But there was something pitiful about Nelda. Sometimes she appeared actually waif-like. It pleased her to learn the child was musical. When her own loneliness had been most unbearable, Amanda had filled her dreary hours with music, which had helped to ease the hungry ache for her dead mother and her seagoing father.

As Nelda played, Amanda found it difficult to

believe that the ten-year-old girl was untrained at
the instrument. Her hands, small as they were,
covered the strings expertly and strummed a
melody what was neither simple nor common-
place. Spellbound, Amanda found herself sinking
into pure feeling to the strains of an aria from, she
was sure, Handel's *Rinaldo*. The overtones were
lilting, sprightly, and Nelda handled the great, six-
and-a-half-octave instrument with ease and grace.
During the first minute or two, Nelda smiled
happily, dimples flashing in her cheeks. She had
absolute control of the harp, which would have
been a stunning accomplishment for a much older
child. Amanda recalled that Mozart had mastered
the piano at six; that other child prodigies were
listed in the history of music. But actually to see a
little child playing a harp like an expert was
breathlessly exciting.

The hairs on Amanda's arms stood straight up.
She had always appreciated the message of music,
but she couldn't get over the age and size of the
child who was able to draw such depths of feeling
from the strings.

"And this is another melody," Nelda said
solemnly. "I don't remember *everything* Mama
played well enough to do it myself, but these are
what I remember best. I think there are words that
go with this one: something about 'the heavens are
telling.' "

The strings sounded again, and Amanda recognized the airy, somewhat folksy sound of Haydn.
Then the message became darker. Again there was
heartache in the message. A quality of sobbing
that was as bleak as the rush of wind through the
willows in winter. Amanda shuddered. She was
reminded of a woman's voice raised in anguish,
desperately lonely and searching. The melody

ended on a haunting note so eerie that Amanda could do nothing but look at the small girl. Finally, realizing that Nelda expected her to say something, she spoke weakly. "And you—you've never had a lesson? Nobody taught you how to make your fingers fly like that across the strings? Why, Nelda, you're marvelous!"

Nelda's eyes sparkled for a moment with pleasure, then went grave. Her next words came as a shock. "That *Andrew!* He won't shut his mouth long enough for me to play for Papa. Or anybody else that's grown-up. He keeps *talking* all the time. Sometimes I just want to *kick* him, the nasty little varmint. That's why I wanted you to hear me play while he's gone." Then the sunny features changed from childish spitefulness to sadness. The soft mouth drooped and the blue, blue eyes turned introspective. "You know that last song I played for you? The one that sounds like a lady crying? Like she's all lost and scared and everybody died and went to the funeral?"

Amanda nodded, knowing she couldn't have expressed the message of Nelda's last song nearly as well.

Nelda's eyes grew narrow. "Well, I'll tell you this! I won't *ever* play that song for anybody unless I like them a whole lot. Because that was the way I felt when my mama got killed."

Amanda spoke through suddenly stiff lips. A cold wind seemed to be blowing across the back of her neck in spite of the warm bedroom. "Killed?"

Nelda's face was contorted with painful memory. "Oh, yes. She got killed. Just like Andrew's mama. Somebody killed them both in their beds at night. They were strangled while they slept. That's why I get so scared sometimes. Would you let me come in here when I get too scared to sleep? I promise not to make any noise or take up too much room in your bed. I'll scootch myself up real little."

3

"Of course you may come to me when you're frightened, Nelda," Amanda said as soon as she could get her breath. By using every ounce of self-control, she was able to keep the grinding terror out of her voice, but she couldn't keep her hands from shaking. On the outside, she felt her flesh shrinking. Under her skin, her muscles and bones felt as though they were melting and falling like blobs of wax on the floor. She swallowed, and continued in a slightly firmer tone. "But surely you must be mistaken about the way your mother died, Nelda. And Andrew's mother, as well. Who told you such a dreadful thing?"

Nelda shrugged. "Everybody knows it. Papa does too. Some folks say he killed them both."

"But people just don't—" Amanda stopped, her voice a croaking protest in her throat. She knew there was no sense in explaining to Nelda that people simply aren't allowed to go around killing two wives and getting off scot-free. She wanted to hurl herself from the chair, dash down the hall, pound down the stairs and leave the house forever. Only the bitter fact that she had nowhere to go kept her from doing just that. Besides, she told herself as she fought to keep down hysteria, she must pull herself together in front of the child. It wouldn't do to go screaming off in mad fright. Because even though Nelda had seemed on the surface to be unruffled by the monstrous idea of her father committing murder, Amanda knew the girl might be pretending. From her own experience, she knew some children are excellent actors.

Nelda sat quietly behind the harp, her big eyes full of woe. Her fingertips swept across the strings. "I shouldn't have told you," she said in a low voice. Then she punctuated her words with a flat chord. *Trummmmmm!* "He said not to tell anyone." Another chord followed the quick rush of words. *Frummmmmm!!*

"Who told you not to tell anyone?" Even as she asked the question, Amanda knew what the answer would be.

"Papa." Nelda looked wistful. Sorrowful. Again she swept the harp strings, using the same morbid chord. *Trunnnnng, trunnnnnngggg, trummmmm!!* "Because he said if you found out you'd get scared and go back to England." *Runnnnnnnng.* "Like that other lady did. She only stayed two weeks." Three more chords, all with a mournful quality that added to the funeral sound of the child's voice. *Dummmmmmm-dai-dawmmmmmmmmmm!* Blue eyes grew stormy and tears spilled silently down rounded cheeks. "I didn't mean to tell you, Miss Kendall. Honest I didn't. The words just kind of slipped out. Would you . . . would you please not tell Papa I told you? Because then he'd be sad. Andrew and I need to have our lessons. But mostly, we just want you to stay." Another harsh slap of the palm of the small hand left the sound of

discord vibrating in the room as Nelda rushed
from behind the instrument and threw herself into
Amanda's arms. "Oh, please! Don't go away! I'm
so lonely and so scared!" Her arms tightened con-
vulsively around Amanda's neck and the small
body jerked as Nelda sobbed brokenly.

Amanda's throat ached with sympathy. She held
Nelda's body close to her breast and spoke soothingly, barely aware of what she was saying. Her
sympathy was strong, and before she thought, she
heard herself promising not to tell Nelda's father
about the accidental slip of tongue.

"But will you stay?" Nelda looked up at her be-
seechingly. Her face was white and tearstained.

Amanda nodded. "Yes, I'll stay. I promise I
won't leave soon. Not for weeks, if I go at all." And
she thought with bitterness that it was an easy
promise. There was no one to turn to—no place to
go.

It took her a while, but finally she soothed away
Nelda's tears by singing and rocking. When
Nelda's long golden lashes at last closed in sleep,
Amanda looked down at the small face against her
breast and wondered if she could find a way to
take Andrew and Nelda with her when she left
Whispering Hills.

After she had placed Nelda on the bed, Amanda
went to the window where she looked toward
Lochard Whitcomb's house. The last few moments
of quiet had brought a little order to her scattered
thoughts, but she was still stabbed with alternate
anger at David Whitcomb, rushes of renewed fear
and a deep sense of despair.

As she looked out of the window in the direction
of his brother's house, her mouth curled in bitterness and shame. *David knew I'd soon find out
about his past two wives and the scandalous circumstances of their death. He went out of his way*

*to put me under his spell with his eloquent words
and grand gestures beforehand. Well, damn him!*

Amanda was shocked at herself for even
thinking a swear word. Even under such trying
circumstances. She clenched her fist in anger. The
fact that she had already begun to care for him
added coals to her burning shame. She felt she had
been taken for a fool.

Time was passing and soon Andrew and his
father would be home, she realized. She was disturbed enough now to take matters into her own
hands. What she was about to do was distasteful
to her, but she reasoned that since Nelda knew the
circumstances of her mother's death and
Andrew's mother as well, everyone else on the
place did. She made up her mind to come out point
blank and ask Becky, the maid. With her shoulders
square and her eyes blazing, she left the sleeping
child.

It had occurred to her that David Whitcomb
must think her downright stupid to believe he
could charm her into marrying him with a shadow
of murder hanging over his head. She made up her
mind what she'd tell him at her first opportunity.
She'd say, "Mr. Whitcomb, it may be the custom in
America to rush into a proposal of marriage less
than three weeks after a lady and gentleman have
met one another; but I consider it an insult for you
to have asked for my hand in marriage so soon.
Especially since you know my background and the
customs in England. But more important, I am
outraged that you think I'm so gullible I would
consider someone who is under suspicion of
having killed his first two wives. Why, you're a
Bluebeard!"

In the keeping room, she found the cook straining honey. "Have you seen Becky?"

"I think she's in the garden, Miss Amanda,"

answered the cook.

"The flower garden?"

The cook's big face glistened and her wide mouth broke into a grin as she laughed long and hard. "Lawsy no Miss Amanda. She's in the veggables. Miz Sarah done took a hankerin' after a mess a beans, and wasn't nobody else to get 'em for her."

"Miss Sarah?" A movement in the dark, cool shadows of the keeping room caught Amanda's attention and she turned, finding herself gazing into a pale, ageless face framed in snow white hair. She knew she must be looking at the cousin David mentioned, and forced a pleasant smile to her face in spite of her agitated state of mind.

The cook went over to the frail woman and put her dark brown hand on the pale white one. With exaggerated mouth movements, the cook spoke. "This here's the teacher for the young'ins, Miz Sarah. You say how-do to Miss Amanda."

Alert blue eyes went swiftly from the cook's broad face to Amanda as understanding dawned. In a voice devoid of expression, the woman said, "How-do-you-do-I-am-glad-to-know-you."

Amanda crossed the stone floor and took papery dry hands in hers. "And I am glad to know you, too, Miss Trueblood."

The cook said, "You gots to git up real close to her, Miss Amanda, she blind as a bat, less'n you close up. She gots to see your lips move. She don' know what you say less'n you moves you lips a whole lot when you talk."

Feeling awkward, yet sympathetic toward the poor woman, Amanda repeated her words as the cook instructed. Then she remained where she was for a few seconds out of politeness, even though she wanted to find Becky and ask about the two dead Whitcomb wives.

It was difficult to carry on a conversation with the deaf-mute woman, especially with the cook interrupting.

"She cain't talk much, Miss Amanda, but she right bright. Trouble is, she get started talkin' and she don' wanna shut up. Lonesome-like, you know. But if you wants Becky, I just saw her go down by the chicken yard. Lemme handle Miss Sarah. I know you is busy."

After Amanda had made an apology to the little woman for being in such a rush, she turned her face away, saddened at the expression of quick understanding in those sad blue eyes. As she strode purposefully in the direction of the chicken yard, she kept seeing the loneliness in those eyes, the message that had come so succinctly in spite of the woman's near lack of verbal communication. "That's all right. I know I'm a chore to be near and probably a bore. But I do wish you'd stay a little longer with me so I could get to know you better."

Becky's yellow dress billowed for a moment at the side of the barn, and Amanda called her name, but apparently the servant didn't hear. She ran through the pasture toward the barn when she saw that Becky was headed in that direction. Again, she called Becky's name, but a cow bawled close by, which probably drowned out her voice, she thought as she hurried to catch up.

Becky seemed to have been swallowed up in the dim, hot vastness of the barn. Amanda glanced around, her nose wrinkling at the smell of manure. The heat was oppressive. She could hear chickens quarreling among themselves, the grunting of pigs, a munching, crunching sound and the restless stamping of a horse. Over all the farm sounds, she could hear voices, and called out again. A great flapping of wings and loud quacks

filled the air as she disturbed a rooster, which had
flown in her face, then a gaggle of geese. Her feet
slipped in straw as she went deeper into the
interior of the big barn. Gradually her eyes
became accustomed to the dimness and she was
about to call Becky's name again, but was stopped
by an enraged shout and several coarse swear
words.

There was no mistaking Becky's voice, even
though it was not sweet and gentle as it usually
was in Amanda's presence. Nor were her words
ladylike. Judging by the angry spill of colorful
phrases, she supposed Becky was talking to her
husband, and that she obviously believed the
husband was guilty of philandering.

"Now, lissen, woman, I ain' 'holden to put up
wid none o' your fat lip. I nebber done no—"

"Talk to *me* about fat lip, will you?" There was a
slapping sound, then Becky's voice shrilled again.
"I show you what a fat lip is, you. Dat's what I do
less'n you settles down and straightens yo'se'f up,
does what I tells you to do."

"Don' hit me again, woman! I had enough sass
out'n you!"

"Shut up! I hit you all I wants to. Beat you silly
head off'n you ape face. You turnin' out like de
rest of dem no 'count niggers that lives in de compound instead of in decent houses like dey got self-
respec'. Here we got us a chance to live good! You
livin' high on de hog, right now, Jimson, and you
do what I say you live better. Whut if you lived
across de ribber in Kentucky? You bought and
sol', bought and sol' till you end up hung, dat's
what. You a bad nigger. Ain't nothin' in this world
worse 'n a bad nigger. And just de other day I say
to Miss Amanda whut a good man you is."

"Becky, now Becky, now look heah, you put dat
pitchfawk *down*, you heah me?" The man's

rumbling voice shot up to a scream.

"You a fancy-footin' it wid dat no-good slut, I fix you good!"

Too stunned to move or speak until then, Amanda stared open-mouthed toward the loft. But when the talk overhead in the haymow turned to such things as the man commanding the woman to put the pitchfork down, she knew she had to do something. Through her mind rushed an unbidden picture of Becky in the act of shoving a pitchfork through her husband's belly. She opened her mouth and screamed. "Becky! Beck-EEEEEEEEEEEEE!"

There was a flurry of sound overhead, then a dull, thumping sound. Fervently, Amanda hoped it was the pitchfork falling harmlessly to the hay. Becky answered, her voice startled, but back to normal.

"Is that you, Miss Amanda? My *lands!* What on earth are you doing out here, and you not long out of your sick bed!" Becky's bare feet appeared, firm on the pegs that ran up the wall to the loft. Then came her ankles and the hem of her yellow dress. When she jumped to the ground not a hair was out of place on Becky's immaculate head. Her face was wreathed in smiles as she spoke with concern for Amanda's welfare. "I'll bet you scared of those old geese. They won't hurt you. Shoooooo-eeee," she yelled as she flicked her apron in the direction of the geese. "Get on out of here." She turned back to Amanda. "My, my, Missy. Not hardly able to be up and around yet, and comin' all the way out here to the barn. You been here long?"

"No," said Amanda. "And I wasn't really afraid of the geese. I just wanted to speak with you about something, Becky, and the cook told me I could find you in the garden." She was so embarrassed over what she'd overheard that she was pleased to pretend she'd heard nothing.

Just inside the barn door, Becky scooped up a pan full of green beans where she'd left them on top of a dusty shelf. Then she put her hand on Amanda's arm and guided her around the rooster. "He's a mean old devil, that red one. Flies up in a person's face and screeches his head off. Now, what did you want to ask me about, Miss Amanda?"

When she was out in the sun again, Amanda was relieved to see a tall, black man come ambling out of the barn when she looked back. She blinked her eyes against the suddenness of the sun, realizing she'd wondered in the back of her mind all along if Becky had run her husband through with the pitchfork before she came calmly down the pegs.

"Uh—about—I think we'd best wait a bit, Becky," Amanda answered.

Intelligent brown eyes looked questioningly into Amanda's gray ones. "You mean my man. You want to wait till he cain't hear us. You see the ghost or something?"

"What ghost?"

"You've not seen it. If you had, you wouldn't be asking 'What ghost.'"

Amanda stumbled over a bumpy ridge in the pasture, and Becky reached out a strong hand and kept her from falling.

"It's about Mr. Whitcomb, Becky. I know you've been here for a long time, and you—I really feel very badly about asking you this, but I don't know anyone else well enough to turn to."

"He pop the question, did he?"

"Yes." Amanda was aghast. She wondered if David had talked over with the servants the possibility of marrying her.

Becky laughed warmly. " 'Bout time. I thought I saw all the signs of a man in love. Time he gettin' himself a wife, too. I told him a long time ago it isn't natural for a man to be without a woman. Twenty-five years old and never married! My, my."

"But . . . Mr. Whitcomb is thirty. And besides, he's had two wives already."

"Oh. You mean Master *David!* I thought you meant Master *Lochard* asked you to marry up with him. He looked like he gettin' ready to. Hung aroun' outside your door when you were sick and all . . ."

"Becky, please! I must ask you to . . . Becky, just stand still for a second. I *must* know how Andrew and Nelda's mothers died. Nelda told me everybody knows they were strangled in their beds at night. And that—her father—might have done it. I just couldn't believe . . . ."

"Just you *don't* believe," said Becky. "That's not the truth, but I know who told little Missy. Master Andrew did. That boy a *sight* how he do make up stories."

Although Amanda was relieved at the servant's words, she still had to ask. "But how *did* they die? What *were* the circumstances?"

There was a definite space of time before Becky answered, and when she did, her voice was reluctant. "That was a bad time around here. A terrible bad time."

Amanda shook the woman's arm. "Is that all you're going to say? You *must* tell me, Becky."

"No ma'am. I mus'n't. You have to ask Master David."

Try as she would to get the woman to say more, she would not and Amanda finally gave up in defeat. She planned to ask David Whitcomb to spend a few minutes with her alone when he came back from Corydon, but she didn't have a chance to do so. Governor Jennings had ridden back to

Whispering Hills with David and Andrew. Amanda met a tall man with thick dark hair and big expressive brown eyes. He had a generous, kind mouth, and when he spoke it was in the manner of a gentleman.

"Miss Kendall has come from England, Governor," said Whitcomb. "We have a mutual friend. You've heard me speak of Jeremy Tomlinson . . . the solicitor was kind enough to find this lovely young lady for me so my children won't grow up in ignorance. Let us go into the drawing room. Miss Kendall is, unlike most women, interested in politics."

A spark of respect shone in the Governor's eyes as he smiled at Amanda. "It's a rare thing indeed to find a member of the weaker sex interested in government."

Amanda wanted to say, "Speaking of government, exactly what are the laws of this strange new land concerning murder?" But instead, she went into the rose drawing room with the two men and forced herself to take part in the conversation. Soon she found herself highly interested. Governor Jennings told her Indiana had been a free state even when it had been a part of the Northwest Territory.

"And exactly what was the Northwest Territory?" she asked.

David Whitcomb took a map from a drawer. With a quill pen, he pointed out Illinois, Indiana, Ohio, Wisconsin and Michigan. "This was the Northwest Territory, Miss Kendall. At the end of the Revolution, this parcel was received into the Republic. Opposition to slavery became general around 1805, before Indiana was a state."

It was pleasant to be in the company of learned men again, and Amanda was reminded of many such times in her own home, before her father

died, when guests of all stations in life were
frequent visitors. She learned even more about the
question of slavery, and for a half hour or more
she almost managed to put her agitated thoughts
out of mind. Lochard Whitcomb, who had been on
a trip to Cincinnati, returned and stopped by the
big house before going on to his own place. David
asked his brother to stay for supper, and Amanda
excused herself so she could dress appropriately
for the occasion. A general flurry of excitement
was all through the house, which she assumed had
to do with the Governor's presence.

While she dressed, spending more time than
usual over her toilette, she realized she was
pleased and a little excited herself. Somehow,
knowing David was a good friend of Governor
Jennings helped to calm her. She told herself it
was doubtful that a man of Mr. Jennings' stature
would continue to befriend a wife-murderer.
Besides, she'd learned they'd known one another
since early childhood; so it followed that the
Governor probably knew the circumstances of the
Whitcomb deaths. Still, the nagging mystery in the
house continued to fret her.

David had asked her if she would act as hostess,
however, and she was too well bred to allow
herself to even contemplate bringing up a
personal matter after dinner. Governor Jennings
would remain at Whispering Hills overnight,
which meant she would be forced to spend a night
worrying and wondering, but she was determined.
Tomorrow she would throw her manners aside
and demand to know the truth.

When she was on her way down the gracefully
curving staircase, Lochard Whitcomb stood at the
bottom looking up at her. His handsome face was
lighted with a smile, and he held a package in his
hand. "I brought gifts for the children, and I

brought one for you, too. Please open it now. They have theirs already, of course." The candelabra, already lighted with candles, shone down on his hair and burnished it an even brighter shade of chestnut. "I'm afraid I have quite spoiled my brother's children. They know their Uncle Lochard's pockets are always filled with gifts when I return from a trip." His voice changed subtly, and became more intimate. "Someday I hope to have children of my own."

Amanda looked up into his marvelously expressive eyes and felt her heart turn over. When she opened the package he'd put in her hands, she gazed in wonder at the beautiful string of pearls that gleamed from a velvet-lined box. "Oh! I can't —accept—a gift like this," she said. In her own jewelry box she had a pearl ring, left to her by her mother. These were exquisitely matched and glowed with the inner radiance of authenticity.

"Of course you can accept them," said Lochard. "You must wear them tonight. They'll look just right with your beautiful gown. We'll say this is a small token of my pleasure in seeing you well again."

"No, I simply can't accept . . ." Amanda cut herself off, aware of David Whitcomb, who just then opened the door from the library. His eyes glanced from Amanda to his younger brother, and his expression was inscrutable. "Oh, Lochard," he said, "Jonathan and I were just discussing the land you're interested in up around Paoli. Won't you join us? You, too, Miss Kendall, if you'd like. You look lovely, my dear."

His voice seemed a shade annoyed, she felt, as she murmured that she wanted to check on the children. Actually, she'd suddenly remembered seeing a family Bible in the rose drawing room, and on the spur of the moment she decided to see

if there was a record of births and deaths. Lochard
withdrew to the library while Amanda ran lightly
upstairs to put the pearls in her room. She knew
she could not accept the necklace, but there would
be a time to return it properly. For just a second,
she looked at herself in the blue green gown and
held the pearls against her throat before she
returned them to the box. She was thinking of the
crushed look that had come over Lochard's face
when his elder brother spoke to her in a
proprietary manner.

Back downstairs, she felt it was a good time
indeed to look inside the family Bible. The household staff would be gathered in the kitchens,
putting the last touches on dinner. Her employer
and his brother were talking to Governor Jennings
in the library, and the children were eating their
supper in the nursery. She had already told them
their bedtime story, admired the toys their Uncle
Lochard had brought them from Cincinnati, and
bade them good night.

Without making a sound, Amanda crossed down
the great hall and turned right into the rose
drawing room. No candle had been left burning, so
the room was in near darkness. For a second, she
was afraid to light a candle, knowing someone
could walk in the room and catch her snooping.
But she rationalized that if someone did unexpectedly come upon her, there would be nothing
wrong in her looking at a Bible. She groped
toward a table where she knew a candle waited in
a holder and searched around with her fingertips
until she found a flint. When the taper burned
yellow, she gasped as she saw a face across the
room, then almost laughed out loud in nervous
relief as she realized she was seeing her own
reflection in a mirror.

The first Bible she opened was in German, a

language Amanda was unfamiliar with. She dropped it quickly on the rocking chair and reached for the other one. Holding the candle close to the back pages where she found handwriting, she skimmed over the first notations, disinterested for the moment in past generations of Whitcombs. It didn't take long for her to find what she wanted.

The records had been faithfully kept in a neat, but flowing script. Andrew was born in 1805. He was two when his mother died in January of 1807. Charity married David Whitcomb in March of 1807. Nelda Ruth was born less than three months later, on May 23, 1807.

Even though she's suspected to find just about what she did, Amanda couldn't ignore the ache in her heart at seeing everything written out in black and white. She wasn't exactly clear about how babies are conceived, but she knew how long it took for one to get ready for birth. Therefore, she thought with accelerated breath and pounding heart, it was reasonable to assume that Nelda had been on her way *before* Celeste died. A six-month infant had very little chance of survival. Amanda had known of babies born just a month or two prematurely and they'd expired. *And they're tiny when they come early,* she thought as she stared at the registered weight of Nelda Ruth. Nelda had weighed eight and a half pounds, obviously a full-term infant. *Well, he shan't marry me, and have me on my death bed while he's carrying on with another woman,* she thought indignantly.

The silver candle holder made a loud thud when she put it down. She closed the Bible and returned it and the one printed in German to the round, marble-topped table where it had been, then bent to blow out the candle. Her mouth was pursed and she'd drawn in her breath in order to expel it, when she heard a low moan and simultaneously felt a cold breeze blow across her back. She turned, looked over her shoulder and made sure nobody was in the room with her. Although she didn't believe it, she tried to convince herself the moan had come from outside the room, the cold breeze caused by the opening of another door somewhere in the house that had caused a draft. Again, she bent over and started to blow out the candle. A movement seen from the corner of her eye caused her to turn her head in that direction, but she remembered being startled at her own reflection when she'd first entered the room. Then, with hammering heart and a dry mouth, she realized that the mirror was now in back of her. It had been to her left when she'd first entered the room.

There was a rustling sound then, like dry leaves, she thought as she fled. Or taffeta skirts. Her knees were knocking and she was so weak with the terror that gripped her that she had to cling to the doorframe for support. The hall was just as it had been when she'd gone into the rose drawing room, brightly lighted by the great candelabra that hung from the ceiling. She wanted desperately to gather enough strength to cross into that brightly lighted, friendly hall instead of standing there clinging to the doorframe. Her back prickled and she felt as though eyes were looking at her malevolently from the room she'd just left. Cold sweat was on her forehead, and her backbone felt weak as water. Slowly, very slowly, she forced herself to take a step toward the hall, willing her legs to hold her up as she let go of the doorframe.

The chill breeze came again. Involuntarily Amanda looked over her shoulder. She saw the glimmering form of a young woman. It glided across the room from the fireplace, misty, yet almost lifelike. A crown of golden hair glowed for an instant; then the wispy, disembodied form disappeared. Just before the cloud-like image dispersed completely, the candle Amanda had left burning toppled over, sputterd against the Bible she'd just held, and went out.

4

The wave of terror that gripped Amanda was so great that for a moment she staggered, clutched at the doorframe, and felt the floor reel under her. She had never been prone to swooning spells during times of stress although most of her female acquaintances fainted away at all sorts of incidents that ranged from seeing a mouse to overhearing something scandalous. In spite of her recent illness, she refused to give in to the beckoning spiral of darkness that loomed all around her and threatened to engulf her. She knew she was about to swoon out of sheer terror, but she was determined to not give in to what she had always considered a silly female weakness. With pounding heart and ice cold hands, she remained upright, managed to turn away from the horror in the room and somehow keep the scream that was tearing at her throat from coming out. A second later, she groped her way to the hall and found a chair, where she sat on the edge trembling violently. Amanda had been taught all her life to not give in to impulse. Influenced by her father's code of behavior more than any other, she'd learned at an early age that one simply does not allow dignity to fly out the window. In her mind was the knowledge that a dignitary was visiting Whispering Hills. There were also the children and the servants to consider. If she gave in to the tendency to scream and behave in other ways in a manner she'd been brought up to scorn, she would appear foolish, which was something her father had always disdained. "Foolish women," he'd been wont to say, "are advocates of the devil." He'd spoken those grim words many times during Amanda's early childhood. When she stepped on a spider. When she'd cut her finger with his carving knife. When she had a slapping, hairpulling, scratching fight with another little girl. Her Nanny had disagreed with her father often, saying he wanted to have a daughter who behaved like a boy instead of a girl, but the captain remained firm in his belief that it wasn't necessary to be a weakling just because one happened to be female.

Such memories somehow helped to calm her quaking hands. She even smiled a little ruefully at the idea of seeing a ghost. From the wide range of books she had studied, Amanda had learned something about the strange powers of nature. Her father had always told stories about the eerie— but completely explainable—happenings which were witnessed out at sea. There may have been a very logical explanation for the sights and sounds she had just witnessed, Amanda reasoned. Her nerves were ragged from the events of the day. Her own mind, coupled with a bit of mist blown in by the wind, had conspired to play tricks on her.

Just then Lochard Whitcomb's long shadow fell upon the door of the hall and Lochard himself appeared at the doorway, his handsome face and figure outlined by the candle-lit Rose Room. "Amanda?" His voice was pleasant, yet he spoke her name questioningly. "Amanda! It *is* you. In the darkness of the hall, I wasn't sure. What happened to the sconces? They were burning brightly a moment or two ago."

She forced herself to speak in what she hoped was a normal voice. "A gust of wind blew them out, perhaps. I had just stepped into the library, and the candle that was burning in there went out too."

"Supper will be served momentarily," he said as he offered his arm. "It will be a pleasure to have the presence of a lovely lady at table again in Whispering Hills." He told a passing servant to see to the wall sconces and chandelier in the hall as he escorted her to the dining room. "Did you wear your pearls?"

Her lips felt wooden, and she knew her face must be drained of color. It was an effort to speak of ordinary matters, yet she forced herself to carry on. "Mr. Whitcomb, I cannot accept such a costly gift. It isn't seemly."

Lochard's hand at her elbow moved away. She felt him stiffen, and when he spoke again his voice was angry, although he didn't raise it. "I should have known my esteemed brother would take advantage of my absence. He wasted precious little time with you. The glance the two of you exchanged when I first saw you after I returned was not lost on me." Suddenly he laughed, and put his hand back on her elbow, once again assuming the courtly manners that had attracted her when she first met him. "Ah, well, such things happen to the second son. David has a way with him when it comes to the fair sex. Pray keep the pearls anyway, my dear. You may tell your future husband they were a gift to celebrate your engagement."

Amanda's eyes glittered with anger, and this time she drew away from Lochard's hand upon her arm. "Sir, I find your casual understanding of an engagement between myself and your brother most odious. No such event has taken place; indeed, I would find it most improper to consider marriage to a man about whom I know little or nothing, a man I barely *know!*"

Lochard stopped dead in his tracks and turned her so she faced him. He laughed. Then he said gently, "Forgive me, Amanda. One of my many faults is my tendency to jump to wrong conclusions. However, for the sake of my own good graces in your eyes, I might add that I know David, even though you claim you do not. When it comes to courting lovely ladies, he allows no dust to gather on his boots. Further, it was David who conveniently saw to it that I had business in Cincinnati. Family business, I must admit, but nevertheless it was *I* who was commissioned to go. He's enamored of you, for which I can't blame him. You're a lovely girl, Amanda, and David my brother is a lonely man who was ill-favored twice in marriage. Besides, I saw the way he looked at you there upon the stairs." Lochard was smiling tenderly down at her as he spoke, and suddenly his countenance grew concerned. "Why, Amanda! Your face is deathly pale. Have you become ill again?"

"No, no," she said quickly. "I'm quite all right— I just—perhaps I came down the steps too fast. I've not been up and about very long. But I'm perfectly all right now."

Lochard apologized again, then added, "I'm afraid my loutish behavior contributed to your pale face and trembling hands. I promise,

Amanda, to cause you no consternation in the future."

Relieved and willing to allow Lochard to take the blame for the paleness of her face and the trembling of her hands after her chilling experience, Amanda smiled, accepted his apology and stepped inside the dining room.

A linen damask cloth covered the dining board as always, but in honor of Governor Jennings the cloth was finer and a great deal of care had been lavished on the table setting. The heavy silver service gleamed under hundreds of candles in the chandelier, the wine and water goblets sparkled and the handsome cobalt dinner plates added to the general air of festivity. The Governor and David Whitcomb entered the vast room from the parlor at almost the precise time Amanda and Lochard entered from the Rose Room. Both Governor Jennings and David bowed courteously to Amanda while Lochard seated her at the foot of the table. When the three men were in their places, with Governor Jennings in the seat of honor, David asked Amanda to give the blessing.

She was not prepared, although she realized with a little jolt of her conscience that she should have been. In spite of her surprise at David's request, she felt she had not hesitated long enough, though, to let the gentlemen know she felt at a loss for words.

"Dear Lord, we are grateful to Thee for all Thou hast given us this day, for all the goodness Thou continually showerest upon us, Thy humble servants. We come together in Thy presence to partake of the bounty Thou hath provided in Thine infinite goodness and mercy and we ask that Thou bless this food and bless this house, Almighty Lord, keeping all frail humans from evil, from fear and from those hostile forces of darkness who continually strive to gain control of this, Thy world. These things we ask in the name of Thy beloved Son, Amen.''

After she had spoken of the evil she herself feared, Amanda wished she had not worded the blessing in just that manner, but a glance at her companions' assured her that she'd not unwittingly stirred their curiosity.

Her intentions were simple. She wanted to present an untroubled atmosphere in the dining room. To not introduce any of the horrified thoughts that were settling in her own brain. Simply to get through supper without giving way to dark fears that kept inserting themselves into her mind, then to retire to her room as soon as she could courteously do so. There she would write a letter to dear Mr. Tomlinson and tell him she could not stay in America after all.

During the meal she made some discreet inquiries pertaining to transportation and trembled when the Governor said, "Oh, my dear girl, I'm sure your own recent experience coming overland must have told you this new land is sadly lacking in travel conveyances.''

"Oh, yes,'' she answered quickly. "I found the stage most difficult as well as abominably slow. I was just wondering if I happened to hit upon a bit of bad luck.''

David Whitcomb looked at her solemnly. "You aren't thinking of leaving!''

"Oh, no!'' The lie left her lips in what she hoped and prayed was a convincing manner. "I was just wondering, that's all. I simply cannot see how this land will ever be populated when it's so difficult to get from one place to another.''

"Well, these things take time. America is a big country,'' said Governor Jennings. "And new.''

"And raw," said Lochard unexpectedly. "I'm afraid Miss Kendall has been quite shocked at the uncivilized behavior of many people. Especially on the frontier. Our manners are rough compared with England."

"Perhaps necessarily so," said David. "Here we've little time for the proprieties. If this land is to become a great power, we have no time to spend on any but the most basic graces. Now to dine like this in comfort and friendship is one thing, but to waste time on balls and all the other fancies one may indulge in back in England is too time-consuming for the present. I, for one, would like to see more culture introduced in America. More books, more music. Yet a country still in its infancy is much like a baby—one must learn to crawl before one can walk. We speak of such things as better roads and more efficient means of travel among ourselves, but we must concentrate on taming the land first. As word gets back to the Old Country about what is available in this wonderful land, we'll not lack for immigrants. Then we'll think of the niceties. Although I might add, my dear Amanda, that having you here is a great boost to the morale of the household." He picked up a platter of roast pig. "Even the servants know that a woman in the house will not tolerate an unkempt home, ill-prepared viands. It pleases me greatly to look upon sparkling crystal and a spotless dinner cloth, just as it pleases me to be in the presence of a female who is not only beautiful and charming, but also intelligent. Pray tell us what was taking place in England when you left, Amanda. I'm sure Governor Jennings will be glad to learn firsthand of the politics and economy of the Mother Country."

Grateful to have her mind occupied by conversation, Amanda spoke lengthily about what she knew of England's economy, including the impact of the war Great Britain lost to the Colonies. She blushed when Governor Jennings chided her gently by saying the States were no longer the Colonies, for which she apologized prettily and said, "But in England, many people believe it is only a matter of time before this new land will come back to the sheltering arms of the Mother Country. You see, it's still hard for a lot of thinking men and women to believe the war was really lost to America."

"But we've had our independence for years," objected Lochard. "Great Britain has always had the attitude that no fledgling country can survive. I should think everyone over there would now realize that we're fast becoming a strong nation. In time America will be a real power in the world. Why, this land is *enormous* compared with the size of the British Isles, and our national resources are untapped."

"But mostly unpopulated," said David dryly. "And when you say we've had our independence for years, my dear brother, you're speaking from the mouth of a youth. This is only 1817. Although I cannot say I agree with the attitude of my friends and relatives across the sea that this country will come back home spreading tales of woe, I can well see why the older folk believe we'll never make it on our own. The term, Mother Country, is well chosen. All parents feel threatened when the children leave their nest. England felt threatened by the attitude of the colonists. We turned our backs on parental guidance."

"Parental *guidance!*" Lochard shouted angrily. "Taxation without representation! What England was doing to us was bleeding us blind. And I'm hardly a youth, David. I'm a mere five years your junior. You speak as though *you* were carrying a musket back in '76. Our father did, but you weren't even born at the time."

It was Governor Jennings who gracefully put an end to the sudden burst of words at the table by using his considerable tact. Then he smiled and said he was glad, no gainsaying, that patriotism still bloomed in the hearts of young men. "I understand there is a wave of anti-Nationalism among the younger generation."

"It'll pass quickly enough," said Lochard, "when the young men find themselves suddenly saddled with responsibility."

"Speaking of responsibility, Lochard," put in David softly, "what happened to your romance with Miss Eldridge? I was under the impression that you were seriously considering settling down with a wife. You did see her when you were in Cincinnati, I suppose."

Lochard shot Amanda a look she couldn't fathom, but when he spoke his voice was controlled. "Miss Eldridge has the mind of a poppet and the heart of a knave. I saw her in Cincinnati, of course. And learned something about that young lady I would never have believed if she hadn't told me with her own lips. She prefers to return to Europe to live. Plague take her. I told her it would be good riddance, too, you may well believe. Her reasons for disliking America are of the most shallow nature imaginable. Imagine! She said there are no bon-bons to be had in all of Cincinnati, and every time she goes to shop for dress goods she comes home weeping with dismay because nothing is to be had that she considers suitable. Why, there are plenty of shops in Cincinnati where one may purchase the most elegant satins and silks—velvets, too. I found Miss Eldridge quite boring." After he made this statement, Lochard again turned his handsome hazel eyes on Amanda. "It's refreshing indeed, to meet a lady who thinks of something other than furbelows and fripperies."

Amanda blushed. She now was aware that life in Whispering Hills was impossible for another reason than the fear that the Master had murdered his wives. Another reason, she thought, for leaving before she became too much attached to the children, was the rivalry between Lochard and David. It was obvious that the brothers held dissident views on most everything, and the fact that she would be the center of yet another contention between them was not pleasant to contemplate. It made her uncomfortable to be practically courted in the open by both men, something that would have thrilled her to the core a year or so ago. But she wanted no part of it. As soon as the dinner was over and the men retired to the library to smoke their heathenish tobacco, Amanda went to her room instead of remaining at table alone with her coffee.

Once there, she lit every candle she could find before she sat down to compose a letter to Mr. Tomlinson. As soon as she had penned the customary greeting, she burst into tears and fell across her bed, the resident of her recent terror overcoming her along with a wave of nostalgia for her own country. "I'm homesick," she whispered to the pillow where she buried her head and sobbed.

Some time later, she awakened to the sound of footsteps outside her bedroom, but although she sat up in bed with a pounding heart, she realized no reputable ghost would make such a racket. Then she heard David Whitcomb's voice and knew the hour was not as late as she'd thought. "Good-night, then, Jon. Get a good rest. You'll find a drop or two of rum in your room for a nightcap." Her employer didn't speak in a loud voice, but his natural speaking tone carried extremely well. Amanda didn't hear what Governor Jennings said in reply, but she heard the sound of his voice. Since most of the candles she had lighted earlier had burned down, she decided to get up and put out the rest. While she was padding barefoot across the wide expanse of carpet, she heard what she assumed were David Whitcomb's footsteps in the hall again. They paused in front of her closed door.

She froze where she was, her hand just about to snuff out the faint glow of the one remaining candle in the room, and waited to see if he would knock. If he did, she wasn't sure if she should answer. Not only was it unseemly for a young woman to be alone in her room with a gentleman, but also Amanda admitted her fear of the man to her secret self, although she was woman enough to be almost as excited at his interest as she was fearful of his true nature.

Moments later a soft knock sounded. She reminded herself that certain birds will allow themselves to be charmed by snakes, knowing full well that the snake will destroy them. Yet, that thought was not quite daunting enough to keep Amanda's hand from turning the knob and opening the door.

"I had hoped you would still be up. I haven't disturbed you, have I?"

"I was just writing a letter," Amanda replied. "To Mr. Tomlinson."

"To tell him of our engagement?" David asked hopefully.

Amanda met his gaze, then looked away. She suddenly felt as if the entire household was secretly eavesdropping on their conversation. "I only promised that I would consider your proposal, Mr. Whitcomb. I certainly would not inform Mr. Tomlinson of my consent *before* I informed you."

Amanda expected him to be taken aback by her reply. Instead, he looked merely amused. "You will forgive me for being so presumptuous, but a determined suitor is ever hopeful. Something tells me that you have given the matter further thought though."

"Yes—I have," Amanda admitted haltingly.

David frowned attractively, his dark eyes still lit with amusement. "Oh, my dear . . . judging from the tone of your reply, my prospects don't sound very good."

"Well . . . I . . ." Amanda faltered. She didn't feel comfortable turning down David's proposal standing in the doorway of her room. She wasn't at all sure if this was either the time or the place to try to gather her scattered thoughts.

"Please let me come in a moment and discuss this with you right now." David did not speak with his usual gruff confidence, but a soft, imploring tone that somehow swayed her.

Brushing aside her concerns about the propriety of the situation, Amanda opened the door to him and stepped aside.

He strode into the room and ran his hand through his thick hair in a worried, distracted manner. "I fear that you have been speaking to the servants about me."

Amanda closed the door and faced him. "I have tried . . . but no one would answer my questions," she replied with a frankness equalling his own.

He stared at her a moment, his hands folded behind his back. "The most remarkable thing about you, Miss Kendall, is that you don't quite realize *how* remarkable a woman you are."

"I am only trying to be honest with you, sir."

Even in the midst of such open conflict, the way he had of looking at her stirred something deep and undeniable. Instead of staring straight into his eyes, Amanda looked down the carpet again.

"Well, honestly answer me this then—what are these questions you have about me? It's about my past marriages, isn't it?"

"Yes, it is."

"Well, go on," he urged her, the slight edge of anger in his tone.

Amanda took a steadying breath. David paced the length of the room like a caged tiger. When she finally got up nerve enough to speak, he had his back to her. "The circumstances of their deaths . . . Charity and Celeste . . ." she began. He stopped walking and turned to look at her. She could go no further.

"Afraid to say it?" He smiled grimly. "Then let me do it for you, Miss Kendall," he offered with mock gallantry. "People say that I murdered both my wives in their beds. Strangled them. They are very accurate with the details, these gossiping old fishwives. Or perhaps you have heard a newer, more elaborate version?"

Now that the topic had been brought out into the open, Amanda suddenly felt as if the whole notion of David Whitcomb murdering anybody was just plain ridiculous. If there was even one shred of truth to the story, could he speak in such a detached, almost joking manner about it?

"I would like to hear *your* version of it," Amanda said, meeting his gaze.

"The truth is simple, though certainly far less colorful than local folklore. Celeste, my first wife, suffered from tuberculosis. She was such a vibrant person . . . it was a shattering experience for us all to watch the illness gradually taking hold. . . ." A look of pain flashed across his eyes and Amanda felt sorry she had pressed him to speak of his past.

"David . . ." she cut in, calling him by name for the first time. "You needn't speak of these matters if they are upsetting to you."

"No—we'll set this straight between us now. When we are married, I want no shadows of the past coming between us." *When* he had said, Amanda noted, not *if*. "Celeste died a natural death," he continued quietly, "finally choking on the phlegm in her chest, as is common with such an illness. Becky, or any of the servants who were here at the time, know this to be true." He stopped his pacing once again and glanced over at her. Amanda felt a renewed sense of embarrassment at making this proud man confess his past to her in such a manner. It was a great strain, she realized, to be cast in the role of judge and jury rolled into one. But as David had suggested, her entire future rested on the outcome of this conversation. She walked closer to him and rested one hand on the mahogany bed post.

"And Charity?" she asked finally.

He looked away. "The truth about Charity is still a mystery to us. We believe an intruder murdered her as she slept. She was found in the morning by one of the maids."

"Found in the morning . . . So you were not even home at the time?" Amanda asked innocently.

"I was at home . . . in my own room," he corrected her gently. "You see . . . Charity and I didn't have a conventional marriage. We were not intimate wth each other as man and wife. In respect for her dear, departed soul I cannot add more at this time than to say that ours was an agreement of mutual convenience."

Amanda suddenly recalled her suspicions that Nelda was conceived before David and Charity were married. Now it occurred to her that perhaps David was not Nelda's real father.

"The sheriff is still investigating the circumstances of her death. That is why her room must remain unaltered. This is all we know of the matter. Perhaps it does not clear me entirely in your eyes, but please remember that this is not the lawless frontier. If there was one shred of evidence to suggest that poor Charity had met her death at my hand, I certainly would not be in this room right now, discussing these matters with you."

Feeling quite drained from the conversation, Amanda sat down on the edge of the bed. "Of course not," she said.

Everything he had told her was easy enough to verify. There were certainly records of Charity's murder at the court house in Corydon. As for Celeste, any of the servants would tell her the same story as David had, she was sure. She felt a total fool now for thinking him capable of such heinous acts. What could he possibly think of her! Her cheeks felt hot with shame and she pressed her hands to her face.

An instant later, he was sitting beside her. "Amanda, please . . . All this talk has upset you, hasn't it? You still don't believe me innocent, do you?"

She turned to him. "Of course I do . . . I'm so embarrassed for even suspecting otherwise. After you've shown me nothing but kindness and respect since I arrived here . . . How insulting for me to have even put such questions to you. You must hate me now."

Much to Amanda's surprise, instead of agreeing with her, he suddenly smiled. He reached over and took her hands in his. "You can insult me as much as you like, if that means you will agree to marry me," he teased her. "Do you?"

Amanda looked into his dark eyes and took a deep breath. *I am a woman without family or fortune. Alone in a strange country, possessing nothing but a pearl ring and my position in this household. Here is a man of wealth and property, respected and admired by all who know him. And aside from all these very practical reasons*, Amanda thought, *I love him very much. How can I not choose to marry David Whitcomb?*

"Yes, David . . . I will marry you," she said slowly.

"You will never regret it, Amanda. I promise you." Moving closer to her, David took her in his arms and kissed her, first very gently and tenderly then with increasing passion as Amanda began to respond to his embrace.

Without knowing exactly how it had happened, Amanda soon found herself lying across the bed, clutching David's broad shoulders as her senses swam under the onslaught of his kiss. His mouth moved from her lips, to rain delicate kisses across her cheeks and eyelids. Then his lips moved lower, down the smooth curve of her neck to the soft swell of her breasts, which were exposed by her low-cut gown.

Her eyes closed, she buried her fingers in his thick golden hair, clutching his head to her breast. With his fingertip, he outlined the hardening nipple of one breast and then the other, through the thin, bluegreen silk, his warm mouth moving with languorous passion.

Amanda felt herself caught in a whirlpool of indescribable pleasure. A pleasure so fiery and intense it was close to pain.

She wanted somehow to give David the same feelings of ecstasy he was giving her, but she didn't know how. Taking his face gently in her

hands she urged his lips back to her own. She
kissed him deeply, urgently, as if a hunger that
had been lying dormant within her for years had
suddenly been awakened by his lovemaking.

With obvious effort, David lifted himself up and
looked down at her. "Amanda, my darling . . . I've
looked for you all my life. I can't wait to make you
mine," he said gruffly. He stroked her slim waist
and the swell of her breast with a possessive hand.
"Promise you'll marry me tomorrow morning."

"Tomorrow? . . . But that's so soon . . ." Amanda
felt dazed. Her hair had come loose from its pins
and was spread out on the silk comforter around
her head. David wound his fingers through one
long strand and pulled her close against the heat
of his body.

"I would marry you right now, but the Governor
is probably sound asleep in his bed. Tomorrow
morning will have to do. In the garden. It will just
be us and the children." His head dipped down to
kiss her lips. "Say you will agree," he whispered
seductively.

David was afraid that she would change her
mind, she realized. He was worried that if she gave
her too much time to think, her mind would fill
with doubts all over again. Amanda framed his
rugged, beloved face in her hands. Little did he
realize that she was afraid of that too. Ironically,
her fear made her push forward, instead of turn
back. "In the grove where you proposed to me,
David. I think I would like us to be married there."

David had no words for her then. His eyes
became so brilliant she thought he was about to
cry. He pulled her close again, his mouth meeting
hers in a searing, soul wrenching kiss that
expressed his feelings with passionate eloquence.

They were married the next morning in the

garden, just as David had promised. The Governor was delighted to stay on an extra day in order to officiate. The sun shone brightly in a cloudless, azure blue sky as Amanda spoke her vows. David, his golden hair ruffled by a light breeze, stood proud and tall at her side. Nelda and Andrew, dressed in their Sunday best, looked on in happy amazement at the sight of their father marrying their beloved governess. Lochard was also present. Wreathed in smiles, he played the role of the rejected suitor admirably, Amanda thought. She wondered if his easy acceptance of the situation was merely an act that masked disappointment. Or, if his advances toward her had really been quite meaningless after all.

She had made her choice, Amanda realized as the ceremony was concluded and David leaned down to lightly kiss her lips. Then the others crowded in and she accepted their heartfelt congratulations. "Shall we return to the house, Mrs. Whitcomb?" David asked, placing her hand in the crook of his arm.

Amanda, suddenly feeling the full impact of what she had done, could only nod in answer to her husband's question. He stared down at her, his gypsy eyes glowing, his expression unreadable. For better or worse, I have chosen David Whitcomb as my husband, she thought.

After the ceremony, a special lunch was served up at the house. The table had been laid with the best china, crystal and silver; the centerpiece was a fragrant mass of fresh flowers. The mood was bright and lighthearted, as if it were a holiday. In a sense, it was, since David had given all the field workers the day off in honor of the occasion.

After the meal was finished, the Governor regretfully took his leave. David decided to ride with him as far as the western border of the plantation. Some roads had been washed out there with recent rains and David thought it best to accompany his friend. Amanda was relieved at the chance to have some time alone in order to sort out her thoughts.

She spent the rest of the afternoon with the children. Nelda and Andrew were plainly delighted to refer to her now as their stepmother and seemed to go out of their way to fit the term into their conversation. They were making a game of it almost, Amanda noticed, but it was one that was very pleasing to her.

When David finally returned to the house, he and Amanda took a walk alone in the garden. It was almost sunset and Amanda realized that they had never walked together at this hour before. Nor had they ever been so quiet in one another's company. But it was a comfortable silence, she thought, one that made her feel closer rather than more distant from her new husband.

A light supper had been laid for them in the dining room, and it was served with a decanter of claret. Amanda did not care much for spirits, but as the time to go upstairs with her husband approached, she found herself accepting even a second glass of the smooth wine. She was more than a little apprehensive about her wedding night. She had no idea what to expect, or what would be expected of her. David's embraces so far had been wonderful. But she knew there had to be more to it than that. It was at times like this when Amanda felt the absence of a mother, sister or female confidant most keenly. As Amanda had dressed for the wedding ceremony that morning, Becky had tried to initiate a conversation about such matters. But Amanda had been too embarrassed to discuss the topic openly with Becky. Now she wished she had not been so quick to cut the conversation off.

When supper was over and David finally led her upstairs, she soon realized that she had no reason to worry. He walked with her to the doorway of his bedroom, then quite considerately left her alone to prepare herself for bed in privacy. Her belongings had not yet been moved to the master suite. But her best nightgown, of sheer cotton batiste trimmed with cream-colored lace, had been laid out on the bed for her. Amanda undressed, washed, and combed out her long hair. Wearing only the gown, she sat tensely at the foot of David's huge bed. Finally, David knocked softly and entered the room. She looked up at him and her heart turned over at the sight of him. There was pure passion and even a strange kind of reverence in his eyes as he approached her.

Instead of sitting next to her on the bed, he went down on his knees, so that they were eye to eye. "My sweet Amanda . . . you are so very beautiful," he whispered, gently stroking back a strand of hair from her cheek. "Don't be afraid," he implored. As he tenderly embraced her, Amanda felt her fear melt away. In its place, the mysterious embers of desire began to glow deep within her. As he continued to gently kiss and caress her, she felt a passionate side of herself awakening with each sensuous touch.

He had returned to her wearing only his shirt, breeches and boots. His stiff white collar had been removed and several buttons on the linen shirt left open to reveal golden swirls of hair on his chest. Her eyes half closed, Amanda slipped her hand inside and touched him, as he was touching her, at first very tentatively. "Amanda . . ." he sighed and she felt his big body shudder in her arms.

Lifted in David's embrace, she was soon stretched out on the bed. Quickly shedding the rest of his clothes, David lay down beside her. The single candle in the far corner of the room gave his lean, muscular body a golden hue. As he pulled her close, she delighted in running her hands along the smooth, hard contours of his broad back and shoulders. He sighed with pleasure at her slightest touch, answering her with deep, soul searching kisses and murmured endearments as his passion mounted ever higher.

With the straps of her gown pushed down to her waist, David's warm mouth trailed down the curve of one shoulder to the soft peak of Amanda's breast. His lips and fingertips played her body as if she were an instrument of desire. Mesmerized by his touch, she felt herself spiraling deeper and deeper into a whirlpool of pleasure. She had never imagined feelings so intense, ecstasy so exquisite.

Finally, the gown was slipped off her and she felt the delicious weight of David's body stretched out on top of her. With utmost control, he slowly entered her. His body began to move within and Amanda clung to him, the slight pain quickly giving way to feelings of powerful, soul-shaking pleasure. He kissed her deeply, whispering words of love and praise that made Amanda feel cherished and desired. Surrendering totally to the moment, she gave herself to the deep rhythm of their lovemaking. Soon, she felt herself borne away on sensations so fiery and unreal that for a moment, she thought she was going to lose consciousness.

She heard David call out her name and a strange voice that was her own answered him. David clung to her as she trembled in his arms. At almost the same moment, she felt the powerful climax of his passion.

For a long time afterward, neither of them

spoke. David shifted to her side, his head still resting heavily next to hers on the pillow. He kissed her cheek. "You are a wonder to me," he whispered. Lifting his head, he stared down at her. In the dim light, Amanda strained to make out his features. She lifted her hand and touched his face. "I didn't hurt you, did I?" he asked with concern.

Amanda shook her head. "You made me feel wonderful."

He dipped his head to kiss her lips. "You are truly my wife now, Amanda. And I am your husband. You were meant to be mine. I knew it the moment I saw you step off the ferry."

"Oh, David . . ." Amanda wanted to believe him, but couldn't yet accept the idea that he had set his sights on her from the very first moment they'd met. "Surely you waited at least until dinner time before you decided to marry me?"

"No, Mrs. Whitcomb. I wanted you from the first moment I saw you. With every fiber of my heart and soul . . . Just like I want you now," he whispered.

He drew her into the heat of his body and Amanda once again surrendered herself to his lovemaking. Afterward, she rested her head on David's chest and fell into a deep, contented sleep.

How different her waking had been from that first dreamless sleep. Now she sat alone in the wide bed, thinking over the events that had brought her here and wondering what the future would deliver.

Amanda was not the least bit superstitious and had never believed that dreams—good or bad—could foretell the future. Yet, the nightmare that had visited her more than once the night before had been so vivid, it was difficult now for her to put aside her sense of foreboding.

When a knock sounded softly on the door, Amanda jumped. "Who is it?" she called out.

"I have some breakfast for you, Miss Amanda," Becky said. She opened the door a crack and peeked in.

"Oh, come in, Becky." Amanda got out of bed and walked over to the dresser in order to tie back her hair. "My, that smells good. I'm starved."

Becky put the tray on a table and removed the snowy cloth. "There, now. Tea and hot biscuits, good rich butter and fresh honey that Miz Sarah strained only yesterday—I had a feeling Master David was going to leave you with a big appetite." She gave Amanda a knowing look that made her blush. "A newly wed bride has to keep her strength up."

"Now, Becky . . ." Amanda turned, her brush still in her hand.

Becky only laughed at Amanda's prim expression. "Being on your honeymoon ain't nothin' to be ashamed of. Why Master David ain't shamed. He was downstairs before dawn, whistlin' like a lark and putting away his meal like a young boy. He woke up Andrew too and is off to the fields. Be back by noon, though."

"Has Nelda had her breakfast yet?" Amanda asked, thinking that the child could come in and share the overflowing tray of biscuits and honey.

"That little Miss Nelda is a sleepyhead today," Becky replied. "She's always up at the crack of dawn and here it is, almost eight-thirty and she hasn't stirred out of her room." Becky shook her head and went about the business of plumping up the big feather pillows while Amanda sipped her tea. "I guess I'll have Matilda go in and wake the child when I'm through here."

Unaccountably, Amanda put down her cup and threw on a wrapper. "I'm going to the nursery,

Becky. Perhaps Nelda has fallen sick in the night." She knew, even as she covered the distance between her room and the nursery that her sudden alarm about Nelda's welfare was unreasonable. The dream she'd had at dawn, she realized, may have contributed to her feeling of anxiety for the child. But still, she knew she would feel better once she'd looked in on the little girl and found her in her usual good health.

The door to the nursery stood slightly ajar. Amanda opened it wider and slipped in, not wishing to awaken Nelda if she still slept. The apartment was designed so the school room—sitting room was in the middle of the two bedrooms where the children slept. Nelda had the bed-chamber to the East of the house and Andrew had the other. The morning sun shone brightly into the middle room, flooding the parquet floor with dazzling gold. Something on the floor glittered so brightly that Amanda put her hand up to protect her eyes. She stooped to pick up the small object and at a glance knew it was a miniature of Nelda's mother. There could be no mistaking it—the features, the hair, the eyes were identical. The lovely frame was exactly like the one Andrew had shown her of his mother, and it was the gold frame that had reflected the sunlight into her eyes. She was sorry to see the glass that protected the painting on ivory had been shattered, but she didn't realize the full import of finding the miniature on the floor with the glass broken until she opened the door that led into Nelda's bedroom. The normally neat room was a shambles. Rose colored satin draperies were half torn from their rods, pillows and bedclothing were strewn about the floor, and Nelda's little desk and chair had been overturned. The wardrobe where all her little frocks hung on hooks was almost empty. A few frocks lay strewn about the floor, petticoats and drawers flung in a disordered heap of bright colored ruffles and bows. Just as Amanda was about to whirl from the room to run for help, she saw the pool of blood upon the floor.

Her eyes widened in mute terror. There was no doubt in her mind that the dark red sticky substance was blood, for even though it was partially congealed, she was nauseated with the smell of it. Horror stacked on top of horror. For there in the middle of the pool of blood was one long golden curl that had been cut from Nelda's little head, the blunt ends, where it had been shorn, saturated with the blood.

5

In spite of her father's attitude toward fainting females, Amanda felt weak and giddy as she fled the room. By the time she reached the hall outside the nursery door she could fight the waves of overwhelming blackness no longer. She fell in a heap on the floor. Seconds later, with an awesome sense of having been unconscious for a long time, she struggled to her feet, grateful for the support of Becky's strong arms. Becky's voice, kind and considerate, had a calming effect. "I saw you fall, Missy, but when I ran to you, it seemed more like a swoon. I do hope the sickness isn't coming back on you. You're so pale and so . . ."

"Hush! It isn't the sickness," cried Amanda. "It's Nelda! She isn't in her room, and oh! God help me, she's been taken."

"Taken, ma'am?" Becky crossed herself, her features twisted in sudden grief. Amanda realized the servant misunderstood, that she believed the child was dead. She shuddered and once again felt the threat of darkness descending.

"No, no, she isn't dead—that is, she might well
be, but, oh, God in heaven, the blood! And her hair
in it! Let me go, Becky. I've not gone daft. Go and
see for yourself."

"But your trembling, Missy," said Becky. "I
can't quite . . ."

"Be gone with you," shouted Amanda. "I'll not
give way to foolish female vapors again. I had a
dreadful turn, but we must do something!"

Becky finally seemed to realize that Amanda
was neither delirious nor demented. She left
Amanda's side and her voice rang out in a
shattering scream within seconds. The room
spoke for itself, Amanda thought as she pounded
down the hall toward the steps. Becky followed
close on her heels, but it was Amanda who had the
presence of mind to ring the big bell on the back
porch. Amanda rang the bell fifteen times before
she left the back porch and ran up the stairs to her
room, where she threw a gray morning dress over
her gown and smoothed her disheveled hair.

She instructed all the servants to start an
immediate search of the premises, then waited for
David Whitcomb to come in answer to the
summons of the bell. The minutes crawled by with
heart-rending slowness and with each tick of the
big clock in the great hall Amanda breathed a
silent prayer that what she feared had taken place
in the little girl's room had not really happened.

Becky was silent as she remained with Amanda.
She stood looking out toward the hills, a dark
figure of control who gave Amanda a sense of
sharing her growing terror. David's cousin Sarah,
who had not heard the ringing of the bell but felt
the vibrations, came down from her room with a
question in her eyes and asked in her monotone
what had taken place. "The bell . . . some-thing-
has-happened . . . somebody-rang-the-bell . . . what-

has-happened . . . won't-somebody-tell-me . . .
please . . ." There was no rise in Sarah's voice at
the end of her question, no fall of voice to desig-
nate the end of a sentence. In spite of the difficulty
of communicating with her, Amanda was stricken
with empathy toward the sweet-faced, wistful-
eyed woman. She tried to explain, but she hadn't
learned to form each word in the kind of exaggerated lip movements necessary to make the
older woman understand. Becky explained
Nelda's disappearance to Sarah while Amanda
watched the road in front of the house with
anxious eyes. And kept trying to convince herself
any number of things could have happened to
Nelda, that she'd *not* been murdered in cold blood:

For instance, she could have cut herself while
using a pair of scissors. Children are sometimes
careless with scissors, and a very small wound will
bleed considerably. But the hair in the blood, the
ends all saturated—no! Don't think of it just now.
Or Nelda could be playing a childish prank. Maybe
she's run off to hide, possibly out of sorts because
Andrew went riding with their father. Since
Amanda had already seen a narrow margin of
favoritism of boy over girl in the short time she'd
been at Whispering Hills, she had an idea Nelda
felt slighted at times and tried to hope with all her
heart that Nelda wanted to gain attention by
throwing the household in a turmoil.

Her thoughts were interrupted by Lochard, who
arrived in a cloud of dust, the hooves of his horse
ringing against the clay of the road. Almost as
though she were watching the scene from a great
distance, Amanda saw Lochard dismount and send
his horse toward the stables, already dashing
toward the house. His face was white, his eyes
concerned as he burst into the room. "The bell! I
heard the bell. What happened?"

In order to keep her voice from breaking, it was necessary for Amanda to speak crisply, almost coldly. "I went into Nelda's room to see why . . . she hadn't come down to breakfast. She's an early riser." She swallowed, fighting back the threat of hysteria that was very close to the surface. "She wasn't there. The room is in a shambles, and a pool of blood, partially congealed, is on the floor close to her bed. One of her curls, the ends dipped in the blood, was cut from her head." As she spoke, she literally held on to the thin edge of reality by curling her fingers into her palms in such a tight fist that she cut the skin of her palms with her nails.

Without saying a word, Lochard turned on his heel and ran up the steps. Overhead, his footsteps thundered loudly, and with that small corner of her mind that wasn't concentrating on all the things that might or might not have happened to the child, Amanda heard his voice cry out in alarm, before he returned to the hall. His presence filled the room with a reflection of her own shock and fear, but Lochard appeared icily calm. "My brother. Where is he?"

"In the fields. Andrew is with him. I hope and pray Nelda is with them also."

"So do I. David will have heard the bell. They'll be back soon." Lochard turned to Becky. "You didn't see Nelda this morning?"

"No, Master Lochard. I didn't see her. I thought she was still asleep. I would have seen her if she'd been up. Little Missy always wakes up with a coming appetite. She didn't come down today at her usual hour."

Amanda remembered the dream, the awakening at dawn to the echo of a scream. She cursed herself silently, wishing hollowly that she could live that moment over again. She'd never rationalize

away the abrupt awakening, turn the memory of a
scream into the substance of a dream. Instead, she
would get up and go immediately to . . . She cut
off her useless desire to go backwards in time and
answered Lochard's questions to the best of her
ability. When he realized she could add no more to
what she'd said, he told her he would go back to
his own place and get the dogs.

"Dogs?" Amanda looked at him blankly.

"Hunting dogs. I'll take them upstairs—give
them Nelda's scent. Maybe, just maybe . . . At
least it's doing *something*," he said harshly. At the
door, he turned and looked at Amanda with
thoughtful eyes. "Think. Before David returns
from the fields, try to think of anything you've
seen since you've been here that might have some
bearing on this terrible thing."

Amanda nodded, but she had already been
mentally laboring along those lines and everything
she thought of was too horrifying to contemplate;
too far-fetched to consdider. The most shattering
of all her shadowy, only partially formed suspects
was too monstrous for her to allow her mind to
dwell upon. Yet, there it was, filtering stubbornly
through the dazed condition of her brain. *Andrew*.
Oh, no, she told herself as she wrung her hands
and looked for the hundredth time toward the
road for David.

But still . . .

During those weeks she had been in resident at
Whispering Hills, she had seen young Andrew's
contempt for his sister manifest itself in more
ways than one. It was true that the little boy
usually behaved politely toward his half sister. At
times he was loving and kind, his bright eyes en-
couraging her as he spoke to her gently while explaining things to her. But Amanda had seen a
quick flash of hatred in his eyes more times than

she cared to remember. On two different occasions she had spoken to the boy harshly, reminding him that gentlemen do not strike ladies. Nor speak abominably to ladies, as Andrew had done so often, which usually resulted in reducing the little girl to tears. Andrew was continually baiting Nelda with accusations of being stupid, just as her mother had been before her. He called her a dumb-bell, a sissy-britches and other names that Amanda didn't consider proper.

Andrew was exceptionally adult in many ways and he was brilliantly cunning. She knew there is an exceedingly fine line that separates the genius from the madman, and she most emphatically did consider Andrew Whitcomb a genius. During those few times when she had talked to him of books, he'd stunned her with his store of knowledge; but most of all she was concerned over his lightning-quick ability to charm everyone around him after a totally horrendous display of temper. Andrew was accustomed to getting his way. Nelda was almost as badly spoiled, but in her heart of hearts Amanda knew that David Whitcomb loved his son more than he did his daughter, and she believed the father had done his son a disservice by usually giving in to the boy's whims. It chilled her blood to think of the possibility of a child murderer . . . yet try as she did to keep such notions at bay, she didn't succeed. The fact remained that Nelda had been taken from her room, leaving chaos behind and a pool of blood on the floor. It was all too evident that a violent struggle had taken place, which also pointed to someone small in stature. For Amanda didn't believe a small girl of ten years could have tried to protect herself to such an extent if her assailant had been an adult.

Another possibility loomed that was equally as

horrendous as considering Andrew as suspect. The ghost. Amanda shook as with the ague as she contemplated a shadowy figure that belonged in another world creepling into a child's room to do damage, possibly commit murder. Of course she kept telling herself that Nelda might be in good health—there was still the chance she had somehow gone off to the fields with her father and brother . . . or was hiding for some reason of her own. But Amanda didn't think so. The mute evidence in the bed chamber pointed too strongly toward foul play.

Amanda's mind leapt hopefully to another idea. Perhaps Andrew and Nelda had merely exchanged a few cruel, but childish, blows that morning before Andrew came down to ride out into the fields with his father. They could have tussled as children will do, she tried to convince herself, which could have resulted in pulling down the draperies and upsetting everything in the room. Then Andrew could have cut off one of Nelda's curls in a fit of temper and the little girl might not be wounded at all. She tried very hard to make herself believe Andrew had been the victim of bloodshed, knowing he was out of harm's way and with his father; therefore if he'd suffered a wound it would be a slight one. She realized people can bleed copiously without much damage. A cut finger, for instance, could have dropped a good bit of blood on the floor. Or a bloody nose. She knew Nelda was quite capable of using her small plump fists just as she knew Andrew was capable of provoking her to extreme anger. She drew a trembling breath, knowing that if there had been a fistfight between the children, Andrew would not have come out of it unscathed. The evidence of Becky's fingernails and possibly teeth would be on his body somewhere.

If not Andrew, who she fervently hoped was innocent of whatever dreadful event had taken place in that room, then who? Amanda asked herself the question as she paced the floor and looked again toward the road. It seemed to her that hours had passed since she had first looked in the nursery apartment, then gone down and frantically tugged at the bell-rope. Becky was a pillar of strength. She kept reminding Amanda that less than a half hour had elapsed since Amanda rang the bell. "It only takes Master Lochard five minutes to get here from his place; but Master David could be most anywhere on the plantation. There's thousands of acres, and only the dear Lord above knows where they rode to."

"But he can hear the bell, can't he? You did say he could hear the bell from anyplace on the plantation, didn't you?"

"Yes Missy, now *do* sit down and rest yourself. There's nothing we can do except what Mr. Lochard is doing, and there he comes now, with the dogs. They're smart animals. Can trail a fox or a coon better'n any hound dogs I ever heard tell of. And there's Master David, too, ridin' hell-bent-for-election."

A flood of relief overcame Amanda as she raced for the front door and ran across the wide verandah. Lochard, mounted on his proud black steed, was speaking to David, the brace of hounds pulling at their chains. From the porch, she could see David stiffen in the saddle, then look toward the house, his face white with shock. Andrew, a quarter-mile down the road, was flaying his mount with the whip, his face a study of alarm. Cutting through the urgent voices of his father and uncle, Andrew called, "What's wrong? Why did the servants ring the bell?" The galloping hooves of his horse drowned out his father's words. Unable to restrain herself, Amanda ran down the steps, intent on looking into Andrew's face for telltale signs of a recent struggle.

The boy jumped from his horse to the ground, and David, shoving Amanda aside, went with Lochard up the wide steps and onto the porch, where the brothers entered the house, the hounds baying excitedly. Andrew looked up at Amanda. "They didn't say what happened. All I know is that something's wrong with Nelda. She's been hurt? What are the hounds for?"

There was not a mark on Andrew's face, Amanda saw with relief. Nelda's fingernails would have left their mark there if she'd struggled with her brother. She told Andrew the truth, what little she knew, and she watched his face closely to see how he took the news of what certainly looked like tragedy had befallen his half-sister. At first, Andrew went paper-white. Then his face flushed with hot blood and his dark eyes went wild with hatred. His young voice rang shrill and full of mingled fear and rage. "I'll kill anybody that hurts her! She's *only* a baby!" Then the little boy burst into tears. Amanda held him close, her own tears very close to the surface as she gave him what hollow comfort she could.

"Hush. Hush, darling. It may not be as bad as we think. We're not sure she's been hurt. We don't know where she is, but there's a possibility she's just run off somewhere—that she's hiding. Children have cut their own hair before, and I suspect they'll keep on doing it as long as there are scissors. What we have to do is help search the house for your sister. And keep calm as well as we can until she's found."

Andrew gave her a tremulous smile, but his eyes were still big with fright. "You're sure she'll be found, then?" All of his adult mannerisms were suddenly gone. He was very much a child of twelve as he took his handkerchief out of his pocket and blew his nose, willing to accept Amanda's carefully chosen words.

The tramping of feet overhead sounded like thunder. The baying dogs, still straining at their leashes, soon bounded down the steps, with both men clattering after them. Lochard disappeared toward the back of the house while David went to join the servants, who were still diligently searching every nook and cranny in the big house. Amanda was glad to accompany young Andrew in a search of their own. He'd said solemnly, "If she is hiding from us, I bet I can find her. We've played hide and seek lots and lots of times. She knows some really good hiding places, too. And I bet I can get inside some little bitty place where grown-ups can't." Although she was glad to do something—anything at all to loosen the tension of fear that was upon her, Amanda understood all too well the eager way the hounds had rounded the corner of the stairs, their silvery tongues baying with excitement. The dogs were following the scent *away* from the house. Further, if she could believe the rapidly dwindling sounds of the baying animals, the scent they followed was taking them periously close to the river. With an anxious eye, taking care to not allow Andrew to see what she was about, she looked out the window from the landing that led to the second floor. The view afforded her a wide expanse of back lawn, and she saw Lochard and his pack of hounds disappear down the hill that led to the river.

"Come on," called Andrew. "We'll look in our mama's room. Once Nelda hid from me in her mama's clothes press, way up high on a shelf." The boy ran on up to the second floor, and Amanda came behind, her heart aching with new horror.

She was thinking of the river, swollen after rainstorms up above Whispering Hills; storms that had unleashed heavy run-off that had brought the river almost to flood stage. While the servants continued to shout to one another from various parts of the house, Amanda searched all the upstairs rooms with Andrew, constantly telling herself to not dwell upon the dreaded possibility of the river.

They searched carefully the room Andrew's mother had occupied before her death, looking in that one first because Andrew said it would be the most likely place for Nelda to hide. "Because, don't you see, the last time I couldn't find her, she hid in *her* mama's room. She'd know I'd look there first."

There was an eerie hush inside Celeste Andrea Maria's room as well as a closed-up mustiness that hinted of death. Amanda drew back the draperies and noticed the subtle fragrance of lilac, something Andrew had already mentioned. She felt a chill travel up and down her spine when she surveyed the orderly quiet of the room, the golden comb and brush, the hand mirror that beautiful Celeste had once used for her looking glass. From some hidden recess of her memory, Amanda recalled an old superstition: A looking glass captures and holds the spirit of those who have died. She considered such superstitions ridiculous, but she admitted to her secret self a sense of being in contact with the unknown when she lifted the mirror and looked at her own face. She was pale, and her gray eyes looked back at her soberly, anxiety in their depths. She jumped at Andrew's voice at her elbow. "Did you think Nelda might be hiding under Mama's looking glass?"

"No, I just . . ." She felt foolish, caught out in a

silly gesture. He darted into the dressing room where he crawled under his mother's gowns, then asked her to look on the top shelves. "Nelda's a very little girl. She might be up there, buried under a pile of Mama's hats."

Amanda looked. She even moved the stack of plumed bonnets, decorated with all manner of ribbons and jewels, then put them back in the neat stack the way they'd been. Andrew was leaving his mother's room, heading for Charity's which was across the hall. The door was closed, and when Amanda opened it, Amanda was momentarily stunned by the darkness. The draperies were heavier than they'd been in the other room they'd just searched, and made of richly piled velvet, through which no ray of sun could filter. When she drew them back, she noted that they were lined with a thick fabric that matched the red velvet, and fashioned in such a way to cut out all light.

"Nelda's mother suffered with migraines," said Andrew importantly. "That's why she liked it dark."

"Migraines," he tossed over his shoulder as he crawled among the boots and boxes. "Her head hurt her bad sometimes. Then she wanted it to be dark."

Perhaps because she'd looked at the contents so neatly arrayed on the dresser in the first Mrs. Whitcomb's room, Amanda went swiftly to dead Charity's and surveyed the marble top. The silver brush and comb were neatly in line alongside a dainty mirror with hand-painted angels on the back. And as she had done in the room they just left, she forced herself to pick up the looking glass and peer into it. Again she saw nothing but the reflection of her own face. She was about to put it back in place when she saw something that didn't belong in the room. If everything had not been in such immaculate order, she would never have noticed the fragment of red paper that lay half under the commode. It looked as though it had blown there, and as she stepped forward to retrieve it, with only a sense of wanting to remove something that obviously didn't belong there, the piece of red paper fluttered from the breeze created by her skirts.

At first, Amanda didn't understand the meaning of what she saw written on the three-cornered scrap of paper.

Her lips moved when she read it over again, as though by whispering the ominous message she would lend credence to the misspelled words and unlearned writing in the diabolical statement:

Master Whitcumb
    If yr pinin to sea yr dawtter again in this hear life take the red taffety bag with the drawstring used by NELDAS MOTHER, the same to be found in this hear rume. Put inside it ten thousand spannish dollars and leave it down by the River at a plase whar you weel sea 4 big rocks all stacket up Togither in a pal. Do Not try and pull no triks as We will be Watchin and if So yr littel dawtter will leeve this Life. Her curl of hair is left behind to show that We Meen Biznes. Put money in poke and take to the place instruktet before the witchin hour this nite. Do as We say and yr girl will come to know harm she will come hoam by brekfus in the mornin.

6

Amanda would never be able to recall leaving the bedchamber after she found the shocking, blood-chilling note. Nor would she remember her mad dash down the stairs. Later, Andrew would talk about how his stepmother had grasped his hand so hard that he thought she would break it. He would relate how her feet had seemed to take wing and fly, rushing him along with her as she ran down the steps toward the rear of the house. And he would say that her voice, deathly calm and distinct, must have shattered the very timbers of Whispering Hills as she cried out for David Whitcomb, his father. Her own memory failed her utterly concerning those first seconds of extreme stress after reading the ransom note. When she grew aware of her actions, she was in the main kitchen of the house, where she told Herbert to go and fetch Master Whitcomb.

The big black husband of Flora, the cook, asked no questions.

"Yes, ma'am," he said as he started toward the river at a fast pace. "He gone to see whut Mastah

119

Lochard turn up wid dem houn's.''

"Tell the master I will be in the library,'' she said to Flora as she turned and with decisive step marched through the vast rooms to the library. She continued to hold Andrew's hand firmly in her own as though she feared he would be stolen, too. She chose the library because of the privacy, because of the heavy carved doors that would muffle the words that would be spoken once David Whitcomb returned to the house.

During the moments they waited, Andrew was able to withdraw his hand from Amanda's after he'd asked her three times to release him. Rubbing his knuckles, his own expression a match for the apprehensive one upon her features, he started to leave the room. Sharply, she called him back. "You are not to leave my side. From this moment on, you are to be with me or your father at all times, do you understand?''

"All right. But what did you find up there? What caused you to cry out like that, then dash down the steps, yelling and screaming for my father? I saw nothing in my stepmother's room that could have given you such a turn.''

"Your father will tell you if he deems it wise,'' said Amanda. And then her hand touched the bodice of her morning dress, where she'd put the piece of red paper with its terrible message. Although she didn't remember any other details about leaving the bedchamber, she knew she'd stuffed the paper into the front of her dress. The sharp edges were at that moment cutting against the delicate skin of her bosom, but she was determined to not remove it until Nelda's father was in the room and he had locked the doors from prying eyes and curious ears. For common sense told her that all the servants would be listening to see what had caused such a turmoil. That same sense of

caution insisted that the paper should be read by
the Master of Whispering Hills, that he should
make up his own mind as to what steps should be
taken before any servant or other member of the
household should be made cognizant of the
contents of that hideous note. Her reasons for
insisting that Andrew stay near her were instinctive. With one child gone, stolen from her room
with a demand for ransom left in her stead, there
was an unspoken threat to the one who remained.

Heralded by a clatter of footsteps, both David
and Lochard burst into the library. Both men were
out of breath, their eyes bright with what
appeared at first glance as hope. One look at her
pale face must have told them they'd hoped in vain
that she had good news.

David's voice was harsh as he grasped her by
both shoulders. "Tell me! Even if it's the very
worst, I must know."

"It might be more terrible than you can bear,"
she said slowly. Her glance wandered from David
to Lochard, as she realized with any icy chill that
anybody could have written that awful note,
including Lochard. *Nobody* was free to suspect
now that Nelda's disappearance had taken this
bizarre turn. Her gray eyes met and held the dark
brown ones of the Master of Whispering Hills. "I
must speak to you in privacy."

"*Speak*, woman," cried David as he gave her
shoulders a slight shake. He looked demented, his
hair falling down on his face, his stubble of beard
making him appear villainously unkempt.

Her eyes remained firm on his. "I insist that I
have words with you alone, David. Believe in me,
please." Her words were torn from her throat in
agony. "What I have to tell you is for your ears
only."

For a second longer, David continued to stare

angrily into her face, then he shrugged, turned to
his brother and asked him to leave the room. "And
take Andrew with you." Turning back to Amanda,
he asked, "I take it that's what you want? To be
completely alone with me? I have no secrets from
my brother and my son."

She nodded to show she understood although
she hated the cold superiority in his voice. Then
she spoke quietly. "I'm well aware of your heartfelt fear concerning your daughter's welfare, and
you should know that everyone in this household
save those who were instrumental in her disappearance share your crushing fears, including
myself. After I have spoken, it will be your choice
as to whether you will relay this abominable news
to others. But right now, I can do and say only
what I must do and say."

Lochard continued to stare at her, his eyes
bleak, his mouth trembling as he spoke to Andrew.
"Come, Drew." Then to David he said softly, "I'm
sure your wife has a good reason to speak to you
alone." Yet the look he turned on Amanda showed
that he was hurt to the quick.

With head erect, though she was hard-pressed to
speak the words, she said, "And remain close by.
Take Andrew and go to the Rose Room." It was all
she dared say, but felt she must consider Andrew's
safety above all. Yet common sense told her if
Lochard was instrumental in the stealing plot he
would never dare spirit Andrew away so soon
after she'd taken the initiative to leave the boy in
his care.

Without another word, Lochard took his
nephew by the hand and they left; but she refused
to say a word until the heavy library door was
closed and bolted. Then she reached into the
bodice of her dress and removed the red paper.
She turned and gave it to David, her enforced calm

disturbed by the glitter of something akin to hatred in his eyes. In spite of his inclination toward liberal speech, the times he had spoken of admiration for her intelligence and learning, Amanda felt he resented the unaccustomed high-handed attitude she'd just shown. Yet she'd known of no other course she could have taken. She watched his face as he read, then re-read the message on the paper. A vein in his left temple throbbed, and his lips compressed. Then he spoke, but quietly. "Where did you find this?"

"In the bedchamber of your second wife. Even though the servants had already searched in there, I was restless. Andrew and I wanted to do something constructive. The children are accustomed to playing hide and seek, and although I didn't really believe we'd find Nelda, I went along with Andrew's suggestion that we search for her. He's young, after all, and doesn't realize the full import of a missing child, of a blood-saturated curl upon the floor of her room. I don't know where the ransom note was lying initially, but I think when Andrew and I opened the door it must have blown from where it had been secreted. It caught my eye where it fluttered under the commode. If it had been in plain sight, I can't believe the servants would not have seen it before I did."

"Except for Becky, none of the servants can read," he told her grimly. "I doubt that any of them would have noticed a piece of paper with writing on it, even if it had been sewn to the counterpane." He paced the room while she told him she had mentioned nothing of the ransom note to any of the servants. "For it has occurred to me that someone of the household must be responsible. The red taffeta reticule that is to be found in . . . the second Mrs. Whitcomb's room would not be of general knowledge. I myself didn't know of a red taffeta reticule among your late wife's effects, so it seemed to me that someone who has access to the house, someone who knows what is to be found in your late wife's chamber must have stolen your daughter."

He nodded, the lines of his face reflecting his deep fears. "Perhaps not, though, Amanda. Whoever did this diabolical thing might be extremely clever. Clever enough to deliberately attempt to throw suspicion on a member of the household." He studied the writing minutely, his eyebrows drawn down in a heavy frown. "The words might have been deliberately misspelled in an attempt to throw suspicion on the unlearned man . . . while the perpetrator of this crime could be well-versed in reading and writing."

"But the red taffeta reticule," said Amanda. "I still say the note had to be written by someone who knows such an item is in the bedchamber where he left the note."

"True, but that isn't to say the man who stole my daughter necessarily lives on the place. I've recently had the floors in all the upstairs rooms refurbished. Also painted. The working men could have seen the red purse in the clothes press . . . or the dressing room, wherever it was kept."

"You just don't *want* to believe a member of your household has done this dastardly deed," she said quietly. "And for that I can't blame you. However, you surely can see that until the child is returned, you must operate upon the theory that *all* are suspect."

"Including my brother," he said coldly.

"Including your brother," she answered just as coldly.

He smiled, but there was no hint of merriment behind it. "And next I suppose you say my son is also suspect."

She hesitated, not wishing to add coals to his already burning ire. She understood that his anger was natural, and it was born of unspeakable fear and was inflamed by circumstance instead of by herself, although she was the recipient of his awesome anger right then. If she told him of her earlier suspicions of Andrew, she was afraid he would explode. Although he was keeping a firm grip on his emotions, she knew how quickly a man who is laboring under shock and unnamed fears can erupt in blazing action. Yet, in order to take every step necessary for the protection of the missing child, she felt she had to answer his question about Andrew truthfully.

With trembling lips, her voice barely above a whisper, she said, "Children do have their disagreements. And I've spoken to you before of the rivalry between Andrew and Nelda. All children quarrel, and I'm sure you must remember having exchanged blows with your own brother when you were youngsters. I was involved in fistfights with other children myself. David, I must tell you that at first I seriously wondered if Andrew might be behind this. I don't think he is a monstrous child who wouldn't think twice about killing his sister, though there are such children in this world. But we must consider all the possibilities. And we must remember that your son is precocious indeed. He reads all manner of books and his imagination is well developed. I don't mean to censor the child because of his imagination, for I, too, have a tendency to make up fantasies. I think it is far-fetched to even *consider* a twelve-year-old boy being behind this monstrous act, but as I said before, we must consider *all* possibilities. Leave no stone unturned. When your son returned with you from the fields, I looked at his face for telltale scratches. Even though he's older and bigger and stronger, he doesn't get off scot-free when the children fight. There's not a mark upon his face, but I can't say what might be upon his body. It wouldn't be proper for me to strip him down, no more than it would be if I were to ask your brother to strip down to show me if there are marks upon his body. Yet, there is evidence in Nelda's room that a mighty struggle took place, and I can't believe her assailant managed to quell her fighting spirit without getting a scratch or two for his pains."

"What you're saying is that I must look for the mark of Nelda's fingernails upon my son's body. And my *brother's!*" The way he spat out the words and the look he turned on her was proof of his disregard for her suspicions.

"I'm not saying I believe either your son or your brother guilty," she said hotly. "I'm merely saying there's a possibility. Ten thousand Spanish dollars is an incredible amount of money, which makes it ridiculous to believe a child wrote that note. Just imagine the difficulty a little boy would have in hiding such a sum! However, I feel you owe it to them and yourself as well as your little girl to remove those you love best from even a faint suspicion."

"Then you, yourself, are not above suspicion, I take it?" David's eyes burned.

Amanda gasped, taken by surprise. "I hadn't thought of that, but yes," she said gamely. "I, too, should be cleared of suspicion, just as your brother and son should."

To her utter shock, David's voice broke and he sobbed. Amanda had never seen a man break down before. Mr. Tomlinson's eyes had grown misty when he'd attended her father's funeral with her, and again he'd grown tearful that day in his office when he'd spoken to her of his financial losses. Seeing David in the throes of grief and fear made her want to cover the space between them; to ease those wracking sobs by holding him to her breast as she would comfort a child. She quickly walked over to him and gripped his hand in hers.

"Forgive me," he said as he turned from her in embarrassment. "I'm sure you are blameless in this matter. It's the not *knowing* about my daughter that torments me. Not knowing whether she lives or *dies*. I feel so helpless." He smacked the red paper with his open palm. "A man who would steal a child from her little bed—who would leave such a note as this—is capable of doing anything. My mind reels with all sorts of possibilities. She could be dead now. The gold that is demanded in return for her freedom, her very life! is nothing to me compared with my child's welfare. Of course I will take the money to the appointed place. But I have no proof that she is not already dead. Or worse. . . ."

He buried his face in his hands. Amanda's heart hammered. "Worse?"

"There are all sorts of things that might happen to a pretty little girl of ten years. There are places where a young girl can be sold into slavery, to be used for the most hideous vices, by men who have no conscience. A well-bred gentle-woman such as you could not know of these hell-holes of vice where a virgin child is used for the most despicable of purposes."

"But she's just a little child! Hardly more than a *baby!*"

"Exactly," said David Whitcomb grimly. "Which is what I mean when I speak of practices so diabolitcal that death would be a welcome release for many unfortunate children who are stolen away from their homes."

"Don't allow yourself to dwell on those things," said Amanda, feeling faint. "Believe me when I say I will do all I can to help . . . and that I . . ." The firm control with which she had marshalled her forces dissolved under the only half-realized questions he'd aroused in her feverish brain. "Oh, David, if only I had this morning to live over!"

"What do you mean?"

She told him of awakening at dawn, her unreasonable panic, then the memory of having heard someone cry out. "But I thought it was merely the crow of a cock—that I had used the cry to fabricate a dream. That same dream you woke me from last night. Now I'm confident that I heard Nelda crying out for help—probably at the very moment when she was being taken from the house. Over and over I have cursed myself for not arousing from my bed, for not going to her room right then and making sure all was well."

"Don't worry yourself by thinking of what might have been," he said. "I, too, am tortured by that kind of reasoning. If I had not been anxious to ride out to the fields this morning, perhaps this thing wouldn't have happened. You see, we mustn't waste valuable time by looking backwards, wishing we had the opportunity to do things over again. What's done is done. And you've behaved splendidly, Amanda. It galls a man to be told what to do by a mere slip of a girl, even if she is his wife. But I see the wisdom behind your decision to tell nobody of the ransom note. Only we two know the true circumstances. The two of us and the diabolical fiends who took my child. We'll do as you suggest, however." A shadow of a father's proud smile hovered on his lips for an instant, made more heartbreaking by the haunting fear in his eyes. Then he said, "I, too, have seen Nelda in the peak of her fury. She fights like forty demons from hell; one of the many reasons she needed the guilding of a good woman. I've often worried about her growing to womanhood. With her tendency to flail those little fists of hers at the slightest provocation, what manner of man would take her to wife?" He licked his dry, feverish lips. "Now I pray God only that she be given the chance to grow to womanhood! Yes, we'll do as you say, Amanda. Examine the flesh of every man and woman on the place for the signs of a frightened child who tried to protect herself. Then we must let it be known why we did it. For when I go to put the gold in the place where I must, all hands must remain well away from the site."

The great house was silent, like a place of mourning. Two hours had passed, during which time David had caused every servant on the place to be closely examined for skin abrasions about their person. No mark of any kind was on anyone. Subdued voices, with an undertone of distrust and anger, rose now and then from the servants, who formed themselves in little groups of resentment. They had all been stripped and examined, the females by Amanda, the males by David. Andrew, sent to Amanda's chambers after his father had examined his young body, cast venomous glances at her from under his long lashes. Only Becky, who submitted without outward signs of anger to the close inspection of her body, and Lochard seemed to hold no resentment over the indignity.

At noon, David knocked at Amanda's door. His face was drawn, the lines deeply etched in worry as he entered. "I'm going to call all the servants together to let them know why they've been examined. I'd appreciate your presence."

"Me, too, Papa?" Andrew ran to his father's side.

"You, too," answered David. "Then you'll know why what was done was necessary . . . and why you must not, under any circumstances, go out alone.

You'll sleep in our room tonight." David turned back to Amanda. "Then there's my cousin Sarah, who is demanding to know what is going on. In our haste, I'm afraid we forgot Sarah, Amanda. She's an old woman, and I dislike submitting her to the indignity of a search, but it must be done."

Amanda thought he looked evasive, but she stood, agreed to carry out the task and asked where Sarah's chambers were.

"In the West wing," David answered. "Her voice began to jar on my nerves. I'm afraid I was abrupt with her just now." He ran a nervous hand through his thatch of unkempt hair, his eyes upon the clock on the mantle piece. "Great God, I can't believe that it's only noon. It seems hours since you handed me that note." He was turning to Andrew, his voice tight with sadness, when Amanda left the room to go to Sarah Trueblood where she would spend one of the most difficult hours of her entire life.

Although Sarah was not mindless, as David had pointed out earlier, she was unlearned in social behavior due to her inability to hear or speak. It was necessary for Amanda to form each syllable with utmost care when she spoke. She tried again and again to make herself clear. The old woman had never been asked to take off her clothing before and submit to a close inspection of her skin, so she didn't understand the patient, repeated words that Amanda tried so hard to make her understand. She wished for Flora, who had little difficulty in communicating with the old woman. Or Becky, who could converse with her almost as easily as the cook. But of course it wouldn't be right to have a servant undertake what Amanda knew must seem like a most unforgivable invasion upon her privacy.

If only, she thought impatiently, *someone had*

taken the pains to teach Sarah how to read and write! Not only would the old lady have the comfort of finding new worlds in the written word, but she could communicate easier. In vain, Amanda tugged at her own clothing, then pointed at the garments Sarah wore. Sarah smiled, getting the meaning of Amanda's gestures all wrong. "No-this-frock . . . does-not-need-to . . . be-laundered . . . I-just-put-it . . . on-today. . . ."

"No, no," shouted Amanda, ashamed at her tendency to scream into the old woman's ear. She knew Sarah had never heard the sound of anybody's voice, that shouting didn't help in the least, but she was powerless to keep her voice down as she tried again to explain. Finally, she went to the door and beckoned for Sarah to follow. The index finger raised and curling forward was obviously something Sarah understood. With little mincing footsteps, the white-haired woman followed Amanda down the hall toward the East wing. As a last resort Amanda decided to use quill and paper to draw a series of pictures. In that way, she hoped she would get her meaning across. Before she was inside her own room, however, she realized both she and David had been carried away by the shattering horror of Nelda's disappearance. Feeling very foolish, she realized they'd not stopped to realize that Sarah couldn't have written the ransom note. She couldn't write, couldn't read.

David and Andrew were in Amanda's room when she entered with Sarah. David said he had spoken to the servants, explained what had happened to Nelda. "The servants are no longer resentful about the search. Every one of them assured me that they will go to any lengths to help in any way they can. I told them the grave danger they'd be adding to Nelda's own danger if they ventured out, even by chance came close to the place where I'm to pay the ransom." His eyes shifted to his cousin, and in a voice that was tight with an emotion Amanda couldn't identify, he asked if she bore any scratches on her body.

"I couldn't make myself clear. She doesn't understand," said Amanda. "Anyway, she couldn't have taken Nelda from her room! Or written that note. She can't write."

"Search her anyway," answered David tersely.

Sarah stood uncertainly in the middle of the room, glancing first at David, then Andrew, then back at Amanda. Speaking to David, she said, "I-don't-know-where-is-Nelda-this-young-woman . . . has-tried-to-speak-to-me . . . about-something. . . ."

Andrew got to his feet. "I'll tell her, Papa," he said manfully. Then Amanda watched while Andrew spoke to Sarah.

"Nelda got taken from her room. Stolen."

Sarah's fingers clutched nervously at the loose skin of her throat. "Not-that-sweet-baby. . . ."

Andrew nodded. "The person who took her left a note." He pointed to Amanda. "She found it. It said for Papa to bring money to the river. At midnight tonight. Then the bad men will let Nelda come home."

At first Sarah Trueblood gazed all around in stunned silence while she digested the young boy's words. Then her blue eyes widened as she went to the window and looked out, her white head shaking madly. When she spoke, her words were shocking in their meaning, made more so by the lack of inflection in tone. "This—" she said distinctly, the word accented by a wrenching sob, "this-house . . . is-cursed. . . ."

When Amanda looked at the frail woman's flesh, she didn't find a mark.

7

Two more hours dragged by. In a house where there was nothing to be done but wait, the stress and strain was beginning to take a toll. David didn't wait well. Lochard, who appeared to bear no ill will toward his brother even before he'd been informed of the reason behind the search of his body, was slightly more capable of withstanding the interminable wait. David paced from room to room, Andrew at his side, now fearful of letting his son out of his sight. When he could bear the house no longer, David went outside.

Governor Jennings, who had come in answer to an entreaty David Whitcomb had sent by one of the servants, was shown into the library where Amanda and Lochard were going back over every hour of the last few days in an effort to shed some new light on the mystery.

Solemnly, Lochard greeted Jonathon Jennings.

"Our thanks to you, sir, for returning so promptly. Yesterday Whispering Hills was a place of pleasant conversation and celebration. Today we've been struck by tragedy of the worst kind.

My brother has gone down to the river. Under the circumstances, one may well understand why he can't sit idly by."

"Good Lord, man, tell me what's happened," said the Governor as he took a seat and accepted the glass of wine offered by sullen Faylodene. "According to David's message, the worst kind of devilment has taken place here. He didn't elaborate, but stressed just that he needed me desperately. For a man of your brother's turn, those were strong words. I wasted no time in riding out."

It was Lochard who told Governor Jennings everything that had taken place in the house that day; from the moment Amanda went into Nelda's room to find the little girl gone, the overturned furnishings, bedding and draperies in disarray, to the finding of the ransom note. Then he said, "Amanda insisted that nobody was innocent until proven so." He turned a wry smile on her. "Such cool reasoning, and from a member of the fairer sex, too. I'll admit I was somewhat affronted when my brother insisted he inspect my hide to see if Nelda had inflicted scratches. He should have told me why first. I'd gladly have stripped down to the buff in order to show me innocence in the matter. I love my niece and nephew as though they were my own. But I admit the flesh inspection was a good idea."

"How is that?" The Governor leaned forward, his intelligent eyes aglow with wrath that such an abominable coup should have been perpetrated against the family.

Lochard laughed, and all three people in the room were aware of how thin that laughter was. "My niece is a scrapper, sir. I admit it isn't seemly for a sweet little girl to claw and bite and kick, but on the other hand, it gives me great satisfaction to know her assailant must surely have suffered a few scratches. The person who did it must have gone stealthily to her room, and found her asleep. I can't say what manner or means was used to drag the child away, but by the looks of that bed and the contents of the room, she put up one . . . a considerable fight. Now, sir, before my brother returns from the house, I want to speak of something I've not dared to mention to him, it's so grave."

Lochard looked at Amanda. Then he went to sit at her side, where he took her hand in his before he spoke. "It's quite possible that this has occurred to my brother. Very few things escape his attention, even pertaining to matters of less importance than the abduction of his daughter. However, he is distraught, so he may not have thought of it. It's this: Nelda is a ten-year-old girl, completely in possession of speech. Further, her memory is excellent. What means of protection has this child-stealer used in order to insure that . . . once she is left to go free, she won't name her abductor?"

The thought had occurred to Amanda, but she didn't say so. By Lochard giving the hidden fear she'd harbored the substance and meaning of words, the realization that Nelda's life was in even worse jeopardy than suspected on the surface somehow was made more real.

"He could have used a blindfold," said the Governor. "Let's hope that was the case." Then he said he wished to see the room.

Amanda and Lochard accompanied him upstairs, while he asked several questions, including the matter of the intimate search. "And you say there are no scratches on the skin of anybody in the household."

By then, Amanda, Lochard and Governor

Jennings were in the nursery, where everything had been left exactly as it had been. Becky had wanted to clean up the mess and scrub away the blood on the floor, but David had insisted she leave it be, explaining that even though there appeared to be no clue in the room as to what had taken place there, they well might be overlooking something. He'd hoped that Governor Jennings, his friend and confidante as well as his legal advisor, would be able to shed some light on the tragedy.

Jennings blanched at the sight of the blood on the floor. It was dried now and the golden hair looked even more ghastly. After some minutes of intent inspection, the Governor turned away, his face set in stern lines. "And the hounds led you to the river, then lost the scent, Lochard?"

"Yes, sir. So it appears that whoever took Nelda from her room must have had a boat of some kind waiting."

Amanda refrained from voicing her most horrifying fear that Nelda had never reached the river alive. Men who would be callous enough to do such a cruel thing to a child would hardly hesitate when it came to disposing of their victim. She believed that the abductor would know the father would pay the ransom without proof that Nelda still lived. She also knew there was a method of dragging the river, had read of it in the newspaper. It was done in England when a child was believed to be drowned. As yet such an operation hadn't been mentioned, but she felt reasonably sure that David had considered the possibility of finding Nelda's dear young body down there under the roiling, swollen waters.

David and Andrew were entering the house by the front door when Amanda, Lochard and the Governor descended the steps after visiting the scene of the crime. As the hours passed, he had become more and more haggard, but a look of hope grew in his eyes when he saw that Jennings had arrived. Amanda was stricken with compassion for her husband, knowing that he was now at the point where he was grasping at straws. She could well understand how he would put false hope in the Governor's presence, however she knew Jennings was kind and considerate, a learned and true friend . . . but a mere human. She wished there were some method of better surveying the evidence in Nelda's room; some as yet unknown method of crime-detection that would point an accusing finger at the person who had done such a foul deed, then voiced her question thoughtlessly:

"Isn't there something else we can do? There should be *some* way a criminal can be found and brought to justice! I've read of certain practices in other countries. It's done for thievery, possibly designed to work upon the guilty person's mind. A rock is heated until it's quite hot, but not impossible to hold in one's hand without burning. Only the guilty person is burned. I *still* say this was done by someone who has knowledge of this house. Somebody who knows a red taffeta reticule was among Charity's possessions. Someone who knows Mr. Whitcomb's habit of rising early and riding out before dawn."

They had gone back to the library, unconsciously seeking the feeling of closeness it afforded that was lacking in the other, larger rooms of the house. A fire had been built in the library because of the chill rain that had started falling. Gusts of wind hammered against the window pane; the wind grew more intense as each second ticked by with torturous slowness.

"Waiting," said the Governor thoughtfully,

"worrying and not being able to do anything, is the most extreme torture known to man." He turned to Amanda. "I'm inclined to agree with you, Miss Kendall. Only close friends of the family would know of the existence of the red reticule in the late Mrs. Whitcomb's possessions."

"But what of the men who repaired the flooring? The painters, too, could have seen the possessions in Charity's room," said Lochard. "I remember when you had the work done, David. All the contents of Charity's dressing room were piled upon the bed and dresser, then placed in the middle of the room. The men then placed heavy cloths over the belongings in order to protect the hats and furs and things. Also, has anybody considered the possibility of a sneak thief? I'm afraid we don't take proper precautions at Whispering Hills. Witness the tragic death of Charity."

David spoke abruptly. "We *do* take proper precautions at Whispering Hills, Lochard. *Especially* since Charity's death. But we mustn't forget that to a man bent upon mischief there is no such thing as a locked door. There are ways to get into a house by those professional criminals who make it their life's business to sack and pillage."

Jennings spoke soothingly. "There's no use in becoming sharp with one another. Nerves are raw at a time like this. And certainly, it's most understandable that a man is unwilling to believe his friends, members of his family or trusted servants capable of such a heinous crime."

"Even so," said Lochard, "you should have a pack of dogs on the place, David. That's another thing. Does anybody remember hearing a dog bark during the night?" He made an impatient gesture. "Those two great friendly puppies you keep would no doubt graciously show a footpad into the house, bowing and scraping like jackdaws. I, for one, intend to take immediate steps to bring in a pack of the most vicious hellhounds available. I'll leave some here at Whispering Hills, the others I'll take to White Rose. It may be like locking the barn door after the horses have escaped, but even though I haven't the riches of my esteemed brother, my home is my castle, and I value what I have."

"Stop!" Amanda stood up. "Nothing is to be gained by bickering."

"I beg your pardon," said Lochard.

"My fault, I'm sure," echoed David. "My nerves are raw. It would seem that I can't hold my wits about me when I keep worrying about the fate that could have befallen my daughter. Have any of you considered the possibility that she's already dead? I tell you, a man who would stoop to barter with the life of a child would stop at *nothing!* He might have murdered her when she struggled with him. Carried her lifeless body down to the river and thrown it in, weighted down with stones. I'm going *mad* with the worry."

"Then go and have the river dragged," suggested Lochard. "I'll go with you. I'm not her father, true. She's not blood of my blood, but I loved Nelda as though she were my own. We'll have the servants lace together poles. If we're to do it, we should be at it, man, for with this new rain, the river will continue to rise."

David held up a hand. "Again, I apologize. To all within the room." He gazed into the sparking fire, his broad shoulders shaking. "No, we'll wait until tomorrow morning. See if she's released unharmed. If that happens, I'll get down on my knees and give thanks to God Almighty for her safety. It would seem to me that if we're being watched—which I suppose we are by the perpetrator of this crime—it would appear that I've given up hope of getting my girl back alive. If he hasn't already killed her, he might do it at the first signs of dragging the river, for then he'd conclude that I won't carry out his instructions."

There was silence in the room, interrupted only by the snapping logs in the fireplace. Amanda spoke first. "I can see your point. You don't know what manner of man you're dealing with, and it's reasonable to believe a madman, one who is willing to gamble with his life by carrying out this dreadful plan, might well conclude that you're not going to pay the ransom."

"A point well taken," said the Governor.

Amanda sighed, her jangled nerves more edgy than they'd been. She excused herself, saying she must go upstairs and lie down for a while. All three men stood as she left the room, and Lochard accompanied her, saying he would like to try the hounds again. "It's really no use," he told her as they left the library. "Even a hound with the best nose in the world can't follow scent on water, and this rain will wash away the trail that led them to the river. But I can't sit still any more, nor can you. Come with me? We'll go over every inch of ground on the place. Who knows but what we might find something."

She knew if she tried to rest her nerves would become more raw than ever. In spite of the torrential rain that poured down from the skies, the ever-blackening clouds and the distant thunder that was growing closer each second, Amanda decided to go out with Lochard to search the grounds once more. She dashed upstairs to get a heavy cloak and a matching hood. Lochard said he would wait for her at the foot of the steps.

The second she opened the door to her old room, Amanda felt the unaccountable chill; knew without knowing how she knew that she was not alone in the room. A fire burned merrily in the grate and since the heat of summertime had been upon the land before the rains that had been falling all around Whispering Hills had finally darkened the skies, the fire, she knew, should have dispelled what little chill was in the room. Instead, she felt an icy breeze that made the hair at the nape of her neck crawl as a thrill of pure terror raced up and down her spine.

She glanced around, frozen in nameless horror. She felt as though the very walls had eyes; that somebody was staring at her from every conceivable place in the room. Yet there was no item out of place, no visible form to show her beyond a shadow of a doubt that the room was inhabited by anyone other than herself. Speaking aloud, she admonished herself to not behave like a wretched fool. But she regretted having closed the door. She was afraid to turn around and open it, fearing that unknown quality, that unnamed *presence* that seemed to fill the room. She had an idea that if she did turn her back on the gloom in the room that unseen hands would grab her from out of the atmosphere, that an icy entity would speak her name.

It's just the rain that makes me so edgy, she told herself as she made her foot step firmly toward the clothes press. *Just the rain and the lowering skies. The rain hammering at the window pane.* A flash of lightning zig-zagged across the muddy looking sky through her window, followed closely by a peal of thunder so loud that her ears rang. Outside, she saw the top of the appple tree in the yard bend under the onslaught of the wind and rain. Even though she knew it was impossible to go out in that storm, she was determined to force herself to get her oiled cloak and hood just the same. Somehow, the action would mean that she was defying the fates; or to be more explicit, that she would show herself she was not really afraid of a ghost she could feel but not hear, sense but not see. *Anyway, storms like this don't last forever,* she thought as she opened the door to the clothes press. *An outing in the fresh air will do me good. Refresh my mind so I can think. When the storm clears, Lochard and I will walk out, and who knows? We might find some trace of Nelda.*

Her actions were jerky as she reached in and took the oiled cloak from the hook. The hood was in her trunk, and she tried to laugh at herself for being afraid to cross the carpet and open it. With a defiant bang of the lid against the wall, she ruffled the garments in the trunk, cast them in wild disarray as she hurriedly clawed around and found the oiled hood. It was in her hands and she was sprinting toward the door, mindful of the increasing chill in the room when she stopped dead still.

"No!"

Her word of protest was instinctive as the batting of an eye when an insect flies into the face.

"Oh, no!"

Trembling so violently that her lifeless fingers dropped the hood and cloak she clutched, she stared at the apparition that built up in front of her eyes.

The thing was misty. Opalescent and shimmering. Something down at the bottom next to the carpet swirled round and round. Amanda was aware of the swirling, fog-like, yet glowing motion, but she was unable to take her eyes from the thing at eye level. A slightly larger than life-size head and shoulders formed in the mist. The head was crowned with golden hair that framed a lovely face. The mouth, opened, but no words came out. The eyes appeared wounded with some grief so all-encompassing that they gave the impression of hopelessness. Two pale hands stretched forward from wispy bare arms. Amanda, rooted to the spot, tried to cry out in her frozen terror but she couldn't get the tiniest sound past her tight throat. While her heart thumped and her eyes grew even wider in her abject terror, she saw the hands fold themselves together under a wispy, transparent face in a beseeching attitude.

"Charity?" The fearful name was torn from Amanda's throat.

Subtly, the expression on the entity's face changed from a burning quality of despair to a sweet-sad, tremulous smile of hope. Once more the wraithlike hands clasped under the misty chin. Then the entire apparition faded from the room as though it had been smoke, dispersed by the wild gusts of wind outside the window.

8

It took an eternity for Amanda to move her leaden feet forward, to grasp the cold door knob and fling the door open.

The warmth in the hall came as a shock. For seconds, she could do nothing but lean against her closed door, her chest heaving as she struggled for breath, for she felt exactly as though someone had struck a heavy blow in her chest. Her lungs labored as her heart throbbed, and all the time she fought for breath and tried to still the wild hammering of her heart. She refused to believe that she had seen a ghost. Again, she blamed her own frayed nerves for playing tricks on her. She kept seeing that face as it had been before her. It was just that she was so anxious and disturbed over Nelda's disappearance, she told herself as she went back down the stairs.

Lochard was waiting for her at the bottom, his handsome face tilted upwards to catch first glance of her. "I was beginning to believe you'd changed your mind. Decided to take a nap after all."

"I would have let you know," she answered, surprised that her voice didn't sound jagged and harsh. It was an effort to behave as though nothing untoward had happened, but then she realized if her countenance showed added strain it would be considered natural under the circumstances.

"They've laid the table. I'm afraid we all forgot about lunch. I'm too worried about Nelda to have much of an appetite, but we should all try to take some nourishment. Besides, the storm has grown in intensity. It's now too inclement to consider taking our walk."

She stared at Lochard, the sound of his voice registering seconds after he'd spoken. At first she didn't understand what he meant. Then she remembered her cloak, thought of the way her numb fingers had dropped it when she'd seen the wraith. Right then, she wondered if she could ever be able to enter that room again. "Oh. My cloak. Yes." Her lips formed the expected words with some effort. "The storm increased when I was in my room, which was why I didn't bring my coat after all."

"Then we should join the others at the table. I'm most concerned about my brother. He's already been through more tragedy during his lifetime than half a dozen men should suffer."

"How sad, but true," Amanda replied, thinking of the untimely deaths of both of David's wives. Particularly, the unsolved mystery of Charity's death. For all she knew, it was possible for a mother to cross the barrier of life and death in order to protect a child. Had the dead woman's spirit been attempting to communicate with her? Had the same villianous hand that ended Charity's life also abducted Nelda?

She wanted to ask Lochard more about Charity's murder, but before she could find the right words, Amanda's thoughts were interrupted by the clear ringing voice of a woman.

"Lochard! How *wonderful* to see you! And how dreadful this rain is, it's spoiled my bonnet, I'm afraid. William and I were out driving, and it was our intention to stop by your house to exchange a greeting before we came calling upon dear David and the children, but your servant said you weren't at home. A most surly brute, I must say. He wouldn't even give us the courtesy of saying when you'd return, nor did he ask us in, and the rain coming down in simply *torrents!*"

Becky, her face registering disapproval of the small girl who had run quickly to Lochard and placed a delicate white hand in his, walked behind a sallow-faced youth, who was apparently in attendance on the beautiful creature dressed in several shades of blue silks and satin. In one glance, Amanda took in the graceful little figure all encased in elegant clothing, from the top of her bright golden head to the tips of her fragile little shoes.

When she'd spent a great deal of time on her toilette and was dressed in her very best, Amanda believed herself to be only passingly attractive. When she had thrown on the first thing that came to hand and had barely taken the time to twist up her hair in a plain topknot, she knew she was quite plain. As she surveyed the dimpled girl who smelled of French perfumes and had the bearing of a pampered darling, she felt suddenly unkempt and bedraggled, gaunt as a witch and twice as ugly. She also felt quite tall and ungainly, a big, awkward girl who towered head and shoulders over the fragile creature before her whom Lochard introduced as Miss Deirdre Bennet. "And this is Mr. William Bennet," Lochard added politely. "Brother and sister. From Corydon."

"Oh, my dear," cried the little creature who was still pressing the feathers of her hat in place, "I'm sure nobody would believe William and I are husband and wife. William is just a mere child, aren't you, dear brother?" She gazed at the sallow-faced youth with her enormous blue eyes, the lashes fluttering as she dimpled. The brother's cheeks flushed as he looked nervously at his shoes. Then Miss Bennet, finally sensing that something was amiss, said, "Oh, Lochard, dearest, I do hope William and I aren't interrupting anything between you and—ah . . ."

"Mrs. David Whitcomb," Amanda said smoothly, extending her hand. Although she still felt like a drab charwoman in comparison to the richly garbed Deirdre, Amanda took secret delight in watching the other woman's eyes widen and her jaw go slack with shock.

"Excuse me . . . ?" Deirdre said, unwilling to believe what she had heard.

Lochard coughed uneasily. "Amanda and David were married just yesterday. A small ceremony with only the family in attendance. It was a very happy moment for us all."

"I'm sure it was." Deirdre would not take her eyes off Amanda. Amanda could only guess at the uncharitable thoughts that must have been running through the woman's mind. Such a hasty marriage between a governess and the master the house might well mean that a child was on the way. "How impetuous of David," Deirdre said then, as if to confirm Amanda's suspicions.

Amanda only smiled and graciously nodded her head. Let her believe what she wants, Amanda thought. I am still the mistress of this household and she, only a guest. The realization made Amanda hold her head a bit higher. "I would have preferred a longer engagement. But David was most insistent that we marry."

"Let me offer *our* congratulations," William Bennet said then. He stared pointedly at his sister. "We are delighted to hear such happy news, aren't we, Deirdre?"

"Yes, of course," Deirdre echoed in a simpering tone. "I will have to congratulate David personally," she added, evidently still quite shocked.

Behind the young man and woman, Becky continued to glower. "A light luncheon is served in the dining room," she said pointedly.

"Oh, but merciful heavens, my brother and I would never dream of *intruding*," squealed the fair Deirdre. Her manner of speaking left no doubt that she secretly believed she could never intrude, that source of constant delight to anybody within hearing or looking distance. Then her china blue eyes looked at Lochard with an entrancing show of wonder. "But isn't it late to be eating the noon meal?"

"We've been greatly upset in the house this morning," said Becky in a none-too-polite voice. "There wasn't time to think of food."

"Oh, my!" Deirdre rolled her eyes in theatrical concern. "Nothing tragic, I hope."

"My niece has been abducted," said Lochard.

Deirdre Bennet's long golden lashes fluttered up and down. Her eyes seemed to wheel around in her head. "Not that sweet child! Not that sunny dispositioned little moppet! Oh, Lochard, my heart bleeds for you—really, I must leave immediately—ah, William and I, that is. Come, William." She put a pensive index finger to her chin, reminding Amanda very much of the studied movement of a stage player. "But first I must express my concern to *dear* David. This is an hour when he needs the sympathy and love of all his closest friends," she said pointedly to Amanda.

Amanda remained where she was while Lochard gallantly offered Miss Bennet his arm and escorted her to the dining room. William, obviously feeling ill at ease, shambled along behind them without a backward glance at Amanda. As Miss Bennet's blue-on-blue satin skirt with the darker blue petticoat dancing flirtatiously and fashionably six inches below the hem, disappeared around the corner, Amanda saw Lochard's face as he looked down at her patently concerned, upturned face. It glowed.

Becky stepped forward. "Damn strumpet," she said in an almost whisper. "Paints her cheeks and I swear she cuts the hair off her head and pastes single strands on her eyelids."

"That will do, Becky," said Amanda.

Becky refused to be called down. "Well, she *is!* I never saw the likes of such a show. Thank goodness Master David got sense enough to take you for his wife, stead of that little witch. Now, Missy Amanda, you go on in there and get you a bite to eat. You got to eat you something, keep up your strength. Little Missy gonna come back home, you may lay to that, and you goin' without food isn't gonna bring her back any sooner. Soon as midnight comes and Master David done pay out that gold to the vile critter that took little Miss, mornin' come sure as sin. Then Missy Nelda will come home, not another hair on her pretty head touched."

"I'll join the others in the dining room in a few moments, Becky. Right now I want to speak to you alone."

Becky gave her a tremulous smile. "Better we get out of here, then. You want to come to the kitchen and eat you a bite with me and Flora and her man?"

"Later, perhaps. Come with me upstairs, Becky. I want you to accompany me into my bedchamber. What I have to say is in strict confidence."

"I understand, Miss Amanda. Laws, this has been a bad day from beginning to end, and that's the Lord's truth."

Amanda walked with a heavy tread up the flight of stairs. Before she opened the door to the room where she had so recently encountered what she was willing, in spite of her own convictions in the past that the dead do not return, that she had seen a ghost, she gave Becky a long, level look. In that instant, she had decided to keep Becky locked in until she learned the truth about Charity Whitcomb. She waited until the servant was well inside before she turned the key in the lock.

"Now. With the charming guest downstairs, who will assuredly create a welcome diversion at a time most needed, you and I will speak frankly. I have no intention of letting you out of this room until you've told me what I want to know. Who murdered Charity Whitcomb?"

Becky's dark eyes widened. "Who said anybody murdered her?"

"Never mind. I know she was strangled in her bed. And don't put on an act with me."

"Oh." Becky turned on a wide, vacant grin as she sank into a chair. Then she rolled her eyes and managed to look stupid.

"Becky, don't look at me like that, as though you've suddenly turned into an idiot. I know you're an intelligent woman. You've learned to read and write, and you know exactly how to judge people."

"But what difference does it make who killed Miss Charity? It's over and done with."

"Exactly, but I have a—a hunch that Nelda's disappearance ties in with her mother's death."

Becky's vacant look left her features. She leaned
forward and stared at Amanda. "You do? A hunch,
you say? You mean you have a feeling in your
bones? Well, I wouldn't know about that."

"Well, I do, and I want you to tell me the truth."

"I promised Master David I wouldn't speak of
that terrible time to anybody."

"You'd better speak of it to me. Remember, I'm
not merely the children's governess anymore. I'm
Master Whitcomb's wife."

When she'd begun to wonder if the spirit of
Charity Whitcomb had tried to give her a message
from beyond the grave, she'd been stunned at such
an idea. But the longer she'd toyed with the idea,
the more sense the weird notion made. Maybe she
had seen a ghost, maybe not. But the wild notion
that Charity's spirit was trying to tell her something had led Amanda to other, more concrete and
rational ideas. She knew the servant Becky had
knowledge of the circumstances surrounding
Charity's death. There was, she felt, at least a
chance that a link existed between that cold-
blooded crime and Nelda's abduction. When she'd
told Becky she had nothing to go on but a hunch,
she spoke the truth.

"You won't tell Master David I spoke of this to
you?" Becky's face was troubled.

"Of course not. Trust me, Becky."

Becky sighed. "All right then. He—nobody was
ever plain-out accused of killing Miss Charity. Not
right out in the open, like. Lots of people think he
did it himself. They never fought or fussed,
though. Got along just fine, only—it was more of a
friendly relation, than, well, like man and wife."
Becky's dark eyebrows drew down. "I mean,
Missy, they weren't in love the way the Master was
in love with Miss Celeste. He kind of liked her and
she kind of liked him. But not the way it's sup-

posed to be between man and wife.''

Amanda grew impatient. David had told her as much himself. "But who do you believe killed Charity?"

"Oh, Missy! That's not for me to say!''

"Don't evade me, Becky. You aren't getting out of this room until you've told me.''

Becky looked at the floor. Her voice was a whisper. "He said it was Miss Sarah. Miss Sarah just plain didn't like Miss Charity. Not one whit. But when the Gov'ner came to the house and the sheriff, he never gave his old cousin's secret away. He said to me, Becky, if she did it, she did it, but I promised my mother I would always look after her. I think some coin passed hands. Maybe so, maybe not. Now, Missy, you asked me for the truth, and the truth is what I'm saying to you. That was exactly what Master David said. That if his old cousin killed his wife, then all hell and high water wasn't goin' to bring her back to life. And Miss Sarah, she has these spells when she walks at night. Like she's asleep, but before God her eyes are wide open and blank as planks. Now of course if she did do away with poor Miss Charity, the Master couldn't take a chance on letting her do in somebody else. So ever' night I lock her in her room. She only walks by night when it's full moon, but just to be on the safe side, I lock her in ever' night.''

"You're telling me the truth, Becky?''

"Yes, ma'am.'' Becky's eyes looked straight into her own.

Amanda was silent for a moment. "Why did Mr. Whitcomb insist that both wives' bedchambers remain undisturbed, just as they had been before his wives died?''

"Because he was mad with grief when his first / wife died. I think he couldn't bear to believe she wouldn't come back. See . . ." Again, Becky knit her eyebrows together in an effort to make herself clear. "Like, if Miss Celeste's room stayed just like it was, then he could maybe convince himself she wasn't gone for good, that she'd come back some day. Then when his second wife died, the sheriff said the room had to stay like it was. Something about what they call 'clues.' They said the case would be left on the books until her murderer had been caught."

Amanda could understand that much. She hesitated before she phrased her next question. "One last question, then you may go. Why did you call the subject of Miss Charity's ghost to my attention shortly after I began to regain my strength, then refuse to talk about it when I asked you to tell me?"

Becky's face turned ashen. "Please, ma'am. Don' ask me that."

"I insist, Becky; I must know."

Shuddering, her face contorted in a mask of fear, Becky looked over her shoulder, then all around the room. With pale lips barely moving, she whispered, "You've not seen it again, have you?"

"No," Amanda lied. "Not lately. I don't remember seeing it when I was sick with the fever. But I did see a misty form the other night when I was in the library. It had no substance, and I was in there alone. It didn't come in the door, but more like—well, it appeared to take shape, then float across the room as though it came from the wall. I don't mind telling you I suffered a terrible fright. Whatever it was, a vision or a figment of my imagination, there was enough power in it to snuff out the candle in the library. The candles also went out in the wall sconces and the chandelier of the hall. Mr. Lochard Whitcomb called for lights, if you'll remember, shortly before we went in to supper."

"Yes. I remember that."

"But why did you behave so strangely about the ghost, Becky? Why did you refuse to talk about it?"

Becky appeared to be in the throes of some secret fear. Finally, she said, "Because, Miss. When you talked about seeing a golden-haired woman and named her by name—that is, when you spoke to her that night when you were so sick, I told Master David about it. He told me not to be a damned fool, and for God's sake not to mention it to you. It was too late. I'd already told you about it. But he told me I'd just better not get you all upset with my talk of ghosts and goblins and the like. Then too, I was afraid you'd get all scared and go back to England. I could of cut my tongue out, and that's the truth, for blurtin' that out before I thought. Because . . . you see, ma'am, whenever somethin' real bad is about to take place in this house a ghost shows up. Like . . . like it's a warnin'. Always before, it was another ghost. An old woman that walks with a limp. The Old Master knew about it. He was an old devil, he was. But even so, he knew there were ghosts that walked. He knew about the ghost of Whispering Hills, that old woman that drug one leg. She always showed up when there was goin' to be trouble in the house. He saw her himself the night before Miss Celeste took bad and died. And when he was a-layin' on his own death bed, he saw her again and he looked right up at me—I was there with him to the end— he looked up at me and said, 'There she is. The demon like the hounds of hell, come to take me away.' He was scared to die, the wicked old sinner. Scared to face the hell fire and damnation he knew he had a-comin' to him, and he asked me to pray for him." Unaccountably, Becky laughed. Her face darkened and her brown eyes burned with the same kind of fiery fury Amanda had seen recently in David Whitcomb's eyes. "Imagine! Now, just imagine him askin' *me*, born into slavery and him buyin' and sellin' like we were dogs, yet he had the gall to ask me to pray for him. By then, Master David had the plantation in his hands, a-course, and he'd set everybody free. But that old devil! Crazy as a bedbug for years before he died, but there at the last he got his sense back and was scared to die."

Amanda stood up, went to the door and unlocked it. When Becky had been downstairs for a few minutes, Amanda went down herself. She didn't look forward with pleasure to the unexpected company, but even though she'd disliked the beautiful young Miss Bennet on sight, she'd spoken the truth when she told Becky the fair Deirdre would be a welcome diversion.

Both David and Lochard had brightened considerably under the magic of the young woman. Even the Governor, faithful married man that he was, appeared to be amused by the fashionably dressed visitor.

It was four o'clock in the afternoon when the Bennet brother and sister left, with Deirdre fluttering her long golden eyelashes as she sighed excessively and repeated, "If there's anything— just anything that I can do to help, David, please send a man for me *immediately*. Even during the night, David, dear," she added with a pretty display of dimples and a dramatic touch of her handkerchief to her eyes. "My heart is with you, pray remember that. And I'm sure you know I will be on my knees all night to God, asking for Nelda's safe return."

Andrew, who had remained silent during all the time Amanda had sat at the table, accompanied his father to the door. David turned back into the library and Andrew came to Amanda and put his hand in hers. "Damned bitch," he whispered to the closed front door.

9

Amanda's lips twitched. It was difficult for her to keep from laughing out loud. All the while she was scolding Andrew she found herself silently echoing his sentiments concerning the adorable Miss Bennet. "Not a word of this to your father, young man," she said severely. "He has enough to worry about without having the added knowledge that his son is blatantly disrespectful. Now you march into the library and stay close to your father's side. I must go upstairs to my room for a few minutes."

Andrew gave her a lop-sided grin. "I wouldn't tell Papa I said naughty things about Miss Bennet. What d'you think I am? Crazy?"

"Sometimes," said Amanda without pausing to be prudent, "I think *everyone* is a little fey." She didn't mention her recent doubts about her own sanity, but she was alarmed at the bubbling mirth that kept rising in her throat all the way up to her room. Once there, she burst into great peals of laughter, quite unable to keep her mind from going back over the succinct words young Andrew had spoken about Miss Bennet. She flung herself on the bed and continued to crow with laughter, making sure she muffled the sounds in her pillow. The tears were close to the surface and threatening to overpower the bursts of amusement, however. At last, feeling both exhausted and oddly relieved, she smoothed her hair and considered changing her frock. But after due consideration, she decided to continue wearing the drab morning dress she'd had on all day, afraid David would realize she found it necessary to improve her appearance because of the fashionably dressed Miss Bennet. "Snip," she said out loud as she looked at her solemn face in the mirror. "That's what she is. A conceited little snip, with just about enough brains inside that fluffy head to fill a thimble."

Once again her mouth trembled as another giggle overcame her. She was ashamed of herself until she remembered an old quotation: *Some things are of that nature as to make one's fancy chuckle while his heart doth ache.* She understood how close her laughter was to tears and recognized the sob in her heart as she wished for at least the hundredth time that day that there was something she could do—something constructive that could be done to help find the missing girl. Those other only half-formed feelings of female envy of Deirdre were so shameful that she tucked them firmly back into the far recesses of her mind where she hoped she would forget them.

The clock on the mantel continued to tick and tock, but the time was passing at snail's pace. Impatiently, Amanda wondered if there ever had been a day she'd spent before in her life when the hours crept by so slowly. There had been the long journey over the ocean when each hour had seemed to crawl by with maddening contempt for her own haste. Then had come the uncomfortable ride on the stage that had brought her overland to Indiana. She'd been impatient, anxious to arrive at her destination. It seemed impossible that the journey had been just a few weeks ago. But now she knew the boring hours spent *en route* had been nothing. Not in comparison with the way it felt to be forced to sit idly by and wonder and worry over the fate of an innocent child. With a pang, she realized how much deeper was the abrasive frustration to those who had known Nelda all her life. Those who had watched her develop from a tiny newborn baby to the charming child of ten were suffering out this long wait with much more pain that she, she reprimanded herself.

It was then that she decided to go again and have a look at the child's room by herself. Although she wasn't sure what she would look for, she couldn't get over the feeling that something important, some clue as to who might have stolen the child, might have been overlooked. In her heart she had the idea that a woman might see something that had been overlooked by the men, although she knew it was nothing but slim hope combined with a need to be active that drove her back to the kidnap room.

The upstairs part of the house was silent. It was a waiting, listening kind of quiet that spoke of the tragedy that lay like a pall over the entire house. Each of Amanda's footsteps seemed overloud in the hush of the upstairs rooms and she grew conscious of unease as she walked determinedly on, trying to ignore the intuitive feeling that someone watched her every move. She knew there was nobody in that wing of the house but herself at that time of day. Only she and Sarah were on the entire second floor, and the deaf woman was in the other wing, long ago having retired to her room, fatigued. The servants would be downstairs, the daily tasks of the upstairs maids complete. Before the Bennet brother and sister left, Becky had begged permission from David to help the cook with supper, Flora having given in to a fit of hysterics. At first David had refused on the grounds that the late lunch had barely been touched. But Becky had pointed out that the servants, most of whom had gone about their daily business of working in the fields, would need a substantial evening meal, so David had given Becky permission to help in the kitchen. Faylodene, that sullen wench, had come down with a headache and fever. With much grumbling, Matilda, the pale bronze upstairs maid, had taken Faylodene to the servants' quarters. David insisted. Matilda had said in an aside remark to Amanda that Faylodene could always manage to invent a headache and fever if she wanted to. She begged to stay with the family, anxious to be close to Andrew. Amanda thought about how disappointed the pretty maid had looked when she'd said, "The Master has asked you to stay with Faylodene. I have no jurisdiction in this matter." Matilda had then broken into tears, stressing her great sorrow and worry over the missing child, and Amanda had felt a surge of empathy for the girl. After all, Matilda was a mere five years older than Nelda. They'd played together as children, before Matilda grew old enough to assume household duties. Further, Matilda had been the household servant who'd been closest to the abducted child, having assumed the duties of Nelda's personal maid as well as servant.

As Amanda continued to tread softly down the hall, almost as though she feared disturbing the dead in a house of mourning, she kept her mind occupied by remembering the crushed look on Matilda's face, the way David had remonstrated with the girl. She'd felt he'd been unduly sharp when he said, "Look here, Matilda, you can't do anything to help. Sitting around and wringing your hands while you cry buckets of tears isn't doing a thing constructive. Actually, your air of grief adds to my own fears. We must hope for the best. Now, get on over there with Faylodene and see that she keeps to her bed. The measles are appearing in the community. We don't need to have an epidemic of measles on top of everything else. And even though it's possible Faylodene sometimes makes herself sick, we can't be positive she's doing it this time."

It occurred to Amanda just then that the Master of Whispering Hills had a lot more on his mind than she'd realized. He was responsible for a vast household full of servants and their well-being. He must house and provide viands for numerous field hands as well as those who worked in the house. When disease struck, the Master must cope with it, yet he also had to find time to go over the accounts, keep an eye on the tobacco market, do his own trading and oversee the crops. Little squabbles that broke out among the household help had to be dealt with. As David's wife, she thought with a rising blush to her cheeks, I must do my part to help ease his burden.

She compressed her lips and opened the door to the nursery, half expecting to see Charity's ghost. Or worse.

Nothing was changed in the middle room. Still, as she made her way to Nelda's room, she continued to feel an unseen presence walking by her side. For a long moment, she hesitated at the door where she knew the dried blood would be, testifying to the violence that had been done there. Her lips made an entreaty in a scarcely audible whisper. "If there's someone here with me, some-one I can't see, please make yourself known. I'm sure you must mean well, Charity Whitcomb or whoever you are, and I know you don't mean me any harm."

She waited, but nothing happened. No sign of any kind manifested itself, no knocks, no wraith-like voice from beyond the grave, no misty form. Her hands felt icy cold as she turned the door knob, trying to convince herself she was simply afraid, overimaginative and too willing to believe an entity walked at her side. The eerie feeling didn't disperse, but neither did it grow stronger as she stepped inside the little room.

Trying not to look at the pool of rust colored blood, Amanda got to her knees and looked under the bed. It was dark under there because of the disheveled sheets. She flipped them up on the mattress, then again knelt and peered closely at the polished wood under the bed. No hint of lint or dust was there to call attention to poor housekeep-ing. Nothing. She was about to move away when she decided to run her fingers across the floor, knowing she might not see something as small as, say, a strand of hair, because of the shadow cast by the mattress.

Her searching fingertips came into contact with nothing but the smooth grain of the wood, and then her eyes jumped as she saw a torn-off part of a fingernail. It was almost completely hidden by one of the carved legs that supported the foot board. Excited, she quickly extracted it and held it to the light. Standing, she went over to the window where she looked at the fragment of human finger-nail, her senses suddenly alert. It was crescent-shaped and mostly smooth; but it was jagged on one edge with a little dark red spot of blood at the end where it had clung stubbornly to the skin of a finger, obviously torn off instead of cut away with scissors.

Critically, Amanda compared the hard sliver she held between thumb and finger of her right hand with the nails of her left hand. Hers were pale pink, with well defined moons, the tips white. Her good health was manifest in the even texture of the portion of fingernail that extended slightly over the ends of her tapered fingers. The one she'd found under the bed was thicker, harder, and there were minute fine lines barely discernible to the naked eye. The faint ridges had lain vertically with the nail. It seemed to her that the nail fragment must have belonged to a man, mainly because of the width of it. And it was possible that she had something of no value, she told herself thoughtfully as she dropped it into the palm of her left hand . . . but it was also just as possible that she'd found something of very *definite* value. At least she could hope she had.

While she held it clutched in her hand, she continued to go over every inch of the room with her eyes. Since the fingernail had been such a small bit of possible evidence, she didn't trust her eyes to merely scan the floor from a standing position. Again she dropped to hands and knees, the better to see anything quite small that could have fallen from Nelda's assailant during the abduction. In a corner where the windows met, she found a snarled bit of golden blonde hair. One glance told her the few strands of hair that were caught on a rough place on the floor board were Nelda's, but whether they'd been torn loose from her scalp during that very morning or some other time, she had no way of knowing.

She also found a bit of white cloth. It was under a ruffled frock that had been flung to the floor. No more than a quarter of an inch, the triangle of cloth looked as though it had been torn from a petticoat. Amanda put the piece of cloth with the fragment of fingernail, then went to the windows where she gazed out onto the sodden lawn. The rain was still coming down in torrents. The thunder was in the distance and the play of lightning was too far away to do any damage to the immediate vicinity, but there was a bleakness that caused Amanda to sigh. Desolate gray-green light cast a depressing appearance over everything, filtered, as it was, through leaden skies and the drenched leaves of the stately trees that surrounded Whispering Hills. It seemed fitting to Amanda that even the heavens were in tune with the pall of dread that clung to the plantation.

As she was about to leave the room, Amanda stopped dead still, her heart pounding in her ears. She wasn't absolutely sure she'd heard it, but it had seemed to her in that moment of turning she'd heard a quiet, mournful sob. She listened, but heard nothing but the trip-hammering of her own heartbeat in her ears. She drew a breath and was aware of the shaky sound, the raspy noise of her suddenly dry throat. With all her strength she commanded her heart to stop thundering, determined to remain where she was. She stood perfectly still in the middle of the room, hoping, yet fearful, that the dismal sob would come again. Finally her heart slowed down to normal and she drew another unsteady breath, then held it. Her hands felt frozen. Indeed, her entire body felt encased in a slab of ice. But she remained quiet, moving nothing but her eyes which kept darting about the child's room. At last she heard the sob again. It was muted, but just as mournful as she'd thought. With all the courage she could muster, she opened her dry lips to form a question.

Nothing came out of her constricted throat but a gasp of sheer terror.

God help me, she prayed silently. And felt her throat muscles loosen. "Please," she spoke to the silent walls. "Please, if there is a—a spirit of some-one who once lived in this room, let me know by giving some sign of—your—presence."

With quaking legs and her hands trembling violently, she stiffened herself for the awesome sight of an entity appearing out of thin air, or the sound of a voice. Every heart beat sounded loudly again in her ears, and she waited. And waited. But nothing happened. More than anything, she wanted to flee from that room with the ominous presence, unseen, no longer heard, but insidiously present. She could all but reach out and touch it, she thought as she clasped her hands together at her waist. A *presence* was there. She *knew* it was there! But although she tried to do it, she couldn't force her hands to reach out, afraid of what she would touch.

Once again, she spoke. "A child has disappeared from this room." She spoke in a strained, thin, yet rasping voice. "A child who put up a terrible struggle. If a soul lives on after death . . . if that intelligence or soul or whatever it is called that still lives on after death can make itself known to those who are still living—then it seems to me a mother's love for her child—a missing child— would make it want to show itself now. With a message."

Amanda knew she probably wasn't expressing herself in acceptable terms, but she didn't know how to go about carrying on a conversation with a ghost. Even so, she'd been deeply impressed with that misty form she'd seen on two occasions. If she had really seen the spirit of Charity Whitcomb, it seemed only reasonable to her that if the spirit

was in the room with her, then an appeal to her
mother-love for her lost chilkd would surely help
bring about another appearance. With another appearance might come revelation.

She waited, silently pleading again, but was disappointed. She heard what sounded like a sigh,
but the tremor was breathy and faint, almost
drowned out in a sudden peal of thunder. After the
echo of the thunder died away, she wasn't sure
she'd heard the weak sigh after all.

Once more, she spoke aloud. "I *beg* of you. If you
are in this room with me, Charity Whitcomb, then
at least let me know if your daughter still *lives*!"

A flash of lightning distracted her. It bathed the
room in a glaring light. Involuntarily, Amanda
jumped, then tensed for the thunder which was to
follow. Just before the lightning flashed the room
had been plunged into near-darkness when a
vicious black cloud had appeared in the skies
outside the windows of the room where she stood
trembling. When the thunder came, it shook the
very rafters and sills of the house, numbing her
feet as it seemed to tear the heavy timbers of the
house apart. Yet, even when the mighty thunder
had dwindled to a muttering rumble, Amanda's
eyes widened in new terror as she saw a misty
form spiral upwards from the floor. She felt an icy
blast chill her from head to toe, then blinked as a
kind of luminous pale blue light seemed to
emanate from the swirling, shroudlike strands of
mist. The bluish haze was outlined in a golden
glow. Then, just as silently as the vision appeared,
it dispersed in a trail of silvery vapor.

Transfixed, Amanda continued to stare at the
spot where the tendrils of mist faded away. The
lightning continued to illuminate the room in a
series of phosphorescent flashes that all but
blinded her, and the thunder was one long, unre-

lenting blast of fury that made her head reel. But Amanda was unmindful of the furies of nature at that moment. She had asked the entity to appear. It had appeared. She had held her wits about her long enough to ask it if the little girl still lived. Telling herself she might well be reading the entity's appearance out of desperation, she couldn't shake the conviction that she'd been shown a good omen. The bluish tinge, the golden glow, the silvery wisps. For all she knew, the spirit had not been *able* to speak to her. She didn't know if ghosts could speak. But since she considered those particular colors she'd seen as benevolent, she was oddly relieved. Gold, she'd always heard, was a protective color. Blue stood for purity. And white, or silver, was for hope.

Although she was still weak and trembling, her hands shaking so violently that she could barely hold onto the door knob long enough to turn it, she was glad she'd helped the entity appear . . . if she had.

Now she would go to her own room, put away the small scraps of what might, or might not have been left behind unwittingly by the abductor. Hide them in some place where they would be safe, and wait until Nelda had been returned safely. Then she would speak to David. Tell him about those two little fragments that might point to the assailant and hopefully bring him to justice. The safety of the child, however, was of more importance right then than punishing the abductor.

The door knob kept slipping in her grasp. Her fingers turned it and turned it. It went round and round on the shaft, but it didn't unlock the bolt. She strained, then in exasperation pushed forward, confused. All she knew at the moment was that the friction that should have released the bolt didn't do it. The storm, which had returned in

all its fury just before she started to leave, seemed
bent on tearing the house down all around, but she
was almost unmindful of the lightning and
thunder in her struggle with the door knob. At last
she gave a mighty heave. She fell backwards into
the room, her skirts grazing the blonde curl that
was now firmly embedded in the dried blood. In
her hand was the door knob. It had come loose
from the shaft.

Amanda sat there, stunned, staring at the thing
in her hand. It took her a second to realize she was
locked in.

10

Outrage, then agonized terror flooded Amanda's mind. Involuntarily, she screamed. It didn't matter whether someone had locked her in the little bedchamber by accident or by design. The only thing that was important was the accomplished fact. She was trapped. Locked in a room where violence had been done. A room that was remote from the rest of the house. A room where she'd just taken her courage in both hands and called up a vision from the spirit world. Had it been a force of good or a force of evil? Had it been her own imagination, playing tricks on her again? Was she possibly losing her sanity in this strange house?

She screamed again.

Outside the windows, the wind screamed an answer. Small branches flayed against the window pane. The rain slanted down at an angle. Each time Amanda pounded on the door a barrage of sticks and stones battered against the house. She could hear the same devilish siege taking place in other rooms and realized that the storm had reached tremendous force. An excessively loud crash behind her caused her to stop screaming long enough to glance over her shoulder. A limb, driven by the howling wind, had broken a window glass. Even as she watched, open-mouthed and panting, her eyes rolling in panic, the limb crashed to the floor midst shattering glass. Over and above the intensity of the storm, the showering rain of glass seemed oddly out of place. Powerful rolls of thunder reverberated continually. The shrieking wind was a continual wail. Yet over the wreckage, the shards of glass tinkled merrily, like little Christmas bells. Amanda pounded again and again on the door.

Minutes passed. Or hours. She didn't know which. There was a sense of time without end. Now and then she believed the storm would go on forever. That she would spend her entire life locked in a room where all the world outside was bent on destruction. The sky was as black as pitch, but now and then she saw a glimmer of a malevolent sulphurous color that was swallowed up in the rolling blackness as quickly as it appeared. Great gusts of wind and rain blew in the jagged opening. A rattle of stones and other debris fell upon the floor along with hail. Amanda huddled against the door, unable to keep her eyes off the window. Now and then she saw such impossible-to-believe things fly past the open window that she questioned her sanity. A chair raced by on the furious wings of the gale. Then a piece of bedding whipped around the corner of the house. After that came a tumbling shower of rocks and leaves and sticks followed closely by a white hen whose feathers were ruffled against the onslaught of the wind.

It's a tornado, her numbed senses finally told

her. And again she felt the floor shake under her as a new inferno of sound whipped the house. A mighty shriek, and a mighty oak tree fell, the trembling leaves whipped this way and that by the violent storm. She slumped to the floor, her eyes protected by her arms as she huddled against the door. The cold rain and gusts of wind continued to rage. Another window broke. At last she dared to hope the storm had abated. It seemed to her that the wind was pitched somewhat lower in key and the slanting rain had lost some of its force. She risked a glance over her shoulder, and saw the sky was no longer black. Instead, a peculiar pinkish-yellowish glow was in the heavens. The rain slowed almost to a drizzle, and the awesome thunder once again rumbled in the distance. Now that the thumping items that had been hurled with such force against the sides of the house had stopped, she believed she heard voices down below. She listened, her ears alert to any sound. She believed the house had been in the path of a tornado. And prayed with all her heart that everyone had survived.

David's voice—or was it Lochard's?—called her name. She couldn't be sure with the door in between. All she felt was a sense of relief as she stood up, her frock wet and clinging, and called back. "I'm in here! Here in Nelda's room!" Again, she pounded with the heel of her hand against the door, then kicked it smartly with the toe of her boot.

"Amanda! A-mannnnnnnnnnndah!" The voice sounded again, a plaintive, forlorn call in the gloom.

"In here!" She screamed the words, then hammered as hard as she could against the door. She heard doors opening and closing and footsteps pounding all over the place. Her eyes swept the room in search of the doorknob, but if it was there it was under the incredible pile of odds and ends blown in by the storm.

At last she picked up the limb that had broken the window. It was cold and wet and rough to her hand, but nothing mattered save the need to get out of that room. She beat frantically against the solid oak door and screamed until her throat was raw.

At last an answering knock. "Amanda? For God's sake! Open the door and come out." It was David's voice, raised in either fear or anger. Amanda chose to believe he was angry.

"You fool, if I could get out, do you think I would be in here?" She knew she sounded waspish and didn't care.

"What in heaven's name do you mean? The door is locked from the *inside!*" She heard the doorknob rattling futilely inside the metal lock. "The knob turns, but the door won't open. Now, Amanda, you simply *must* come out of there. You've no idea what we've been through downstairs. One of the kitchens and a pantry were torn away from the house! We've been through a tornado with such force as I've never heard of before. You can't imagine how upset everyone has been! We didn't know if you were alive or *dead!*"

Amanda ground her teeth together. The goose-flesh that covered her bare arms from the elbow down left in the heat of her irrational ire. "David Whitcomb, I am *not* a child," she shrieked. "I have *not* locked myself in here out of some childish fear —or because I want to play foolish games! Do you *hear* me? I *can't* get out! The door knob fell away in my hands."

An audible gasp was heard through the door, then "Good God! You mean someone locked you in?"

"Just let me out," Amanda railed. "The windows are out and it's cold and wet in here! Just break the door down or something! Just stop talking and *do* something!" Raw tears that had been close to the surface all along scalded her eyes. Tears of frustration, anger, and relief.

For a few seconds nothing but silence came from the other side of the door. Then quickly receding footsteps, a distant shout, and returning footsteps. Followed by, "Stand back, Amanda! Get away from the door!"

Blow after blow battered the heavy door. Then a mightly splintering of wood and David Whitcomb stood there, a subdued, pale-faced son at his side. Andrew's small arms wrapped around Amanda's waist as the boy sobbed thankfully against her side while his father gathered her into his arms and held her even closer than the son. "Ah, Amanda, you can't know, you can't possibly know how terrified I've been," he whispered, his voice broken. "To be already rocked to the very edge of sanity over worry about Nelda, then to fear you were lifted into the funnel of the tornado and taken from me. . . ."

"Hush," she said, conscious of curious eyes upon them. Finally she pulled away from him, but clung to Andrew hungrily. It was perfectly all right to hold a little boy close, but she felt too self-conscious to remain in David's embrace for very long. Even if he was her husband now. Meeting David's eyes over the top of Andrew's head, Amanda asked about the other people in the house.

"We don't know yet. Lochard, Governor Jennings and I were in the library with Andrew through the worst of it. My cousin Sarah had wandered down, so she was safe too. The library was protected from the storm. Nothing but the sound and the fury penetrated the walls." He had a pale line around his mouth. "My first thought was of you, of course. Lochard has gone in search of Miss Bennet and her brother. We fear they may have been caught by the storm since it came so suddenly. It's to be hoped they took shelter before the funnel formed in the sky. Anything that happened to be in the direct path that tornado took is lost, I'm afraid."

"This house stood," said Andrew proudly. "Whispering Hills stood solid as a rock. Except the one kitchen and pantry. But that part was an addition, Papa says."

"And Lochard's home?" asked Amanda.

"Some minor damage has been done to White Rose," answered David, "but all the servants are alive and well. There's a good view of Lochard's place from your bedchamber. A few window panes were broken and the roof there will need repair." He left her at the door to her bedchamber. "My fear is for the servants' quarters. And Becky, who became alarmed long before anybody else. She knew that a twister was descending and went out in the thick of it to see to the younger girls. I could cut out my tongue for insisting that Matilda go with Faylodene. Not that I would wish any harm to come to either girl . . . I just wish I'd known we were in for such a storm. I should have told them to come upstairs. Lord knows we've plenty of empty rooms."

It was Amanda's turn to tell David that there was nothing to be gained by looking backwards and wishing one had it all to do over again—as he had told her that morning when she said she wished she'd gone to Nelda when she heard the early morning cry. Before leaving him to change her wet clothing and do something with her wild hair, she learned to her surprise that the most severe part of the storm had lasted no longer than ten minutes. It had seemed like an eternity, but the clock in her room was just chiming the half hour. She stared at it in disbelief. It had been about five of the clock when she'd left the others to go upstairs.

After she had noted the time, or rather the lack of time, that had passed by during the awesome fury of the storm, Amanda unfolded the hand she'd kept closed around the two small things she'd found in Nelda's room. Her fingers felt cramped from keeping the tight grip she'd held on the bit of fingernail and the three-cornered piece of cotton material.

A likely hiding place, she decided after a moment, was a place that was in plain sight. Better than her jewel case or anything else where items of value would likely be found. She settled upon a corner of the clock which was lacquered gold. There was a little indentation where the broken fingernail fit snuggly, and behind a gold rose was where she hid the cotton cloth. Then she turned her thoughts to getting out of the damp, chilled garment and into something warmer.

As she surveyed her frocks, Amanda decided to put on something that would lend a note of cheer to the dismal day, the continuing fear that had crept in long before the wind and rain of the storm. In back of her mind was the remembered vision of Miss Deirdre Bennet, who had fussed so prettily about the damage the earlier rain had done to her hair and her bonnet. She hoped she wouldn't appear to be grasping at the opportunity to dress herself with care in order to look better than she had when Miss Bennet's eyes had appraised her so scathingly. *After all,* she told herself as she prepared the hip bath and stripped the sodden dress away, *this is no time for primping and preening. But still . . . the red dress would be nice. The one with the light blue petticoat with pleats at the bottom.* Gold roses were sewn at the hem of the dress to form scallops that showed off the blue pleats. She looked longingly at the red and blue dress all the while she bathed, knowing it was all wrong for the occasion.

After her bath, she stepped into fresh drawers, a pair of woolen stockings, chemise and corset, her flesh frankly appreciative of the feel of clean dry garments. After the corset came an undergarment of dainty white muslin with six ruffles at the hem. She chose a pair of slippers instead of her usual sturdy boots, still half-contemplating the red and blue frock. Then she stood in front of the hooks where all five of her gowns hung, her nose wrinkled in disdain at the dreary brown slub, the serviceable dark blue and the shabby gray. The red and blue gown beckoned enticingly. Her hand went out to touch the fabric, smooth and silken, but she shook her head. The pale gold would do very well. It was not as drab as the other three but more fitting than the daring gown she'd paid too much for when she'd had it made. The pale gold was fashionable enough without calling attention to itself. It also had a modest neckline instead of the low one, as well as nicely puffed long sleeves. The chill wind still blew, and she was well aware of it as she slipped the pale gold gown over her head.

Once dressed, she removed the pins from her hair and allowed it to tumble down her back. Because of the dampness, the tendency of her hair to form in curls made her frown. Amanda preferred the smooth silky look of straight hair, and believed herself cursed with curls. Every morning she gave her long hair a hundred strokes with the brush and patted it in place, hoping the curls would not spring out of her careful bun. Every night before she retired she brushed it again, hoping someday to brush away the unruly curls forever. With her golden brown curls spilling richly down her back and around her face, she knew she looked closer to fourteen than eighteen, and she disliked the look of softness around her face. She jumped at the sound of a knock at her door, then dropped the brush and a handful of pins as a shrill voice cried out, "Miss Amanda, come quick! Master Lochard is ridin' hell-bent for leather towards the house with a girl in his arms and that girl Faylodene turn up missin' along with Becky, and Matilda hurt bad. Master David say they's not a second to lose, she failin' *fast. They in the dinin' room.*"

Flora the cook was running back down the hall, her big feet already thumping on the stairs by the time Amanda dashed out of her room.

By the time she arrived in the dining room, Matilda had already died. A long, jagged wound was in her chest, exposing the vital organs. Shards of glass still clung to the unfortunate girl's bodice. David, pale and shaken, said the Governor had found the girl unconscious and bleeding profusely, under a tree that had fallen in the yard. "The glass must have been hurled at her by the storm, long before the tree fell," he said hurriedly. "Probably stopped her in her tracks, poor soul." Then he lifted the dead girl in his arms and carried her tenderly toward the rear of the house while Amanda stood speechless, momentarily locked in the horror of looking for the first time in her life on recent and violent death.

Young Andrew drew her away. He was as pale as death himself, and his eyes were brimming over with tears. "Oh, I loved Matilda," he said brokenly. "She was my favorite servant in the house. Miss Amanda, please come into the library. While my papa is with Matilda's mother I have something to say to you. And I know who Uncle Lochard is bringing back on his horse. It's that silly Bennet woman. But Papa told me to get you in the library where nobody will hear us talk." The little boy looked so drawn and shaken that Amanda immediately pulled herself together. Taking Andrew by the hand, she went with him through the house, wondering if the series of tragedies would never end.

The fire in the library was warm, and both Amanda and the boy went to it, drawn to the warmth and at least the semblance of cheer. Then Andrew said, "It wasn't the storm that killed Matilda."

Amanda clutched his shoulder. "Why do you say such a thing?"

"Because Papa said so. I was with him when he helped dig her out from under the tree. She would have died of the wound in her chest even if the tree hadn't crushed her. Papa saw right away that there weren't any other pieces of glass around close by. Just the ones that had been all smashed up when the tree fell on Matilda. I don't know exactly what he meant, but he said the blood on her chest had been there too long. Then something about it being already dried when it had run down her sides. And she'd been drug there. The backs of her shoes—the heels—have got mud all over them, and when the tree fell on her, she was on her back. Papa said it wouldn't have happened that way. Governor Jennings said so too. They looked at her real good when there was nobody there but us three, and when they saw how she was already nearly dead before the tree fell on her, they swore something awful! Then my papa said to me that I must tell you right away. He took her to her parents' house." Then he handed her a piece of creamy parchment paper that had been closed by a blob of sealing wax, saying, "There's this, too. Papa said to give it to you."

Right at that moment, Amanda was in no condition to put her mind on reading anything, but she started to unfold it; saw the seal had already been broken. Just then the library door opened. Amanda's duty was clear. Lochard, his hair wet and his clothing dripping, had Deirdre Bennet in his arms. The girl was unconscious.

"God damn," said Lochard, as he placed the small girl on the sofa. "God *damn!*" His voice sounded more prayerful than blasphemous. Amanda moved closer and saw the unnatural way Deirdre Bennet's arm hung backward from the elbow, the grotesque angle of her foot.

"Move away," she said crisply. "You'll not help her by swearing and staring. What happened to her poor brother?"

"He's all right. Saved his own skin and let his sister damn near perish, the yellow-bellied swine," Lochard said contemptuously. "I left him down the road. One of their horses was fit to ride. I had to shoot the other one. It had a broken leg."

As he spoke, Lochard stood back to give Amanda room in front of the sofa. She examined the dangling forearm and the foot that hung so awkwardly from the ankle and confirmed her earlier suspicions. There was no doubt about it. Miss Bennet had suffered a broken arm and ankle. The break in the arm was a clean one, but the horror of looking at the splintered bone where it protruded from the girl's slender ankle had brought an involuntary gasp of protest from Amanda's mouth. She'd read about broken bones and seen pictures of them, etchings she'd found in musty old medical books back home in England. But looking at pen and ink drawings in a book was not the same as staring at living flesh and bones. All around the ugly splinters of bone the punctured skin was mottled with blackish blood and the swelling flesh was about the color of an overripe plum. "I'll need a basin of water," she said coolly. "And do stop moaning and groaning and using the Lord's name in vain. Get me some linen cloths, too."

"Oh, God in heaven!" Lochard's drenched skin went paper white. He'd seen the nasty ankle wound before Amanda covered it with the girl's skirt. Then he shouted hoarsely. "You're not a doctor! My God, we've got to get somebody here to set that break!"

"True," answered Amanda. In order to speak at all, it was necessary to make her voice cold and crisp. Otherwise, she'd have given in to her inclination to run screaming from the pasty-faced girl on the couch whose bedraggled appearance gave no hint of the fashionably dressed young lady who had come calling earlier. "But there's mud and debris in the wound. Common sense tells me it should be bathed. She has another break in her arm, but I believe I can set that. If she happens to be lucky and remains unconscious."

Lochard spluttered. "Remains *unconscious!* I should think the very best thing would be to bring her out of that faint! Good Lord, do you know what you're doing? Do you have any idea what you're about?"

Amanda took her hands from the girl's swelling forearm and put them on her hips. Then she turned and pinned Lochard's troubled hazel eyes with her own gray ones. Her voice was so brittle it almost broke when she asked in a bell-like tone, "Do *you* know how to set a broken bone? Do you know how to do anything but stand there and ask questions? Now get a basin of water. *And* a ball of soap. I know very little about setting a broken bone, but I've read of a doctor back home who swears sepsis can be averted if measures of cleanliness are used in cases like this. Perhaps it's exposure to the air that causes the sepsis. Nobody seems to know, but this particular doctor makes sure any wound is cleaned with soap and water. Or salt. Sometimes both. It's far better to do *something*, Mr. Lochard Whitcomb, than to stand at this girl's side and bemoan her fate."

When Lochard left the library, young Andrew ventured a long drawn-out whistle. It sounded naughty. "I guess you told him. God's eyes, how did you learn so much? And what's to keep you from falling into a swoon? I'm sure Miss Bennet would have fainted away long ago if she were in your place. But first she'd take care to arrange her skirts, and I dare say she'd fall in a graceful heap to show off her tiny waist to good advantage." He giggled wickedly. "I bet if she knew how awful she looks, she'd have a screaming fit, too."

"Andrew! I'll hear no more of this kind of talk from you," Amanda said dutifully. "You're most unchivalrous. And don't say 'God's eyes' either. For shame!"

"Still," said Andrew, not to be dismissed so lightly when he had a point to make, "you've got to admit that you're not weak and inclined to go into the vapors like most women. Even my mother screamed when she saw blood. Got sick to her stomach, too."

"Be quiet," said Amanda. "I'm listening to her heart beat." She held her index finger on the pulse in Miss Bennet's throat. She'd heard of ominous things like people passing away because of shock and loss of blood.

Lochard returned with the basin and a ball of

soap. Big Flora returned with him, shaking her head and muttering. "Hmmmm, mmmmmmmm! Now, Miss Amanda, I think you'd best step aside so's I can tend to the poor young thing. Master Lochard said you didn't 'pear like you knows much about medicine, talkin' about usin' lots of soap and water and all. Well, I got this here hexin' powder. It's made out of boneset. Good old-fashioned yarb remedies—they's the best, Missy Amanda."

Amanda watched fat Flora dip her hand into her greasy pocket and come out with a filthy rag that had some brownish looking dried stuff on it. "Boneset? What's that?"

"Why, like I said, it's a yarb. Grown on the land. Gawd A'mighty nebber missed a trick, He didn' when he whomped up this old earth. For ever' thaing wrong with a human person, they's a yarb to cure it. I'll take some of this here lard from a pig," she dipped into the other pocket and came up with another greasy rag, "and rub it all over Miss Deirdre's pore broken arm and laig. Then I'll take and spainkle some of this-here dried boneset on it. That'll do until Master Lochard can get her to a doctor, or get one out here."

Amanda stood her ground. "No. No boneset, no herbs, no lard. Afterwards . . . when I've made the wound clean, you can go out and pick some fresh boneset plant. But none of that dried stuff."

"Now wait a minute," broke in Lochard. "What you've read out of books is one thing, but Flora is a lot older than you and she's more experienced in tending the sick and wounded. I'll have you know that. . . ."

Amanda flew into a fury, the only alternative to hysterical weeping. Between clenched teeth, she screamed, "Get out of here! Both of you!" She pointed a shaking finger at Andrew. "I'd rather trust that boy to take care of Miss Bennet than you, Lochard Whitcomb!''

"God's beard, but you're a beautiful sight with your hair tumbling down around your shoulders and fire in your eye," said Lochard in a moment of surprise. But his affronted manhood came flooding back from the momentary lapse and before she could speak, he said, "You sound like Lady Mary when she insisted that piercing the skin with walnuts that had smallpox pus smeared on them would keep a person from getting the disease.''

"And so it does," retorted Amanda. "People with an ounce of book learning now have their children engrafted for the pox as a matter of course. If Lady Mary had been born a man instead of a female, the world would be rid of the smallpox by now. Instead, just a few English families have it done. After all these years since Lady Mary discovered the prevention. *Including* the royal family, if you please!''

Fat Flora tried to shove Amanda aside, but Amanda wouldn't have it. While she pitched a verbal battle over what she felt in her heart was right, a very small part of her seemed to stand to one side and watch, appalled, at the figure she cut as she stood defiance to Lochard Whitcomb. Still another part of Amanda imagined the whimsical nod of approval that would be on her father's face if he only had lived to see her standing up for her beliefs. Andrew lent his young voice to the exchange of words, and finally Flora left in defeat, leaving only Lochard, who stood there glaring. "Very well, Miss Medicine Girl. I leave Deirdre in your young hands. But remember that she's almost the same age as you—and has as much right to look forward to a decent life as a wife and mother. If your wild notions of sepsis doesn't work, Flora uses the boneset and lard on the morrow."

Amanda smiled and had the last word. "I'll warrant that some day, when the world is much older and much wiser than it is now, when women are allowed to have a part in making the laws, anything less than wifehood and motherhood will not be considered, as you say, indecent."

Lochard seated himself and watched suspiciously while Amanda washed the horrid wound on Deirdre's ankle, taking care to soap all around the purplish, already seeping bone that stuck out of the skin. Then she rinsed it and closed her eyes, hoping that a doctor would come soon to push the splintered bone back inside the bleeding, torn muscle. She didn't think she could bear it if she had to do that.

Delicately, with her stomach tight and a tendency to gag, she touched the girl's tiny wrist, then held it firm while she washed all around the broken bone she could feel but couldn't see. Then she closed her eyes, felt her eyelids jiggle violently and swallowed down the rush of hot fluid that rose in her throat. It had a bitter taste. Once again, she closed her eyes so she wouldn't hve to look at what she was doing until it was absolutely necessary. As she grasped the elbow firmly but tenderly, her heart leaped in her breast as though she'd swallowed a bird. A wave of blackness came over her, but she ground her teeth and took a deep breath, willing to die before she'd give into the weakness of her sex. Compressing her lips together in a firm line, she felt for the broken bone, then held the tender flesh of the limp arm between her fingers. One more moment of terror so great that beads of sweat popped out on her forehead. But she knew if ever she were going to do it, the time was at hand. She pressed the two pieces of bone together. Heard the sickening crunch as edge of bone met edge of bone. Seconds went by while she stood there with her back bent, fighting waves of dizziness. Then she said to Andrew, "Get me that piece of linen. Slip it under her fingers. I dare not loosen my grip. The linen must be bound ever so tightly. You think you can do it?"

"Of course," said Andrew.

For a moment, Amanda allowed herself to glance at the intent face of the boy as he pressed the strip of linen under her fingers. She held it in place while Andrew wound it around the small arm. Then she lifted one finger at a time until the cloth bound round and round. Andrew was breathing rapidly and she felt his nervous tension. Her nostrils flared as she smelled his strong underarm odor, realizing he was wet with nervous sweat. So intent on what she was doing was Amanda that she didn't realize that Lochard had left his chair and was watching her closely as she motioned for Andrew to move away. She tied the bandage neatly with thread before she straightened up and looked at Lochard. His face was the color of a pea. A harsh pain that was more like suddenly noticing that a part of her back had been cut away caused Amanda to fall into a chair. Lochard turned away. He said, "Christ!" and she wasn't even able to grin with triumph as he rushed from the room, the hand he'd clasped to his mouth failing to squelch the gagging sounds.

"Good boy, Andrew," she finally said in the wispiest voice imaginable. "You did beautifully." She sobbed, and was aware of the tears falling down her cheeks like rain.

"Oh, stop that," he cried as he pressed a square of linen to her face. "Uncle Lochard would be pleased to see you crying now that it's over."

Amanda giggled. Then she hiccupped, burst into fresh tears and finally bathed her eyes with the linen which she dipped into the basin. After she'd blown her nose she believed she would be all right. There wasn't time to wait and see. Deirdre was stirring, her long golden lashes rising from her waxen cheeks. For a second, the hazy azure-blue depths remained blank. When recognition lighted those beautiful eyes, a scream came from the girl's lips. "You! How did you get here?"

"I live here," said Amanda. "*You* were the one who was brought. In Lochard Whitcomb's arms, I might add."

Disappointment stabbed into the wide open blue eyes. "Lochard? Oh. Not David?"

"My husband was seeing to his household," Amanda said without much more than a trace of spite. "One of his servants was killed . . . in the storm."

"Dreadful," mouthed the lovely girl.

Amanda spoke pointedly. "Also, David is still concerned to the point of distraction about his little daughter."

"Yes, yes, of course. But I . . ." Deirdre made a sitting-up motion. It was then that she became aware of the pain. She screamed, then drew a long, shuddering breath and screamed again as she looked at her bandaged arm. "I'm maimed for life!"

"Not at all. You've a broken arm and a broken ankle. Pray don't attempt to move. I'm afraid you'll be helpless for quite some time. I trust a doctor has been sent for." Amanda had to speak in between Deirdre's screams and moans. Mercifully, the girl fainted again.

Moments later, Deirdre's brother William came in. Like Lochard, he was drenched to the skin, and his expression was distraught. He rushed to his sister's side and blanched at the sight of the bandage on her arm. Amanda poured some spirits into a cup and gave it to the boy. He drank, sputtered, then drank again before falling into a chair.

"I'll go get some dry clothes, William," offered Andrew.

"You'll stay here with me," ordered Amanda. "Under the circumstances," she said to William Bennet, "Andrew simply must not leave my side. I'm sure you understand. But Mr. Whitcomb . . . Mr. Lochard Whitcomb . . . will surely return in a moment or two. Then I'm sure he will find you something warm and dry to wear. Meanwhile, please pull that chair over to the fire and warm yourself."

William rolled his eyes around to his sister again, but the stark whiteness was leaving his skin. His complexion was rapidly returning to normal. He finished the spirits, which Andrew immediately replenished. After he'd taken another sip, he said hollowly, "If she'd only have remained where we were! I'd looked up in the sky, you know. Just scanning it, fearful a bad storm was brewing, but never once dreaming we'd be hit by a twister. If you'll remember, when we left here the sky was beginning to clear. Before then, it had been just a light rain anyway. But when I saw that giant funnel rolling directly toward our carriage, I knew we were in for it. I jumped out of the seat and tried to turn the horses loose. Skip went, but Bitsy was stomping and blowing and kicking, spooked by the thunder. I could see there was no time to work with her, what with her having gone daft at the storm. Then there was the infernal funnel, bearing down on us. Quickly as I could, I just cut Bitsy loose, then overturned the carriage. It was a good shelter. A bush was there by the side of the road, which I told my sister to hold on to for dear life. Deirdre wouldn't stay where I put her. I told her to cling to that bush. Roots in the ground don't get torn up near bad by that kind of freakish wind, I said to her, but she went crazy as Bitsy. I tried to grab her when she crawled out from under the carriage, but she slipped out like greased lightning. Dear God! Went careening down the road right in the path of the storm like a thing possessed. When I caught up with her, she'd already been lifted up and set down by the wind. Smashed against a lean-to, then the lean-to roared off in the wind. God help me, I thought she was dead!

"Well, we stayed there, Deirdre under me. I protected her as best I could, but she kept screaming that I was killing her, poor lass. Then, when the worst of it had passed on by, I started walking, carrying her back towards the carriage. We were almost there when Mr. Lochard found us. And I'll swear, Miss Kendall, the carriage was intact. If only my sister had seen fit to stay there! But she was scared, poor dear. Scared right out of her wits. Well . . . Bitsy fared worse. Lochard had to destroy her. Her leg was broke."

Amanda was shocked to find herself thinking it had been a shame Lochard hadn't shot Deirdre too, seeing that her ankle was broken. Such a thought, even in passing, was most contemptible, and her shattered sense of decency was even more disturbed when she realized she didn't dare meet Andrew's eyes. She felt them on her, dancing with merriment. If she looked at him, they would both burst into great shouts of laughter, she was sure.

Lochard returned, looking much better but a little shamed. Amanda pointed out the wet condition of young Bennet's trousers and jacket;

Lochard took him upstairs and they came back together, with David.

"It would seem that my cousin Sarah spoke the truth when she said this is a house of horrors. Poor Deirdre," said David.

Amanda pointed out that Deirdre was not in the house when she met misfortune. It was also on the tip of her tongue to say if that young woman had listened to her brother she would have been none the worse off for the storm, but she restrained herself.

David's eyes lingered in concern on Deirdre's face. Amanda felt pretty sure the patient was awake again. Or that she hadn't really fainted under the pain after she'd once roused. For, as Andrew had snidely remarked, the attitude of her fragile body was most fetching. In her repose, she'd half-turned her body, which showed off her tiny waist to good advantage. Too, there was something falsely theatrical about the way those long golden eyelashes fluttered, as pain-wracked eyes opened like a flower just unfolding. " David," she breathed. And lifted the arm that wasn't broken in a beckoning gesture. Tears shone in those magnificent azure blue eyes. "Oh, David!" The small voice was brave, no doubt designed to make David believe she gave no thought to her own misfortune. "And have you heard anything of your beloved Nelda? Any new developments?"

"Nothing." David knelt at the injured girl's side. In the silence, Andrew snorted. It wasn't a very loud snort, but it *was* a snort, Amanda thought. And Lochard, his own face a mask of concern, joined his bother in front of the shattered little figure on the sofa who looked at them both with a sweet, brave smile.

The log in the grate snapped. Deirdre gave a

pretty little start. Then she said courageously, benevolently, "Pray don't give a thought to me. I'm sure I'll be quite all right. Oh, that lout of a brother of mine! I *do* hope he wasn't injured. You know, he *quite* went to pieces!" She couldn't see William, who was hidden from her view by the back of the chair where he sat gazing into the fire. "Oh, dear, I'm so troubled about him. You see, I *told* William the safest place we could be was under the carriage. I turned loose the horses and gave them a smart slap on their—ah, posteriors. And I told William to unfasten the carriage and overturn it. I just *knew* we'd weather the storm underneath the carriage. Why, I even pointed out a bush we could cling to, but oh, dear! Poor William! He ran away. I tried to follow him, but had to take shelter against an old shed. It was most frightening."

"Try not to think about it," said Lochard. "Your brother is quite all right. He'd apparently come back and found you, unconscious because of your broken limbs, my dear. He's there in the chair."

Deirdre's blue eyes widened. Her cheeks blushed crimson. Then she closed her eyes and swooned, conveniently, again.

A call outside the door and a hurried knock brought both Lochard and David to their feet. William, too, stood up and went to the library door. Flora stood trembling in the threshold. "Oh, Master Lochard, sir! Faylodene done crawled in from the wet. She done taken leave of her senses."

"I'll go," said Lochard.

"We'll both go," David said in a strained voice. "Don't trouble yourself, William," he told the young man who stood awkwardly by. "Stay by your sister's side. Amanda, keep Andrew here with you."

Andrew protested. "I want to go with you, Papa."

David raised his voice. "Do as I say. Stay with Amanda." In his eyes was a terrible fury.

As soon as the door was closed behind the brothers, small Deirdre opened her big blue eyes. "William, I'm sorry I said it all backwards." She smiled. Bravely. Then winced in pain. "It must have been the fever that made me twist things up. I'm sure I'll never recover. You don't have any *idea* how I suffer! Tell dear father I was a brave girl, William, that I faced the end without showing cowardice."

"Oh, for the love of sweet God Almighty," said William. "You're not dying. You filthy little *liar!*"

While brother and sister squabbled, Amanda remembered the parchment Andrew had given her. So many things had happened that she'd forgotten all about it, but a quick movement of her shoulders made one of the sharp edges dig into her tender flesh. She turned her back on William and Andrew and reached down the front of the pale gold dress. She had an idea that David had written her a note during the nightmarish event of finding Matilda dying of the wound that Andrew swore had not been due to accident. It would be something he wanted her to know concerning either Nelda's disappearance or Matilda's death, she thought.

But it was nothing of the kind. She was familiar with her husband's angular handwriting. David wrote, her thoughts kept spinning, almost straight up and down. There was nothing fancy about his handwriting. Lochard's script was similar, but it had a slant to the right. She even remembered exactly where she'd seen both samples of handwriting. David had written several notations on

the children's school books. Lochard had enclosed
a little note when he'd given her the pearls.

All of those unimportant thoughts kept rocket-
ing around in her mind and she knew exactly why
she was thinking of such trivialities. It was
because she simply didn't want her mind to
register what was written on the creamy parchment.

In the same illiterate scrawl as the first ransom
message, the words screamed up at her:

> *We changed are minds about who wuz to
> bring the money. Yr nuw wife is to do it being
> as you seen fit to call in his honer the
> guvennor of Indiana. Make shure she cums
> all by herself as if you dont yr little dawtter
> will pay for it good and proper. We meen
> biznes.*

There was no signature.

11

Amanda's face felt numb. Frozen. Her lips were dry as tinder and her voice came out in a croak. "You gave me this, Andrew."

He looked up at her, his dark eyes troubled and at that moment looking uncannily like his father's. "Yes, ma'am. You just now read it?"

"Where did this come from, Andrew?"

"Papa told me he found it upstairs. When you were locked in Nelda's bedchamber. Then everything else happened so fast that—"

"Did he tell you not to read it?"

Andrew's wide eyes looked at her for a moment, inscrutable. They grew a little wider as he said, "I didn't—". Then he lowered his eyelids and looked down at the floor. "I was going to lie to you. I *did* read it. But Papa said you're not to worry, you aren't going to do it."

At those words Deirdre raised herself up on her elbow, but quickly sank back down, her upper lip glistening with sweat as a shudder of pain wracked her body. "Oh, my ankle! I just tried to

195

move it, it felt numb until now, oh, my *God!* It's killing me!"

"I told you to lie still," Amanda said coldly.

Lochard came back into the room. "Faylodene is all right. Shaken and slightly battered, but she's little the worse for wear."

Although he didn't say anything else, Amanda sensed that he was holding something back. "Where is Governor Jennings?"

"Why, he just came in from outside. He was the one who found Faylodene. Some of the servants were with him. She'd been pinned under some logs, but she's all right except for a few bruises. My brother is still with her."

"There's been another tragedy," Amanda insisted. "Something you aren't telling me."

Lochard looked at the beautiful little pain-wracked figure on the bed. He held up a hand. "My dear Amanda," he began.

Andrew was using the flat of his hand to drum against the family Bible.

"There's something you aren't saying, Lochard. You might as well tell me." Her eyes darted to Andrew, hoping she'd catch his eyes so she could frown, give him a silent message to stop.

"All right. Yes. It's Becky. She's in bad shape," Lochard replied.

"The storm?" Amanda's eyes locked with Lochard's. He shook his head.

"No, Amanda. David believes she was attacked."

"The kidnapper," yelled Andrew. "I bet Becky caught him, then he hit her. Or stabbed her." During the time he was excitedly speaking, he stopped the infernal thumbing on the Bible.

"No . . . Yes . . . Something like that," said Lochard. He dropped into a leather chair and buried his face in his hands. Just then Andrew began using both hands against the Bible. She knew he was nervous. They all were. But that constant thudding sound was driving her mad. It sounded like insistent drums.

"Andrew! Please," she said sharply. "Stop that!"

He looked at her all innocent. "Stop what?"

"Stop making that noise." It was a command, and in her state of jangled nerves she knocked a candlestick over when she waved her hand in the air. The metal candle holder clattered. Andrew jumped. Amanda was instantly sorry she'd spoken so abruptly, knowing his nerves were raw just like everyone else's. He got to his feet and started to put the Bible back on the marble-topped table when he stumbled over his own feet and sprawled to the floor. Both Amanda and Lochard went to him immediately. He'd hit his head on the edge of the marble top. Before either of the adults reached him, he righted himself, his eyes showing his shame over what he obviously felt was his awkwardness. "I'm sorry," he said.

Amanda touched his forehead with her hand. She felt a bump, but it wasn't serious. "I'm sorry I spoke to you so crossly, Andrew. Grownups sometimes forget younger people have the same tortured emotions that disturb adults. Does the bump hurt much?"

"Naw." Andrew grinned. "I'm just sick and tired of sitting still for so long. All day long I've not done much of anything."

"Oh, now, you went riding with your father early this morning," said Amanda.

"That seems like a million years ago."

"Yes." Amanda was about to say more about the way time had dragged by all day, but Lochard stooped, just at that moment, to pick up the Bible. She'd started to do the same, and they bumped heads. Neither one was hurt, and Andrew laughed.

Lochard gave the Bible to Amanda since she was
closer to the marble-topped table where the two
Bibles were customarily kept. The big Bible had
fallen open, and before she closed it she glanced
down at the page, read what was written there
automatically, then closed it and put it on top of
the German Bible. The entire episode had been
one of those little events that occur so often
during times of emotional upheaval. There was
nothing of any special importance. It could have
happened under normal circumstances and never
be remembered, or talked about again. A boy falls
on the floor and bumps his head, inadvertently
dropping the family Bible on the floor. A man and
a woman stoop to retrieve the Bible from the
floor. They bump their heads together when they
both reach for it. At the time, Amanda was not
aware of experiencing a moment of great
importance, but immediately afterwards she
found herself going back over the trivial happening again and again. Somehow, she had an idea
that an event of great importance had occurred.
Or that her mind had suddenly opened to show her
all the answers, then as quickly closed.

Her thoughts twisted and turned as she tried to
grasp the fleeting moment when she'd felt her
mind blaze into a stunned realization of the truth.
She was positive she'd remembered or stumbled
upon something of tremendous importance. A key
that would unlock the entire puzzle behind
Nelda's abduction. But the long day of one
catastrophe stacked up on another was taking an
unexpected toll. Her mind stubbornly refused to
open again. She tried and tried to remember what
it was that had made her shriek silently to herself
That's it!

Instead, she found herself recalling an event
that had happened to her as a child; something of

no importance, she thought impatiently.

She'd been about thirteen years old at the time. While walking down the street, she found a piece of jewelry that glittered so brightly with ruby and gold colors that she'd been excited at the idea of finding something of great value. For days and days she had scanned the newspaper, hoping she would find a reward offered for a ruby and gold bracelet. In time her father came home from the sea and she showed him the bracelet. He told her it was paste. She stared at him blankly. "Counterfeit," he told her. She didn't know what that meant, either. "The bracelet is fashioned to resemble a thing of great value, but it's not worth a pound. It's glass. Just red glass and pot metal." This had occurred at a time when Amanda was going through a phase of avid interest in words. She looked up *paste* in the dictionary. Then *counterfeit*. Then she found *forgery* as a descriptive word for *counterfeit*. She'd been intrigued at the idea of people printing counterfeit money.

The mind, she decided as she again wondered why she was skipping around from one inane subject to another, *is a strange thing indeed. Now why would I remember that particular time in my life right now?* She knew of no answer, and as she tried to find a reason for the sudden recollection of the paste bracelet, David entered the library and all her thoughts fled.

"Amanda, will you come with me, please?"

She rose to her feet.

He held out his arm. "Lochard, please remain with Miss Bennet and William. And keep Andrew with you."

Andrew said he was hungry. David told his son that Flora and Henry were getting a meal together.

His face was set in stern lines and his manner

was so forboding that Amanda was afraid to say a word, even after they left the library. He paused and put his hands on her shoulders, turning her face toward his. They were in the hall that led into the dining room. She was surprised to see how dark the night had become. A fan of light from the blazing candelabra in the dining room fell on her as she looked up into David's serious face. He spoke in a voice that wouldn't carry beyond her own ears. "Amanda, the time has passed so quickly, yet at the same time so very slowly. It's a quarter after eight. All the time I was away from you, I wanted to be at your side."

"I wanted to be close to you as well," she confessed quietly. He pulled her near and wrapped his arms around her in a comforting embrace. Pressing her cheek against his chest, she heard the steady beat of his heart.

"Listen carefully. The latest demand from the abductor—Andrew gave it to you, didn't he?"

Amanda nodded.

"A devilish circumstance. To have to place my confidence in a twelve-year-old boy. Yet—" David glanced back down the hall toward the closed library door. A shadow moved for an instant in the dark recesses of the hall. It could have been a servant or someone may have stepped out of the library for an instant, she thought, then gone back inside. Abruptly, David spoke in a normal voice. "Amanda, you're beautiful with your hair down."

She remembered Lochard had said the same thing just a few minutes before, but only her husband's words had the power to touch her heart. David's hands on her shoulders clutched more tightly. He whispered. "We'll go upstairs to our room. It's the only place we'll not be overheard. There are two people involved in Nelda's

disappearance. I believe I know who one is, but
not the other—yet. He—or she—may be around
the corner. Any corner, hiding in any room, with
ears wide open. My God!'' His hands left her
shoulders and one arm went to her waist for a
second, guiding her in the direction of the steps.

A ripple of fear washed over Amanda as David
opened the door to their bedchamber. For a split
second, she was afraid of him, knowing he might
have taken his own child, written that ransom
note on the red paper himself. She asked herself
what reason he could possibly have for doing such
a thing and rejected the idea as ridiculous. Nelda
would *never* have struggled with her own father.
She loved him dearly. And there was no sane
reason for a man to carry out such a mad scheme
. . . she caught her breath and realized with a stab
of horror that David Whitcomb could be mad.
Insanity plays no favorites. Her flying thoughts
ebbed and flowed as she heard him grope for the
tinder box. The sparks flew and the candle flared.
The mellow light dispersed her fears just as it
brought light into darkness.

He closed the door after he lit three more
candles, then faced her once again. In a flat voice,
he said, ''That paper belongs to my brother. It
looked familiar when I first found it. I knew I had
seen it before, but there were so many emer-
gencies right after the tornado. The envelope was
weighted by a rock in front of the door to Nelda's
room. I saw it, read my name on the envelope,
broke the seal and read it as soon as I was alone.''

''After you left me in my room to get out of my
wet clothes,'' stated Amanda.

''Yes. Before I went in search of the girls. Then
we found Matilda under the tree. *God!* What a
horrible day this has been! Immediately, I saw
that Matilda had already been wounded severely,

long before the tree fell. Andrew was with me. Just then I remembered where I had seen that parchment. Lochard received it as a gift last Christmas. And there was only Andrew to trust with the duty of keeping it safe. I told him to say nothing to anyone. To give it to you."

"But you trust your brother to watch over your son," Amanda said. "Even when you believe him guilty of—"

"He's far too intelligent to attempt anything with Andrew. Not when he knows I'm aware that Andrew is with him. Then, too, don't forget William Bennet is in that room."

"But your own *brother!*" It was too terrifying for Amanda to believe. "But Lochard had no marks upon his person."

"There's a way marks could have been averted. He could have worn gloves. Or perhaps he didn't do the actual deed himself. It's possible that he hired somebody else to take Nelda from her bed. That was probably it, for I don't think Nelda would have put up a fight with Lochard. He's always played games with both children."

"But what reason . . ."

David sighed. It came from the depths of his soul. "Lochard has always been envious of my position. As elder brother, I inherited Whispering Hills. Factually, his White Rose is every bit as grand as Whispering Hills, but I've always known Lochard resented being my junior. He also fancied himself in love with my wife."

"Which wife?" Amanda allowed that question to slip out before she thought, something that happened often of late.

David stared at her. "Why—Celeste, of course." He broke into a smile that was almost genuine. "Oh. You're thinking of Charity. Well, yes, he wanted her, too. You see, Lochard has always wanted what I want. Coveted what I have. Financially, he's about in the same state as I am. When my father's estate was settled, I wanted to be fair about it. After all, I had no say in the matter of my birth. Not any more than Lochard did. He could have been born the eldest brother and I the younger, except it didn't work out that way. Even as young boys, there was this rivalry between us, something you've said exists between my daughter and son."

He drew another long sigh and his eyes grew somber. "But I never thought Lochard's envy would come to this. In fact, I thought he'd outgrown it. For the past year or so he's seemed quite satisfied with things the way they are. I had hoped he was maturing."

"But you aren't absolutely *sure* it was Lochard who wrote the last letter—the one that said I must bring the ransom money to the designated spot."

"Yes. I am. And Amanda, I have no intention to allow you to do it. That was not my reason for telling Andrew to give you the letter and nobody else. I also cautioned him not to speak of it to anybody but you. My reason for seeing to it that you had it in your possession was because of all the things I had to do. First there was the sad duty of taking Matilda's corpse to her mother and father. Then we had to continue the search for Faylodene and Becky. I was afraid I would lose it."

She looked at the steadily glowing candle flame. "But couldn't that note-paper have belonged to someone else? Can you be absolutely positive it belongs to Lochard? It looks like a rather easily obtained grade of expensive parchment. I've seen the same kind in London."

"Exactly. This paper came from London. It was sent by a childhood friend. Besides, Amanda, I've been to White Rose. I was able to get in without any of Lochard's servants seeing me. In Lochard's study, I found the parchment where I knew it would be. In his writing case. Give it to me. I'll show you."

She turned her back on him and withdrew the slightly crinkled paper, then handed it to him wordlessly. He took it from the envelope, then extracted another sheet from his pocket. "Look closely," he said as he smoothed both pieces on the table by the bed. "This was originally one sheet of paper. It was torn in two. The two pieces fit." His index finger pointed out a small tear at the bottom of the piece that had the writing on it. "You can see this small rip, then the matching tab that fits it."

"There's no doubt," she said in a faltering voice. Then her gray eyes met his brown ones gravely. "But I *will* go, David. And take the money."

"*No!* I can't allow you to put yourself in such danger. I'll go myself."

"There'll be no danger," she said. "Lochard wouldn't dare leave the house at midnight. He'll have to stay close at hand. Otherwise, he'd be giving himself away."

"You forget. He has a confederate. I'm positive."

"How do you know?"

"Becky has been severely injured. I don't believe her wounds are grave. Not severe enough to cause her to be in immediate danger. She's out of her head, and I've been with her this past fifteen minutes or so. Now and then she repeats the same awful words, and when she says them her hands clench and her eyes roll. Her body pitches violently back and forth in the bed."

"What does she say?"

"She appears to be asking someone to tell her where Nelda is. I'd rather you heard for yourself,

Amanda. Besides, you may be able to help her. As soon as the storm was over I sent for a doctor, but God alone knows when he'll come. The tornado has no doubt wrought havoc for miles around.''

"Where is Becky injured?"

"The back of the head. As I said, it's a nasty wound, but if it doesn't turn gangrenous she's got a pretty good chance of survival.''

"I'll go to her at once, of course," said Amanda.

"If she'd only regain consciousness, she might be able to tell us everything we need to know.'' David held out his arms and Amanda allowed herself the luxury of the comfort of being held close, but only for a brief time. "My dear," he murmured as he held her so tightly that she couldn't get her breath. "My dearest dear. Will this long night ever end?"

She stepped away from him. "It will end, David. And in the morning your little girl will be returned safely. I feel quite confident that she will.''

"God knows I hope and pray you're right. But Amanda, I forbid you to walk out into the night carrying ten thousand Spanish dollars. In the first place, you couldn't carry it. In the second place, I won't allow it." He held her close once more. So tight was his embrace that she could feel the hammering of his heart. Then he murmured, "One more proof of a sick mind, designed to drive me even more distracted with worry. Besides, a sane person would know a mere slip of a girl couldn't possibly carry ten thousand Spanish dollars! But my dearest, I would go mad with worry knowing you were walking alone so late at night. So you'll not take this responsibility on your shoulders.''

"Very well, David," Amanda said breathlessly.

But she knew she would. Somehow, she would find a way to get the money and figure a way to carry it. And at the same time she knew she must leave the house long before the appointed time, and manage it so David couldn't possibly restrain her. Her smile was sweet as she asked him which room Becky was in. He told her he'd taken her to Charity's room, and walked with her down the hall.

"I'm glad you aren't going to argue with me about going down to the river in the pitch dark. You're a sensible girl, Amanda Whitcomb."

She smiled at him again, knowing she was every bit as sincere when she gave him her innocent look and nodded her head as Deirdre Bennet was when she expressed concern over anybody but her precious self. At the door, she told David she would rather go into Becky's room alone. "Besides, you must be with your son."

He nodded, brushed her forehead with his lips, and turned away.

A dozen candles burned in the bedroom where Charity Whitcomb had met her tragic death. Becky's dark skin was a startling sight against the snowy pillow and sheets, but Amanda forgot all about that first impression when she saw the way Becky was thrashing around on the bed, muttering and rolling her eyes.

"Becky," she said gently when the girl was silent for a second. "Becky, do you hear me?"

"Yes'm."

"Becky, do you know me?"

"It seems like it's almost cooked all the way through, but I think it's still raw in the middle," answered Becky. "Smells good, though." Then she halfway sat up, flailed the air, and sank to her pillows, her mouth slack as she spoke a string of words so garbled that Amanda couldn't understand.

Gingerly, she put her hands on Becky's head and

turned it sideways. The fine hand of Flora had already been at work on the bloody wound at the back of Becky's head. It was smeared with lard, then coated with some nasty smelling stuff that made Amanda think of damp and mildew and decay. Becky's hair was matted and stuck to the blood where it wasn't greasy with lard.

"I'll get me a rag and I'll mop that up," said Becky clearly. "I always did say milk looks like a lot mo' when it's on the flo' than it do when it's in the jug."

Amanda doubted that there would be water in the pitcher, but she was surprised. There was water, and she found a soap ball in the cabinet under the wash basin. Within five minutes, she'd bathed the evil smelling decoction from the back of Becky's head. While she worked, the wounded servant continued to thrash about on the bed, then fell back into exhausted silence. Then she'd speak of disjointed subjects or call out a name. Amanda didn't recognize any of the names except Jimson, her husband. She screeched, "Didn' I say to carry dem slops out?" Then she spoke in a honeyed voice, again to her husband. "Jimson, honey, you is de best!" After that, she railed long and loud, with only a few of her words clear, then she fell back again to the pillows, her mouth wide open, her eyes closed. For a long while, she lay motionless. Amanda put a hand at her throat and satisfied herself that a pulse still beat. It was strong but erratic, sometimes racing along and then slowing down alarmingly.

The wound itself was not as bad as Amanda had first thought. The lacerations looked superficial athough it was obvious there had been a copious amount of blood. The worst cut was not terribly deep, but the lack of swelling around the battered bone was what gave Amanda the most concern.

She wasn't absolutely positive, but she believed she'd heard a doctor say once that a concussion doesn't make a bump. There were a few small knots on the back of Becky's head, but the place where the cut was the deepest appeared indented when she touched it with her fingers. She knew that might mean a break in the skull. A possible injury on the inside of Becky's head, which would certainly account for the erratic behavior of the patient.

Since there was nothing else she could do, she decided it might ease the poor girl if she bathed her. When she was gently drying the pale face, Becky pushed her to one side and screamed. "I say what did you do with that sweet chile, you sombitch? I'm gonna kill you, you heah me, you don' lead me to her!"

The candles flickered all over the room. As the words came pouring out of Becky's mouth. Amanda had a vision of how she must have stood like a tiger, demanding the man—it would have been a man, otherwise Becky wouldn't have called him a 'sombitch,' she rationalized. But it pained her to think of Becky defying Lochard Whitcomb in her rage to make him tell her where he'd put the missing child. She was so intent on visualizing just how it might have been, that stormy scene between servant and abductor, that she didn't realize the significance of the flickering candles. Then she heard footsteps and knew the candles were dancing because somebody had opened the door.

Lochard's tall figure was framed in the open doorway.

12

"I didn't mean to startle you, Amanda," he said quietly. "I don't think you heard me knock."

She was rattled, but made a hurried attempt to pull herself together. If Lochard had stolen his niece and was holding her for ransom, then everything, including Nelda's very life, depended on getting the gold to the appointed place on time without Lochard realizing he was suspected.

He came over and stood by the bed. She forced herself to smile at him in what she hoped was a friendly manner. "I'm afraid I've washed away all Flora's herbal medicine, but really! Such a stench! And Becky does look a little better."

"I came to tell you supper is ready. Would you prefer having a tray brought to the room?"

"That would be nice." She wondered what David must be thinking of to allow Lochard to wander about the house if he believed him guilty of not only kidnapping Nelda, but attacking Becky.

As though he read her mind, Lochard said, "William is out in the hall with me. My brother has issued a mandate. Nobody is to go anywhere alone." He smiled. "I can remember other days when David wouldn't have cared a fig if I had fallen into the river. Nor would I have cared if it happened to him. We change, thank God, as we grow older. Andrew is already repenting all his sins where Nelda is concerned. He told me a while ago he wished he'd never fought with his little sister, and promised faithfully that if he had a chance to make amends he'd do so. I'm glad Becky appears better. A nasty thing, tornadoes. A man I knew once swore he saw a baby inside a cradle lifted up and carried away in a tornado. Then baby, cradle and all was set down as nicely as you please, in a haystack."

"And how is Miss Bennet?"

"Resting quietly." He laughed. "I'm afraid Deirdre wasn't terribly grateful when she found out you were the one who administered to her. Doctor Graves arrived a few minutes ago. He said you did a wonderful job. As well as he could have done."

His hands were level with Amanda's eyes. Furtively, she cast a glance at his fingernails. None were broken, but that told her nothing. Lochard either habitually kept his nails pared quite short or had recently cut them.

They conversed for a few minutes more. "I meant it when I said you're beautiful with your hair down around your shoulders. Far more beautiful than Deirdre Bennet. Intelligent, too."

She thanked him politely, glad to see him go but hoping she didn't show it.

While Lochard was in the room, Becky had remained mostly quiet. She'd muttered a few times about irrelevant things, then ranted about a gray fox. At least that was what her garbled words sounded like. Now she was quiet again, and appeared to be sleeping soundly. Her mouth was no longer gaping open and it seemed to Amanda that her breathing wasn't quite as labored.

A weepy-eyed Faylodene brought her a tray with biscuit and soup. Faylodene shivered as she looked at Becky. Mindy, who was Flora's daughter, came along. Mindy lingered in the doorway instead of coming inside the room and Faylodene said spitefully, "I was the one that got hurt, but Mindy acks like it was her. I was the one got sent out to the quarters with Matilda. Oh, my back! I bet I die while I'm young."

Mindy, who was a small girl of twelve, peeked into the room. "I'm scared of rooms where somebody got kilt."

"Oh, fiddle-dee-dee," said Faylodene. "If you're scaret of Becky, she ain' gon' hurt you. She's out of her haid. And if it's Missus Charity, she ain' gon' hurt you neither. She wouldn't hurt a fly when she was alive and dey don' change dey ways when dey daid."

Amanda asked Faylodene how she happened to be hurt in the storm and was immediately sorry she'd asked. The girl didn't hesitate to launch into a long and rambling story that made her appear a heroine.

"Well, I tell you. It was like this. You knows when I taken sick with my headache and got all feverishified, Master Whitcomb done say I got to go to the quarters and sent Matilda with me. Matilda, she's daid, but I'm bounden to tell the Gawd's truth, even though it ain't nice to speak ill of the daid. She sneaked out to meet her man, and that's for sure and sartain. So I just stayed there in my bed with my misery and Matilda went out to meet her man, that no-good, low-down Washin'ton, and him got a woman and all. Some folks bein' so high and mighty, I don' care if they is

daid. Don' make what she done right, just cause
she happen to get herself killed. So I heard this
screamin' goin' on, and it was her. Durn near
screamed her haid off. She went to her own house
where she lives—I mean *lived*—with her Papa and
Mama. Then a bit later she commenced this
screamin' an carryin' on."

"How soon after Matilda left you did she start
screaming?"

"Oh, lands . . . I cain't say fo' sho'. A little while, I
reckon. Maybe ten minutes, I tell you I was in so
much agony with my haid! I got these here
migrims, you know, like Missus Celeste Whitcomb done had. Pained me somethin' awful. But it
seemed to me like Matilda she callin' from de back
of de houses where most of de servants live. So I
got out of my sick bed and run toward the sound
of that voice, storm and all. Never paid no attention to howlin' wind, pieces of limbs done
snatched offen de trees sashayin' around over my
pore haid. Oh, Lawdy, Lawdy, I knowed it was a
bad storm! It gettin' dark as de inside of de
debbil's heart out there. Ole sky splittin' wide
open with lightnin', thunder, stuff crashin' all over
de place. . . ."

"I know all about the tornado, Faylodene," said
Amanda in exasperation. "I just want to know if
you *saw* Matilda."

"No'm. Nebber did see her. Heard her yellin'
and screamin', seemed to me like she call my
name, then seem to me like she say somethin'
about shelter. Maybe she say spring house. But I
couldn't make out de words too good. Ole wind
snatch 'em right outa her mouf. But I went out in
de *storm* to see if she was hurt."

"And came right back in."

"Well . . . wasn't nothin' I could do! Not out
there in dat Gawd-forsaken weatherin'. An, Oh,

Lawdy, I got down on my knees and prayed for deliv'rence once I got back inside de house. Ole wood just a splittin' and a screechin'; floor swayin' right under my feet! But I tried to go to that Matilda. Would of he'pped her, too, afore Gawd I would of, if I could of found her."

"Did you see anybody at all during your mad dash out into the storm?"

"No'm. Nobody. Not tell it had slacked down some. Then I went out and fell plump into a pile of logs for de cookin' far. Dem logs been stacked up all nice and neat, but ole storm scattered 'em dis way and dat. Seemed like I started 'em rollin', den first thing I knowed ole logs was on top of me, and me already sufferin' so bad with my pore haid. Den I saw Becky and Matilda, dem screamin' bloody murder. I knowed Matilda was hurt. They runnin', but I couldn' get dem damn logs offa me to save my soul! They had me pinned down to the groun' right on my *laigs!* Pretty soon Mastah Jennings, de Gov'nor, and some other men come along and got me out of there. Brought me to de house and made me go to *wuck!* Jus' lak I nebber been down to de valley of de shadow of death."

"You've a brave girl, Faylodene," said Amanda sweetly. "Now will you please go downstairs and find Governor Jennings? Ask him to come up here and tell him I want to speak to him *alone.* . . . No, wait." She saw the quill pen and ink bottle on the little writing desk. "I'll put my request in writing. That way you won't have to give him my message in front of anybody else. And Faylodene, be absolutely sure that you don't tell a soul that I want to speak to Governor Jennings alone."

Faylodene promised. After Amanda had written the message, she looked Faylodene straight in the eye and said sternly, "When I said I want you to speak to nobody about giving this message to the

Governor, that includes Master David or Master
Lochard Whitcomb. And the other servants.''

"Lawd, Gawd, ma'am, I wouldn't tell nobody!''

Amanda continued to gaze into Faylodene's
sullen eyes, but when she spoke her voice was
gentle. "If you do tell anybody, I will know,
Faylodene. I have ways of knowing things that go
on in this house. *Everything!* I use secret methods
that some people might say is witchcraft. I
wouldn't like to learn that you disobeyed me in
this matter, Faylodene, because it is very, very
important.''

Faylodene shuddered. "Hoodoo! You knows
about hoodoo?'' She took two steps backward.
''Don' you conjure no debbil up aroun' here, Miss
Amanda!''

"I didn't say that, Faylodene." Amanda turned
an angelic smile on for the girl's benefit, then
added, "If you keep our secret, I'll give you
anything you want from my jewel box.''

"I'll take the opal ring, then," announced
Faylodene.

"Very well." Amanda didn't mention anything
about how she'd noticed the contents of her
jewelry box had been rifled. She was well aware of
the servants' tendency to rummage around in
drawers and boxes and nothing had been missing.
She'd not worn her opal ring since her arrival, but
now she knew Faylodene, for one, had looked
inside the little case where she kept her few pieces
of jewelry. She also believed that Faylodene would
keep her promise of remaining silent about the
message to Jonathan Jennings. Mentioning witchcraft had been a spur-of-the-moment decision. The
promise of payment for silence had been in her
mind all along. She handed the hastily written
note to the girl.

At the door, Faylodene looked back at her appre-

hensively, then said, "After things calms down
aroun' here some, would you make me a conjur so
I can get me a man, Miss Amanda?" Mindy, still
hovering in the doorway, tittered.

Amanda nodded her head, but now that she'd as
good as said she practiced the ancient craft of
voodoo (or at least had allowed Faylodene to
believe she did) she didn't look forward to the time
when, as the girl had put it, "things had calmed
down some." She had an idea all the servants
would ask her to do conjures, about which she
knew nothing.

She stood at the side of Becky's bed for a long
moment, deep in thought. Although the dusky-
skinned girl was still restless, she seemed to have
taken a turn for the better. She was resting
quietly, arms down at her sides. Now and then a
small sigh escaped her lips, but the wild thrashing
had stopped, and the torrent of sometimes meaningless words no longer came from her lips. Her
heart beat was no longer so fluttery.

While she waited for Jonathan Jennings,
Amanda allowed her own mind to ramble. She'd
sent the message to him because he was the only
person in the house who could not have been
involved in the abduction. It made her shiver to
realize it, but she knew Jennings was the only
person in the house she could trust. Of course
there was William and Deirdre Bennet, but
Deirdre was helpless and she considered William
too young for what she was going to ask of
Governor Jennings. Aside from that, she doubted
if William would agree to do what she was going
to ask.

The seconds continued to crawl by with infuri-
ating slowness. She'd hoped Governor Jennings
would come upstairs right away, but she knew
Faylodene would have to find him first, and the

house was big. It was getting close to nine o'clock.

Becky's hands moved restlessly. She moaned as though in pain. Amanda bathed her face again, then washed her hands. Remembering the fingernail fragment she'd found under Nelda's bed, she examined Becky's. They were smooth and pink, narrow and rounded at the ends. None were broken close to the quick.

Faylodene's nails were ragged. Except for one long, rather pointed nail, they looked as though they'd all been torn away, which she guessed had happened as Faylodene clawed at the stack of wood that came tumbling down upon her.

So much for that, she thought restlessly, and decided her carefully gleaned evidence wasn't of value after all.

Her patience was running thin when Governor Jennings came. In spite of her impatience to talk to him, though, Amanda felt a moment of irritation that he'd chosen that moment to come in answer to her summons. For just at that very second, she'd been so close to remembering something of grave importance—something that had to do with the ridiculous little scene that had occurred down in the library when Andrew dropped the Bible. If the Governor had just waited a second or two more, she was sure she'd be able to remember it. But now that nagging insight was the same disturbing question that it had been before.

She greeted Governor Jennings courteously, then launched into her request.

13

"No, no, absolutely not. I won't go along with your idea at all, my dear," said Governor Jennings. "David is quite right. It's far too risky to allow you out alone at night. Especially when we know a criminal is out and about. A mad man, who probably would not hesitate to maim and kill. I refuse to go along with you in this."

Amanda pleaded her case quietly, sensing that the sympathetic man who looked at her with such understanding eyes would not listen to her for a moment if she didn't show good sense as well as courage.

"No," he said after courteous consideration. "I refuse to lock David Whitcomb in a room. He and I have already discussed the second communication that demands you bring the ransom money. We are dealing with a deranged person. I will not be a party to what you suggest."

"But Governor Jennings," said Amanda, calling up all her reasoning power, "don't you see we must carry out every request of the abductor? A child's *life* is at stake!"

"Don't you know her father realizes that?"
Governor Jennings spoke eloquently of a father's
love for his daughter. Then he said, "This second
note is proof that we are dealing with a mad man.
Look at you. What do you weigh, a hundred and
five pounds or so? You couldn't possibly carry ten
thousand dollars down to the river. It would seem
to me that a man who would make such an impossible request must be either insane or possessed of
a diabolical sense of humor. Such a ridiculous
demand."

"There are other ways of getting money down to
the river than carrying it. I didn't plan to tote it on
my head. Nor put it in my pocket, Governor
Jennings." She spoke crisply, intending to rattle
the Governor, then swiftly thrust the arrow of her
next statements. "Where does Mr. Whitcomb have
the gold?"

"It's in a strong box."

"But where?"

"I shan't tell you, dear girl. I can see that you're
a lady of determined ways."

Amanda played her last card. With a great fluttering of her eyelashes in the manner of Deirdre
Bennet, she gave him a wistful look, threw in a
long, disappointed sigh, and said, "Then you leave
me no choice. I will have to turn to someone else in
this matter."

"Damn it to hell, girl, there is nobody else you
can turn to."

Thinking of William with his sallow face and his
callow youth, Amanda gave the Governor a look of
calculated determination. "Oh, yes, there is someone else to whom I can turn. And I *will* turn to
him, too."

Becky sighed heavily and said, "Mud on the
sheets—now if that don't beat all!"

"She's out of her head with fever," Amanda explained. Then she smiled sweetly and spoke in a voice dripping with disappointment. "I'm sorry you and I do not see eye to eye, sir. However, I beg of you to not mention my reason for asking you to come up here and talk about this . . . this plan I had. I suppose you'll go to your death bed believing I was behaving in a ridiculous, typically female manner. While I—I shall go to my death believing that you behaved in a manner typical of all males. Stubbornly. Without considering all angles. My heart breaks when I contemplate the possibility of what will happen to a ten-year-old child if every order the kidnapper has given isn't carried out as instructed. I don't suppose you can hold another accountable for the murder of a child under those circumstances, though. You, sir, are the authority on the law." She leaned forward and put her face quite close to his. "But how are you going to feel if Nelda is not returned?"

"My dear, but you are a caution," said Governor Jennings. "With a marvelous ability to get at the hub of the matter. I can understand why David was in such a rush to put a ring on your finger. But no."

Amanda continued to talk. Sometimes she wheedled, but most of the time she drove the point home about the mind of a criminal who would take a child, write one ransom note, then another that specified a different person should bring the money. "You see, sir, we just don't know *what* might set a man with such an unstable mind off. He'll believe he's lost his chance for remaining free. I believe he demanded that I deliver the money because he's afraid David will learn his identity."

Governor Jennings was not without his resources, either. "Then why wouldn't you learn his identity? I'll tell you why. He'd kill you! He plans to kill you down there by the river. And he knows he wouldn't stand as good a chance of living if he tried to kill David Whitcomb."

Three quarters of an hour went by while the first Governor of Indiana and Amanda debated. In the end, she lost.

In her moment of defeat, Amanda kept her dignity although it was difficult to do so. She wanted to stamp her foot and scream and rage at the man for his pig-headed refusal to see things her way. What rankled most was the knowledge that she was being protected because of her sex . . . which was why she felt the second note had been left. She didn't mind being considered no threat to the kidnapper because she was a woman, but she did resent Jennings' refusal to help her because she was not a man.

After Governor Jennings had taken his leave, she sat for a moment in deep thought. Then she went to the writing desk and took out a piece of paper. Before she could set pen to it, the Governor was back again with the doctor.

Doctor Graves was a rotund little man with a shock of white hair and the kindest eyes Amanda had ever seen. He examined Becky with care, then shook his head as he turned away. "You're a young woman of rare courage and amazing knowledge, Mrs. Whitcomb," he said quietly. "Miss Bennet, who is my patient, was lucky you were here to attend her." He smiled. "Because of your quick action when it came to cleansing the wound on her ankle, she stands a good chance of walking again without a limp. All too often, the sepsis that enters a compound fracture such as she suffered gives the patient more lasting damage than the break itself. And I must say you're to be complimented on the way you set the break in her arm.

Have you had experience in tending the wounded?"

"No, sir." Amanda hoped neither the doctor nor the Governor had seen her hastily put the piece of writing paper she'd taken from the late Charity Whitcomb's writing desk under the wrist band of the long sleeve of her dress. "I've mended no broken bones before, but I had a Nanny who used to heal the broken legs of birds. I watched her set the break, then take a splinter of wood and bind cloth to it. Then, too, I've read a few medical books that were my father's."

"Well, you are to be commended." He turned back to Becky, whose dusky face was in repose.

"Now, here we have a different matter. The situation is grave. I am not a learned surgeon; delivering babies and setting broken bones is about as far as my knowledge goes. But I believe this girl has a severe concussion. I wouldn't dare attempt a trephany, which is what a colleague of mine would do, I warrant." His eyes grew pained as he bent over the bed and moved Becky's head to one side. Pointing to the deepest cut on her scalp, he said, "This portion of her skull is shattered. There are several small breaks all around the larger one, and when I probe the area with my finger I find it deeply indented. You've done all there is to do. Keep the patient quiet and continue to bathe the back of her head with soap and water. A sponge bath will have an easing effect, which I see you've already done." He reached into his bag and took out several packets of powders. "If she arouses, give her this sleeping draught in a glass of water. As far as I know, she'll not suffer a great amount of pain, for the brain itself is not sensitive to pain. However, she *will* suffer a great amount of discomfort from the breaks in her skull, and the best thing to do is keep the patient quiet."

"Then do you think she'll—" Amanda didn't like to ask if Becky had a chance to recover. Understanding her hesitation to put the dread question into words, Doctor Graves came to her rescue:

"I don't know. Sometimes, especially when left alone, the body has great recovery powers. Other times—" He shrugged. "Who knows. She is in the hands of her Maker. And you my dear girl, who will attend her." He then told her he must go to another servant at Whispering Hills, who had gone into early labor. "It would seem that it doesn't rain but what it pours. The woman was not due for accouchement for another two months, but the havoc wrought by the storm has brought about early labor. Well, well. With care, the babe about to be born will survive, another link in the great chain of life. Sometimes injuries to the brain cause a great restlessness. It wouldn't do at all for her to get to her feet and walk around. This sometimes happens, with a result of further injuries. I would suggest that when you leave the room you have someone else standing by. If you need me, send for me. I will remain on the place until the little girl has been returned. God alone knows what kind of shape she may be in when she's returned to her father."

Amanda turned to Governor Jennings after she spoke a few more words to the doctor. She asked if he would send Flora or Faylodene upstairs. The Governor nodded. Then he said, "I'm glad to see that you've accepted the folly of your earlier decision. A woman such as yourself cannot be spared in this house."

Amanda didn't argue. She understood his words to mean something entirely different from what he was saying. What he really meant was that men would do men's work and women would do women's work, and her duty was clear. She was to nurse the sick. Years of dealing with her father, who took pride in her intellect but insisted that she behave in a fittingly female fashion had taught her much about men like Governor Jennings, she realized. More than once she had lost an argument with her father. It pleased her to know the Governor believed emphatically that she was acquiescent, satisfied to let the men handle the problem of defying the kidnapper's orders to send her with the money. She nodded her head, gave both the doctor and the Governor a little curtsy and saw them to the door.

It was half past nine.

14

Flora came upstairs immediately after the doctor and the Governor left, with shy Mindy in attendance. Amanda gave Flora the doctor's instructions concerning the care of Becky, then went across the hall to her own room, explaining to Flora that she had some personal things to attend to. Once she was in her room, she sat down at the writing table and began to practice a style of writing that was much different from her own. With only the memory of those ransom notes to go by, she could merely hope that she was doing a passable job of imitating the abductor's handwriting as well as the crudely misspelled words. Some minutes later, she was forced to go back into the room where she'd left Flora and Mindy with Becky. It just wouldn't do to use her own writing paper.

Once she was in the room, she was able to get her hands on Charity's paper by simply pointing out the sleeping draught she'd left on the top of the writing table. But then she changed her mind again, knowing David was aware of the length of

time she'd spent in Charity's room. She knew she
was wasting time by attempting to second-guess
him, but she knew she was not dealing with a fool
—and she had already tipped her hand to
Governor Jennings, although she felt reasonably
sure she'd mollified him into thinking she would
behave herself.

When she left the bedchamber, she immediately
went back to her room, realizing how tense one
becomes when forced to carry out a furtive plan.
She had an idea that Flora and Mindy were listening to the sounds of her footsteps to make sure she
went to her room as she'd said, although she knew
better. For a few seconds, she remained in her
room, then slipped out of her slippers so she'd
make no noise as she prowled about the upper
floor of Whispering Hills in search of writing
paper.

The upstairs part of the house was quiet, and
she shuddered involuntarily as she realized she
was comparing the still, listening silence to the
quiet of a tomb. Her stockinged feet made
whispering sounds as she glided down the hall,
and made her think of the wispy sigh she'd heard
from the ghostly visitors of Whispering Hills.

It took all the force of Amanda's will to open the
door to the nursery. But she recalled having seen
colored paper on a shelf, and had made up her
mind it would be the very best thing for her to use.
The first note from the abductor had been on red
paper, so she thought it would be more convincing
if she wrote the third one on the same kind.

The darkness was a handicap as well as her
nervousness. She didn't dare light a candle
because she had no way of knowing who might be
out in the night. If someone looked up and saw a
light in the nursery, suspicion would be aroused.

It was cold and damp in the middle room where

the children kept their school books and games. Combined with the cool, musty odor was the everyday, normal scent of papers and books, the very usual atmosphere of the room adding to her sense of unnamed fear. A blast of damp air came from under the door that led to Nelda's room, and for a moment Amanda wanted nothing more than to run from the room and forget all about her mission. The light and warmth of the rest of the house beckoned as much as the companionship of other people. As her fingers groped along the shelves in search of the paper she sought, she remembered with increased terror David's mandate about nobody in the house going about without being accompanied by another. Common sense told her no harm could come to her in the nursery; that it would be the last place the vile creature would hide. Yet the moment was not compatible with common sense. Each time her fingers came in contact with a toy or a book, she feared she might touch living flesh and bone. A hand that would wield an instrument to render her senseless, even as senseless as Becky was back there in the room.

At last, her fingers found and recognized the rather rough texture of what she sought. In her haste, she knocked over the entire stack, making it necessary for her to stoop in the dark and return the paper to where it had been. If David did suspect her—or Governor Jennings, for that matter—she knew she'd best leave no traces of her furtive movements. While she was replacing the stack of paper on the shelf, she knocked over a metal object that rang like a bell to her sensitive ears. For a long moment, all she could do was whimper in the darkness, her hands holding the paper to her breast as though for protection.

The long walk back to her room was even worse

than when she'd left it. Every shadow, every doorway seemed fraught with danger. She was trembling from head to toe when she finally entered her own room, closed the door and fell in a chair, too unnerved to do anything but gather her scattered wits about her and command her hands to stop shaking.

Although it seemed as though it had taken hours, a mere three quarters of an hour had elapsed from the time Amanda left Flora and Mindy in attendance upon Becky until the time she returned. By then she had thrown a woolen robe over the pale yellow gown and taken her hair down, hoping to give the impression that she was resigned to spending the night in the relative safety of Whispering Hills. She had slipped downstairs and put the letter on the dining room table, and was in the process of entering the room where Becky still lay in stupor upon the bed.

"Thank you, Flora," she said in what she hoped was a suitably tired voice. "I'm afraid I quite took advantage of the knowledge Becky was in good hands. I meant only to rest for a few seconds, but I must have dozed off."

"And no wonder, Miss," said Flora. "I tell you, it's been one awful day around here, and you right in the thick of it."

Little Mindy, asleep on a pallet on the floor, turned over. Flora said Becky hadn't roused, but now and then she muttered something. Amanda told Flora she was free to go back downstairs. "It will be a long night, Flora. Let Mindy stay where she is. I'll walk with you to the stairs, and I'll be glad enough to have the comfort of Mindy's presence, even though she is only a child and must have her sleep. You should try to rest for a while, too, Flora. Nothing is to be gained by wearing yourself out."

Flora's eyes filled with tears. "I couldn't sleep a wink knowing that sweet child is out there somewhere, God alone knows in what shape she in."

After she had accompanied Flora to the stairs, Amanda came back and took up her vigil at Becky's side. The hands on the clock in the room appeared to have become stuck. She stood up, went to the clock and put her ear to it to make sure it was still ticking. It was, but time seemed to stand still as she waited for someone to come upstairs and tell her that another letter had been found.

It was David and Doctor Graves who came to tell her what she already knew. As she spoke the words of concern, gave David hope and encouragement, she felt consumed with guilt. She knew full well that part of the reason she was not suspected of writing the third letter was due to David's state of mind. He was more distraught than ever and he appeared to have aged ten years.

During the time that had elapsed since she'd left the letter on the dining room table, she'd suffered a hundred doubts. If David had done this terrible deed himself for a reason she couldn't fathom, then he'd know the note she wrote was a forgery. Her mind blanked out when she tried to consider what he'd do, but she believed he'd open it, read it, then say nothing. If he was innocent of spiriting Nelda away—which she believed him to be—then by his acceptance of the forgery, he'd prove it. Still . . . she wasn't able to quell all the sick doubts about whether she'd done the right thing or not.

With a numb mouth and a queasy feeling in the pit of her stomach, she said, "At least, David, you'll know tonight whether she lives or not. Perhaps the person who took Nelda is remorseful. I can only be glad that the message said she'd be returned an hour after you leave the money, though I do find it strange that the place of delivery has been changed."

The doctor had a theory about that. He said, "I rather imagine the kidnapper planned to have a boat on the river. The plans were probably changed because of the swollen river. It's almost impossible to get down to the water's edge. I wouldn't doubt but what the pile of rocks that was to be used for a marker has been swallowed up in the rising river." He sighed. "I only wish to God this thing had never happened. But like you, Amanda, my hopes are high for the safe return of the little girl."

David and the doctor left the room, leaving Amanda alone with her guilty thoughts. Her mind felt on fire with her shame over what she had done, but she still felt she'd done what she must. It seemed painfully clear to her that the abductor had intended her to deliver the gold because she represented the lesser threat than David. Knowing how thin the line between sanity and insanity is, she believed sincerely that if the instructions were not carried out right down to the last letter, Nelda would be murdered. But now she wished she had not interfered, realizing that she would never survive the sense of being responsible if things went wrong.

There was not a second to lose, however, and now that she'd begun, she had no alternative but to continue. She roused the sleeping Mindy, and instructed her calmly, "I must go. If anyone enters this room, scream your head off, do you understand?"

Mindy nodded, either too stunned at Amanda's words to protest, or too numb with sleep to really understand.

It took Amanda and William Bennet a good fifteen minutes to exchange the strongbox of gold for a strongbox filled with rocks and shale. She'd not wanted to press the youth into service, but she had no choice in the matter. The doctor had told her young Bennet had been put up for the night in a guest room while Deirdre slept under opiates in the library. William was stunned at first, then shocked at her proposal. But Amanda quickly convinced him that he had no choice. She told him if he wouldn't help her she would find a way to do what must be done alone. She'd witnessed enough of William's chivalrous manners with his sister to know he was vulnerable when it came to helping damsels in distress, but for good measure, she said, " Besides, I'll tell David this was all your idea if things go wrong. He'll believe me, you know."

William worked with haste, if not willingly, yet they almost didn't get the necessary change done in time. Amanda and William pressed themselves flat up against the shadows of the house while David started off in the opposite direction that Amanda would take. She closed her eyes and saw the forged message under her eyelids.

> *There has been a change in plans. Take the gold to a point beyond White Rose hill where you will cum upon a marker made of stones pilled one atop the uther. There is whar yr to leeve the gold and yr little dawtter will cum home in one our.*

It was twenty minutes till twelve when Amanda slipped from the shadows under the trees next to the back porch. Her black clothing blended with the shadows. For a second, she gave a thought to William, whom she'd instructed to go upstairs and stay with Mindy and Becky. The sky had cleared. A three-quarter moon rode high in the sky. At first she was glad of the light of the moon, but then she began to wish for the darkness, knowing she made a good target as she moved in close to the horse and cart where William had helped her load the box. Her teeth chattered, a jarring note in the night where silence reigned except for nature. The sound of her chattering teeth was loud as the crickets, loud as the thrill of the whippoorwills that called from the leafy trees. Just a little louder than her own galloping heartbeats.

She made a soft sound of encouragement to the horse, then gently slapped his flank. Holding her breath as he lifted his feet and bent to the burden in the cart, she waited for the sound of opening doors in the house, fearful that William had given her secret away. Looking back, she saw the yellow glow of candle light in the back part of the house. For an instant, she longed to be inside the safe walls of a house, to be sheltered from the unknown fearsome journey into the night. Before she turned her face back to the horse, she saw the shadowy figure of Doctor Graves move close to the window. His white hair gleamed for an instant under the blaze of candles in a sconce, and she knew that tall form at his side was Governor Jennings. Both of them apparently believed she was with Becky.

The horse whinnied. Amanda froze, then looked back again toward the kitchen. But Jonathan Jennings and Doctor Graves remained where they were.

I'm all alone. She said the lonely words to herself, then looked up at the starry skies, struck with the indifference of the heavens.

Even though she knew it wasn't more than fifty rods to the river's edge, it looked much farther. The horse plodded along, lifting one foot at a time and putting it down with care. The grass in back of the house was wet and the heavy rain had left the earth spongy. Her own feet sunk into the loam.

How she longed to be held safely in David's arms! Right then, she wondered if she would ever live to see him again, and railed at herself for almost giving in to her own terror. Deliberately, she forced herself to think of other times, other places.

It was then as she remembered the glimmer of insight that she'd known for that glittering, but elusive moment, back there in the library, the intangible, flickering thought that thrust itself forward and immediately withdrew when Andrew dropped the Bible.

"Of course!" Involuntarily, she whispered the two words out loud. For now Amanda knew who had taken Nelda from her bed . . . and who had killed Charity Whitcomb. Her mind ricocheted in several different directions as she neared the river. She was close enough to hear the steady slap-slap-slap of the waves against the bank. The stars were reflected in the water. Even though her senses were alert to the danger of the night, aware that any moment a dark shadow could emerge from behind one of those big masses of rock that lined the ledge, a part of her mind looked forward to a time in the future when she hoped to come down to the river at night and enjoy its mystic beauty with David.

As the horse and cart moved closer and closer to the dark, forbidding river, Amanda began to peer suspiciously at every rock formation, every little bush. She was overwhelmed with the terrifying idea that a dark shape would hurl itself upon her from behind. It was agony to continue.

All around her, she imagined that malevolent eyes were boring holes in her vulnerable body. The back of her head seemed particularly endangered. Shivers ran up and down her spine, and when a night bird squawked, then followed the chilling sound by a rush of wings as it flew upward from out of the darkness, she had to press both hands against her mouth to choke back a scream. Again her teeth started chattering, and she could hear the pounding blood rush through her veins above every other sound.

Since the heavy rain, the river was much higher than it had been before. The rush of the water was loud to her ears as torrents of water tumbled downstream. With a sick sense of new foreboding, she wondered what she should do if the river had risen so high it covered the stack of rocks. Common sense told her that the rocks must have been stacked up to form the marker earlier in the day, and the doctor had mentioned the possibility.

Then she saw a furtive shadow behind a pile of rocks.

Something dark and threatening moved in back of the dark blobs of rough limestone. At first Amanda didn't want to believe she was really seeing a shadowy substance move away from the pile of rocks, but she knew it was happening, and then she knew it was moving around the rocks and heading in her direction. Furthermore, it was made of flesh and blood. During that first shock of realizing she was not alone, her first thought was that the thing that moved from behind the rocks was a ghost. Now she realized that a living entity was a far worse threat than one that belonged to the shadowy world of the dead.

15

Amanda's throat muscles convulsed as the high, thin, piercing scream ripped through her; a scream that was lost in the frantic rush of the water. Then her eyes widened in numb terror. She was unable to scream again. Her breath came in whistling gasps as she stepped backwards, blindly groping for the horse as she continued to stare at the shadow of substance as it moved toward her. Then she heard a whimper, followed closely by a sharp bark. The thing jumped forward, bounded gleefully around in little circles, then barked again in joyful recognition.

It took her several seconds to realize that it was the dog. The big friendly puppy that Nelda and Andrew adored. The animal reared up on his hind feet and put his muddy paws on Amanda's breast as it licked her face and continued to whimper and alternately bark.

"You!" Her voice sounded strange as she patted the big puppy's wet head. "Where have you been?" She realized, even in the wake of terror that had left her weak and wobbly, that the big-pawed, awkward puppy had not been seen all day. She clung to the dog for support as much as in answer to his frantic greeting, before she turned away from him to unhitch the cart.

Because she was still numb with shock and the strong afterwaves of the agonizing moment of fear, her fingers stumbled at the traces. All the time she was untethering the horse she felt compelled to look over her shoulder, glance all around in the darkness, still feeling she was not alone at the water's edge. At last she jumped upon the horse's back, turned him toward Whispering Hills and dug her heels in sharply. In the madness of the moment, she heard herself giggle hysterically as she remembered her old Nanny, who would be shocked to see her riding astride. It was all she could do to hang on, her arms around the animal's neck, her face pressed into his warm hide. The big dog bounded along at her side, the sound of his excited barks loud above the flying hooves.

Halfway up the hill, she was met by what appeared at first glance to be a thundering army. Shouts rang out in the night. "Amanda!" And "Thank God, she's all right!" Greetings merged into greetings along with a goodly share of scolding words and voices in anxiety that sounded much like anger. In the confusion of the moment, all she could fathom was that several servants were shouting right along with David, Lochard, Governor Jennings, William and the doctor. David's arms encircled her as she slid from the horse, then he held her in his arms where he kept her in a tight embrace as he ran up the hill, refusing to relinquish her until she was in the brightly lighted dining room. His face was wild as he looked down at her and said angrily, "Don't you ever put me through that kind of fear again! Do you hear me?"

"Don't speak to me in that tone of voice," she snapped, her voice lost in the voices all around them.

David shook his head. "I'll speak to you in any tone of voice I choose." He was roaring, and he lent force to his words with a slight shake of his hands upon her shoulders. "You little fool! You little fool! Oh, God, if I weren't so relieved to see you I think I'd turn you across my knee and give you a taste of the rod!"

"I refuse to allow you to talk to me like that," Amanda yelled.

"And I refuse to be married to a woman who doesn't give a thought to any other person's feelings!"

"You—you—you—" Amanda was at a loss for words. While she seethed with fury, David spoke of things that had to do with the situation being bad enough without having a headstrong female around the house who took her life in her own hands, deliberately disobeyed him, brought in a young fool who already didn't know his soul was his own, and something about criminal intent when she wrote that third kidnap note and set him on a foolish journey.

The rest of the people had melted away and she realized with overwhelming embarrassment that they'd been shocked and shamed by such unseemly behavior as well as terrified at the wrath of the Master of Whispering Hills. Suddenly the whole wretched, anxiety-filled day became too much to bear. Amanda ground her teeth together and waited for David to catch a breath so he could continue showering abuses on her head. Then she said distinctly, her voice loud enough to reach the farthest recesses of Whispering Hills, "*Oh, shut up!*"

Stunned, David blinked his eyes twice, held her

at arm's length and stared at her. Then he gathered her in his arms and spoke tenderly about other things. Things like not knowing how he would make it if he lost her, things like, "If you only knew how I felt when I rode back and found that idiot of a William waiting for me, his eyes rolling around in his head as he told me what he'd helped you do!"

Amanda's mind twisted and turned. On the one hand, she wanted to remain where she was, safe in the circle of David's arms while he spoke to her gently, tenderly. On the other hand she wanted to give in to the emotions that continued to batter at her during the aftermath of those desperate moments she'd just endured. Much later, she would remember that time when she'd alternately clung to David Whitcomb and listened to him speak, then drew away, her eyes flashing, as she tried to tell him how she felt. She often believed she would have done something dreadful, if young Andrew had not stumbled sleepily into the room just then. What was uppermost on her mind at that instant was the almost uncontrollable urge to kick David Whitcomb in the shins and scream out all her own pent-up fears and furies. But Andrew's voice had the effect of restoring order to chaos. "Papa! I bet I know where Nelda is! She's in the spring house!"

Amanda and David sprang apart. David looked down at his son and shook his head. "No, Andrew. Your sister isn't in the spring house. The servants looked there and so did I."

Andrew was more asleep than awake. He'd been sent upstairs to sleep in his father's bed, with William Bennet for company. He muttered something about being awakened by all the loud talk, and David, somewhat shame-faced, led him back upstairs to bed. When he returned, Amanda was waiting for him at the foot of the stairs, her expression solemn.

"Doctor Graves just told me Becky passed away," she said.

Then she would have told him that she knew who was behind Nelda's disappearance, but there wasn't time. Flora, her breathing labored, her face gray, stumbled in from the outside entrance. In her arms she carried a golden-haired little girl who blinked at the sudden light, then held out her arms to her father.

"Papa! Oh, Papa!"

16

Except for Deirdre Bennet, who slept peacefully under the sleeping draught Doctor Graves had administered, everyone in the house sent up a tumultuous prayer of thanksgiving over Nelda's safe return. Several minutes of joyful confusion followed that stunning, marvelous moment when Flora appeared with the child in her arms, as a cacophony of voices rang through the house, everyone wanting to speak at once.

At length, with David on one side and Amanda on the other, Nelda sat in regal grace while her captivated audience listened in wonder to her story. But first, Flora had to say why she happened to go to the spring house. Her answer was simple. "Why, Lawd, with all this racketin' around and little girls gettin' stole outen their beds and people sick and dyin' on the place, a body has still got to eat, and I'm the cook!" Flora had realized the kitchen was out of cream for the continuous pots of coffee that she and the other servants had made thoughout the long day. "So I went on down to the spring house. Don't matter if the dead of

night, people wants their coffee at a time of
sorrow, and they wants cream in it, too. Well, you
could of knocked me over with a hen's feather, I'll
swear to the living Gawd when I saw that sweet
little chile my ole heart plump stopped beatin'!"

"But we were *there*," said Lochard and
Governor Jennings in unison. "We already
checked out the spring house . . . and the servants
checked it out before the Governor and I went,"
added Lochard in disbelief.

"Well, that precious lamb of Gawd wasn't *in*
there all day long," said Flora. She turned to
Nelda. "Tell 'em, honey. You tell 'em jus' lak you
tell Flora when she got over her shock at findin'
you there."

"The door—" Nelda's words were interrupted
by Flora. "Yes! The door done blow shut by the
wind. Big old pile of bresh up agin it. I had to get
those tree limbs and leaves and things away from
the door where they'd blowed up agin it away
before I could get it open. And my lands! You'll
never know how I felt when I saw this sweet
chile. . . ."

Lochard leaned forward and captured Nelda's
small hand in his. "But honey, you weren't in the
spring house all day. You couldn't have been.
There's no place to hide in there."

"I wasn't hiding, Uncle Lochard," said Nelda
solemnly.

"I tole you-all, she was in there tight as a drum,
couldn't get out no way a-tall," Flora said.

It was then that David held his hand up and
demanded silence. "For the love of God, let Nelda
speak without interrupting her!"

Nelda's story was simple. "I woke up this morn-
ning early, just as I always do. I was about to come
downstairs when Becky came and said she had a
surprise for me, but I had to be very quiet, that I

wasn't to wake up anybody else in the house." In her innocence, Nelda laughed merrily. "She stubbed her toe on the leg of the bed, and Papa, she said some naughty words. I laughed, and she said I'd be sorry for laughing at her, but you know Becky doesn't mean it when she gets cross. Her toe did hurt, too. It bled a little."

"A little, sweetheart?" David's voice was mild, but there was no mistaking the urgency in his question. Amanda, remembering the pool of blood, the matted curl that had been in the blood, felt a cold wave of remembered horror rush over her. "It would seem to me there was *quite* a little blood in your room."

Nelda looked blank. Doctor Graves said he would fill that part in later.

"So I went downstairs with Becky," Nelda continued. " Because of the secret, we used the back stairs. Then we went over to her house and she gave me breakfast before she'd let me have the surprise. It was a doll. A beautiful baby, Papa, all dressed up in the finest clothes, and she said it was my very own. Becky made it out of an apple for the head, and oh, it's so pretty!" The child's expression became perplexed as well as disturbed. "I left the doll there when the storm came. I want to go get it, Papa."

"Later, darling," said David. "Just tell us everything else you can. Everything that happened."

"Well, I went to sleep, Papa. I must have been sick. I don't know why I went to sleep, but the last thing I remember was sitting at the table and seeing everything go all blurry, then Becky picked me up and carried me in her arms to—I don't know. But when I woke up, I knew we were having a tornado. Oh, I was so *scared!*" Her blue eyes darkened as she related the way she had awakened in the little house where Becky and Jimson lived, the house shrieking as the wood suffered under the fury of the storm. The walls shook and the wind tore and wailed while lightning flashed and thunder crashed all around her. In the darkness, with her way illuminated only by the lightning, Nelda remembered being told on several different occasions that if she was ever caught out in a bad storm she was to take shelter in the spring house. She made her way to the door, only to have it torn out of her hands by the winds. The force of the wind had broken out a window pane, and she soon found herself on the floor, momentarily stunned. She explained how she felt fuzzy when she first awakened, with a bad taste in her mouth and her eyes all blurry, and for a few moments it was obvious that the child had become disoriented. Then the door banged open again, and she saw Matilda run in, her hair dripping, her clothing partially torn away.

"I screamed real loud, but at first Matilda didn't see me. When she did, she screamed a lot louder than I did, and grabbed me and hugged me. But I didn't care about getting myself all wet from her clothes, I was awfully glad to see Matilda. She said everybody had been looking for me and a lot more things, but the wind was so bad and all those things crashing up against the house . . . I don't remember all she said. Then . . . Matilda told me to stay there. I wanted to go to the spring house, but she said I'd never get there alive or something like that. I couldn't understand why she went out into it if it was so bad. But she went, after making me crawl under the bed.

"I was too scared to stay there. The storm got worse and worse, so I went after Matilda. I bet I didn't stay under that bed for a second. Then . . ." The child turned to her father, her puzzled expression more pronounced. "Papa, I saw Becky out there in the dark with the wind whipping her clothes. And Matilda. And Papa, it looked like they were fighting! I heard Becky say something like 'you sombitch, tell me where you put that child,' and Papa . . .''

Nelda shuddered and her small body seemed to huddle within itself. "Papa, they *were* fighting! And it scared me even more, but just then there was this awful crash and . . . then I started running. I ran and ran, because I wanted to go into the house to be with you! There were trees down all around and a great big crash happened, then there was an awful roaring sound, and what made me think people were screaming . . . then the tree came down. I just got out from under it in time. It was so big. And I was so scared. And it was so dark. I just—ran to the spring house, because I couldn't get past the tree to get in the house.''

"So you were not in the spring house all day long,'' said Lochard. "That explains why we didn't find you there.''

"Yes. I told you, Uncle Lochard. I was in Becky's house, then I went to sleep.''

"But where were you in Becky's house?'' Amanda's voice was exceedingly tender. "You see, honey, everyone has been looking for you all day long.''

"Why, I was there,'' said Nelda. "Right there in her house. If you looked there, you should have found me.''

"Becky was the one who looked in the servants' quarters,'' said David before he turned back to Nelda and asked her to tell the rest.

"Then, when the storm went away, I tried to get out of the spring house. But I couldn't.''

"I bet you were scared to death,'' said Andrew. "If I got locked inside the spring house I would have been scared.''

"I was more sleepy," Nelda admitted. "And cold and wet . . . I went to sleep for a while. But then, when I woke up, I felt *awful!*"

"I bet you bawled, too," taunted Andrew. "Bawled your eyes out."

Nelda lifted her chin. "I did not. I just waited, Andrew Whitcomb, 'cause I knew pretty soon somebody would come and get me out of there, so *there!*"

Lochard reminded Andrew that he'd sworn he would never tease his little sister again, but Andrew was not willing to remember just then. He said, "Well, I bet she did bawl like a baby." It was obvious that he was not too pleased with his sister's position in the center of attention. His father quelled what could have been an angry exchange of words between the boy and girl by telling Nelda to finish telling her story.

"I *did*, Papa! I don't know any more. Flora came and got me out, and now I'm here."

Amanda wished with all her heart that the simple explanation that Nelda was able to give was all there was to the peril she'd been in. But she reminded herself that Nelda had no way of knowing of the pool of blood on the floor of her bedroom, of her blood-soaked curl, obviously missing from her tangled hair as she leaned against her father's chest. No way of knowing about the ransom notes, the incredible events of the entire day.

After Nelda was put to bed, it was Doctor Graves who filled in the missing pieces.

"Before Becky died, she regained consciousness. This happens often toward the end," he said quietly. "She knew she was dying, poor soul. She told of how she had always believed herself to be just as good as anyone else—how it had rankled with her that she was a servant, while other people lived in the lap of luxury. She explained how she had tried to force her husband to go along with the kidnap plan. But it was Andrew she wanted to abduct and hold for money instead of Nelda. Jimson refused to have any part of such a scheme.''

"But he knew it was Becky," said David harshly. "I'll deal with him later."

"I wouldn't be too severe with the man, David," said the doctor. "He certainly didn't know his wife had hidden Nelda in their own house; and he had no way of knowing the woman had drugged her to keep her sleeping. He knew she'd promised somebody—she wouldn't tell him who—to have a boat waiting at the river at dawn. The two of them were to have escaped in it. Becky told me why the dogs went to the river, but then lost the scent. She took Nelda's clothing, filling it with rocks and dragged them down to the river, knowing Lochard would probably use his hounds. That was after she made certain she had drugged Nelda into unconsciousness. Then, she came back up to the child's room and created all that havoc. That was designed to throw us off. Everyone knew that Nelda would never put up a fight against someone she knew and loved.''

"The blood in Nelda's room, how about that?" It was Amanda who asked the question.

"Chicken blood," said the doctor. "A clever, as well as diabolical woman, Becky."

Amanda said nothing. She'd known it was Becky, but not until she'd had that flash of insight during her trip down to the river. The flash of insight that had to do with what she'd seen in the Whitcomb family Bible. But she understood why she'd thought the minute piece of white cloth might be relevant. The doctor spoke just then about the way Becky had taken the dead chicken to the room and allowed the blood to run from a gash in its throat to the floor. The legs of the chicken had been tied with cloth. Then she added Nelda's curl as a grim reminder of the child's danger.

"But why did she—" David began a question which he answered himself. "I can see, now that I think of it, why she misspelled her words and wrote in an unlearned hand. Everyone knows Becky has—*had*, that is, beautiful handwriting."

There were a few more questions that Doctor Graves could answer. Becky had managed to get the writing paper from Lochard's house long ago, when she'd first conceived her plan. The red paper had been taken from the children's room, of course, just as Amanda had taken it when she wrote the third note. "She felt reasonably sure that her plan wouldn't go awry. You see, once she got her hands on that money, she didn't believe she would have to worry about Nelda giving away her secret. She intended to leave Nelda where she was, in the cabin. In time, someone would either find her, or she would awaken and come to the big house on her own. She reckoned without the flash flood that made the river impossible to navigate, and she also had no way of knowing in advance about the tornado. She was pretty well rattled by the time she left the big house with the statement that she was worried about Faylodene and Matilda. Actually, she went to make sure Nelda wasn't endangered by the storm. Then, when she arrived at the house, she didn't see Nelda. Instead, she saw Matilda, who was just then coming out of the house on the way to the big house. There's no doubt that Matilda's last conscious thought was for Nelda. Becky told me Matilda and she grappled, that Matilda swore she had hidden the child away where Becky would never find her.

Then Matilda picked up the piece of broken glass. That must have been when Nelda saw them fighting in the storm. A ghastly thing! After Becky had run the other girl through with the glass, she tried to drag her away from her own little house, knowing if Matilda was found there she would be suspected. Well . . . we know the rest. The tree fell. Becky had just managed to get Matilda a few feet away from her own house. Matilda was pinned underneath. Becky was hit by a huge limb of the tree as it went down, and the force of it carried her to the clump of bushes where she was found."

The long night had finally ended and dawn was beginning to tint the sky with glorious shades of pink and gold when Amanda and David went upstairs. She didn't think she could sleep, even then. But locked in David's warm embrace, she slept, knowing there was more to Becky's story. Nobody in Whispering Hills knew but herself, and she had not wanted to speak of what she'd read during that confused time in the library when Andrew knocked over the family Bible.

The sun was shining down with benevolence on the havoc wrought less than twenty-four hours earlier. It was one of those golden days with an azure sky quite free of threatening clouds. When Amanda got out of bed, she went to the window and looked out, drawn by the sound of voices on the bright green lawn, down below. Nelda, who looked none the worse after her ordeal, was romping with the dog. Andrew, who likewise showed none of the fearful strain of the day before, was throwing a ball high in the air and catching it. Amanda wished she could spring back into joyful abandon, forgetful of the horror of the past. She was still weary and every bone in her body ached when she moved.

David was still asleep, looking peaceful and untroubled. Amanda put on a wrapper and went downstairs to the library. She picked up the heavy Bible in two hands and carried it back up to the bedroom. Placing the Bible at the foot of the bed, she sat next to David and kissed his cheek.

His eyes fluttered open, his arms coming up to embrace her. "Amanda . . . what time is it?" he asked groggily.

"Time to get up. It's a beautiful day. The children are already outside playing."

He smiled at her and sat up. "How quick children are to put unhappiness behind them. Let's take a lesson from them, Amanda." He squeezed her hand. "From this morning on, we will not speak of the awful nightmare we lived through yesterday."

"I am as eager to put it all behind as you are, David. But first, there is something I must show you." Amanda tugged the Bible onto her lap and opened it. "If you would read your Bible once and awhile, you'd be better off," she said softly.

He looked at her, surprised. "What do you mean?"

"If I hadn't been so—confused and upset yesterday, I would have known it was Becky who took Nelda. I would have known it the second I saw this." She pointed out a single page in the book, one that had to do with the Whitcomb family tree.

David read the first notation. He frowned. Then he spoke quietly. "I meant to tell you about that, Amanda. Before we were married. I'm afraid it's true. Charity was my sister. My half-sister. My— ah, father was well-known for his philandering ways. I didn't know of this until she came to me with absolute proof of her paternity. At the time, I was, as you may well understand, quite shocked. Charity had taken a lover and was already expecting a baby. Her lover was killed in a boating accident, and she came to me for financial aid. She nursed Andrew back to health when he was very sickly. More than anything else, she wanted her own child to have a father. Out of gratitude, I married her so that Nelda would be spared the stigma of illegitimacy. Of course, Nelda knows nothing of this. I can't imagine who could have written this in the family Bible. Charity herself was illegitimate. My father was married to my mother when he . . . fathered her."

"This was written by Becky, David," said Amanda. "It's her handwriting, isn't it?"

He looked at the writing again, studying it. Then he nodded. "But why should Becky—and how did she find out?"

Amanda shook her head. "That's one of the things we'll never know. Perhaps Charity told her. Or she might have learned it from someone else." She thought of the time Becky had spent at Mason Whitcomb's bedside. "But look at what's written at the bottom of the page, David," she urged.

David read the words out loud. "Rebecca Ann, Born December 21, the year of our Lord 1784, to Mason Whitcomb and Evangeline, his slave woman."

For a long moment, David continued to look at the writing in the Bible. "The sins of our fathers," he said slowly. "God in heaven. No wonder poor Becky felt as though she had every right to live in luxury! Becky! That means she, too, was my half-sister! She did have every right to—the bounty of Whispering Hills." He put his head in his hands and sobbed brokenly. When he spoke again, he was somber with grief, sorrow and the guilt that would lie heavily on the shoulders of all those who descended from men who bought and sold human beings. "Doctor Graves left something out last night, Amanda. He didn't want to speak of it in front of the children. I held my poor cousin Sarah to blame for strangling Charity. She never liked her, and she does walk at night during the full of the moon. But it was Becky who killed Charity. She confessed it to Doctor Graves along with everything else. My God, how Becky must have hated Charity . . . and nobody ever knew! Nobody had any idea that Becky was my father's daughter, just as Charity was."

Amanda thought of the day—not so long ago, but right then it seemed ages—when she'd overheard Becky insisting that Jimson do what she told him to do. At the time, she'd thought Jimson was lazy and inclined to spend his time gambling or meeting other women. Now she realized that Becky had carefully planted that idea in her head, not being sure of just how much she'd overheard that day when she'd gone in search of her, to make her tell what she knew of the death of Charity Whitcomb. "Love," she said gently, "is a strong force. I believe Jimson knew, too." She told David what she'd overheard that day when she'd been afraid Becky was running her husband through with a pitchfork.

"I've talked to him. He wants to leave."

"I can see why he doesn't want to stay on the place," said David. "Without the woman you love, there is no happiness."

He reached for Amanda's hand and pressed the palm to his lips. It was the first time he had actually said that he loved her. Amanda felt her heart skip a beat. "And I love you, David," she said softly.

He pulled her down against his chest and kissed her passionately. "My angel girl. When I think of how you smiled at me so sweetly and seemed so aquiescent after I told you I wouldn't allow you to take that ransom money down to the river. All the time, you were planning to ask my best friend to lock me up so you could do it! If anything had ever happened to you, I don't know what I would have done, Amanda. You know, when we married you promised to honor and obey me," he reminded her in a teasing voice.

Amanda smiled. "I've been meaning to speak to you about that, dear. Perhaps we can say our vows over someday when the Governor is visiting again . . . I really don't think it's fair to expect a woman to obey a man *all* the time."

David started to protest, but Amanda put her hand over his lips. "Let's not argue on such a beautiful day."

"Now Amanda . . ." he managed.

Having no other choice Amanda pressed her lips to his and silenced him with a kiss. David's arms wrapped tightly around her and their differences were soon forgotten.

BE SWEPT AWAY
ON A TIDE OF PASSION
BY LEISURE'S THRILLING
HISTORICAL ROMANCES!

2332-6	**STILL GROW THE STARS**	$3.95 US, $4.50 Can
2328-8	**LOVESTORM**	$3.95 US, $4.95 Can
2322-9	**SECRET SPLENDOR**	$3.95 US, $4.50 Can
2311-3	**HARVEST OF DESIRE**	$3.95 US, $4.50 Can
2308-3	**RELUCTANT RAPTURE**	$3.95 US, $4.95 Can
2299-0	**NORTHWARD THE HEART**	$3.95 US, $4.95 Can
2290-7	**RAVEN McCORD**	$3.95 US, $4.50 Can
2280-x	**MOSCOW MISTS**	$3.95 US, $4.50 Can
2266-4	**THE SEVENTH SISTER**	$3.95 US, $4.95 Can
2258-3	**THE CAPTAIN'S LADIES**	$3.75 US, $4.50 Can
2255-9	**RECKLESS HEART**	$3.95 US, $4.95 Can
2216-8	**THE HEART OF THE ROSE**	$3.95 US, $4.95 Can
2205-2	**LEGACY OF HONOR**	$3.95 US, $4.95 Can
2194-3	**THORN OF LOVE**	$3.95 US, $4.95 Can
2184-6	**EMERALD DESIRE**	$3.75 US, $4.50 Can
2173-0	**TENDER FURY**	$3.75 US, $4.50 Can
2141-2	**THE PASSION STONE**	$3.50
2094-7	**DESIRE ON THE DUNES**	$3.50 US, $3.95 Can
2024-6	**FORBIDDEN LOVE**	$3.95

FOR THE FINEST
IN CONTEMPORARY
WOMEN'S FICTION,
FOLLOW LEISURE'S LEAD

2310-5	**PATTERNS**	$3.95 US, $4.50 Can
2304-0	**VENTURES**	$3.50 US, $3.95 Can
2291-5	**GIVERS AND TAKERS**	$3.25 US, $3.75 Can
2279-6	**MARGUERITE TANNER**	3.50 US, 3.95 Can
2268-0	**OPTIONS**	$3.75 US, $4.50 Can
2257-5	**TO LOVE A STRANGER**	$3.75 US, $4.50 Can
2250-8	**FRAGMENTS**	$3.25
2249-4	**THE LOVING SEASON**	$3.50
2230-3	**A PROMISE BROKEN**	$3.25
2227-3	**THE HEART FORGIVES**	$3.75 US, $4.50 Can
2217-6	**THE GLITTER GAME**	$3.75 US, $4.50 Can
2207-9	**PARTINGS**	$3.50 US, $4.25 Can
2196-x	**THE LOVE ARENA**	$3.75 US, $4.50 Can
2155-2	**TOMORROW AND FOREVER**	$2.75
2143-9	**AMERICAN BEAUTY**	$3.50 US, $3.95 Can

Make the Most of Your Leisure Time
with
LEISURE BOOKS

Please send me the following titles:

Quantity	Book Number	Price
_____	_____	_____
_____	_____	_____
_____	_____	_____
_____	_____	_____

If out of stock on any of the above titles, please send me the alternate title(s) listed below:

_____	_____	_____
_____	_____	_____
_____	_____	_____
_____	_____	_____

	Postage & Handling	_____
	Total Enclosed	$ _____

☐ Please send me a free catalog.

NAME _____
(please print)

ADDRESS _____

CITY _____ STATE _____ ZIP _____

Please include $1.00 shipping and handling for the first book ordered and 25¢ for each book thereafter in the same order. All orders are shipped within approximately 4 weeks via postal service book rate. PAYMENT MUST ACCOMPANY ALL ORDERS.*

*Canadian orders must be paid in US dollars payable through a New York banking facility.

Mail coupon to: **Dorchester Publishing Co., Inc.
6 East 39 Street, Suite 900
New York, NY 10016
Att: ORDER DEPT.**